CHRISTIANE HEGGAN

D0030955

BLIND
FAITH

In a game of murder and deception, is blind
faith enough?

Also available from bestselling author

CHRISTIANE HEGGAN

and **MIRA®** Books

Victoria hardly said a word during the trip back to her Bryn Mawr house, but once inside, she fell apart. "Aunt Cecily is right," she said, collapsing into a living-room chair. "Jonathan meant to leave me all along and he didn't have the courage to tell me to my face."

Kelly was beside her in an instant. "Victoria, that's crazy. If he wanted to leave you he would never do it in such a despicable way. Not Jonathan."

"But what if it is him on that tape?"

"It still doesn't prove he left you. Why would he do that?" She took Victoria's hands in hers. They were cold. "You and Phoebe are all he lives for."

Victoria snatched her hands away. "Don't forget Magdalena," she said bitterly.

Kelly didn't know what to say to that. She had run out of excuses for Jonathan and was relieved when the phone on the little console by the window rang.

Victoria sprang out of her chair to answer it. "Hello?" she said breathlessly.

Almost immediately the blood drained from her face. She gripped the phone with both hands. *"Jonathan?"*

"Heggan weaves together several suspense plots into a satisfying whole...."
          —*Publishers Weekly* on *Trust No One*

CHRISTIANE HEGGAN

BLIND FAITH

MIRA

ISBN 1-55166-783-5

BLIND FAITH

MIRA and the Star Colophon are trademarks used under license and registered
in Australia, New Zealand, Philippines, United States Patent and Trademark
Office and in other countries.

Visit us at www.mirabooks.com

Printed in U.S.A.

To Sandi and Dennis,
friends, legal advisors
and fabulous storytellers.

Printed in U.S.A.

One

"Hey, hey, hey!" Kelly Robolo spun the wheel of her bright blue VW Beetle and blasted her horn as a SEPTA bus pulled from the curb and unceremoniously cut in front of her, forcing her to slam on her brakes.

Without so much as a glance in her direction, the driver pushed farther into the congested avenue, bringing the Monday-evening rush-hour traffic on Philadelphia's busy Broad Street to a standstill. Incensed, Kelly hit her horn again. "Jerk!" she yelled, even though she knew the driver couldn't hear her. "I pay your salary, you know."

As the bus drove off and the light turned red, Kelly fell back against her seat and let out a sigh of frustration. She should have known better than to be caught in Center City in the middle of rush hour. But as usual, Dr. Brady had run late and though Kelly had considered rescheduling, she had changed her mind and patiently waited her turn. The sooner the doctor gave her a clean bill of health, the sooner she could go back to work. That he had ordered her to stay

home for another two weeks had probably contributed
to her foul mood.

With nothing else to do but wait for the light to
change, Kelly loosened her grip on the steering wheel
and began to relax. In spite of the noisy traffic jams,
the rude SEPTA drivers and the aggravations Philadelphians were subjected to on a daily basis, Kelly
loved this city. She loved its rich heritage, the un-
sinkable spirit of its people, the diversity of its neighborhoods. She even liked the weather, especially at
this time of year, when the skies were overcast and
the air held a hint of snow.

For a while after her brush with death a few weeks
ago, she had thought of leaving Philadelphia and
starting fresh somewhere else—New York perhaps, or
Chicago. Both had excellent newspapers and with her
track record as a tough, thorough investigative reporter, finding a job wouldn't have been too difficult.

In the end she hadn't been able to do it. She had
roots here, a mother, friends, and a job she loved,
even if it had almost cost her her life.

The sudden feeling that she was being watched
made her glance out her side window. A patrol car
had pulled up alongside the VW. In the front seat,
two uniformed officers stared at her openly, their expression a mixture of scorn and resentment. Five
weeks ago, they would have waved, for Kelly Robolo
was a familiar sight at police headquarters. After thir-
teen years with the *Philadelphia Globe*, she had

earned the respect, and even the admiration, of some of Philadelphia's toughest cops.

All that had changed.

As the light turned green again, the squad car didn't drive off, but swung behind the VW. They were tailing her, she realized, probably waiting for an opportunity to give her another ticket she didn't deserve. In the last two weeks alone, she had collected three of those suckers—one for supposedly running a red light, another for speeding in a thirty-five-mile-per-hour zone and a third for failing to make a complete stop at a stop sign. No matter how vehemently she had argued the bogus charges, the officers had ignored her protests and told her she was free to contest the tickets in court.

There had been other incidents, this time closer to home—a torn mailbox outside her town house, the word *bitch* spray-painted on her front door in big, blood-red letters and two slashed tires on her car. She couldn't prove the harassment was the work of the Philadelphia police department, but who else hated her enough to be so vindictive?

She had mentioned the incidents to only one person—her best friend, Victoria Bowman. Not one to take unnecessary risks, Victoria had begged her to file a complaint with the police commissioner, whom Kelly knew well. Kelly had ignored the advice. She didn't want to compound the problem, or appear wimpy, by complaining to the top man. Besides, after investigating some of the toughest cases in the Delaware Valley for the past six years, she was used to threats, real and implied, and wasn't easily rattled by them.

"They'll get tired of the game," Kelly had told Victoria.

Her cell phone rang just as she turned onto Seventeenth Street. After a quick glance in the rearview mirror, she took the phone from her bag without taking her eyes off the road. "Hi, Ma."

She heard the chuckle at the other end of the line. "One of these days," Connie Robolo replied, "it won't be me, but some committee calling to say you won another Pulitzer. What will you say then?"

Kelly smiled. "It's always you, Ma. You're as predictable as the sunrise."

"I wouldn't have to be if you had called me right after your doctor's appointment like you were supposed to." Then, not giving Kelly a chance to reply, she added, "So, what did Dr. Brady say? Are you all right? Is the wound healing properly? Did he agree with me that hanging wallpaper five weeks after being shot is no way to recuperate? Or did you conveniently leave out that little detail?"

Kelly was used to the third-degree questioning. Even though she was two months away from her thirty-sixth birthday and the oldest of two children, her mother hovered over her as if she were still a little kid.

"Those are the hazards of being born to an Italian family," her grandmother had told her once. "Like it

or not, your life will never be completely your own."
Truer words had never been spoken.

Catching something from the corner of her eye, she glanced into the rearview mirror in time to see the patrol car, its lights blazing, turn west on Spruce Street. She heaved a sigh of relief, grateful for whatever emergency had taken the tailing officers away. "I told him everything you instructed me to tell him, Ma," Kelly replied.

"Stop being such a smart mouth," Connie said sternly, "and answer the question."

"Dr. Brady gave me an almost perfect bill of health."

"What do you mean almost? What's wrong with you?"

"Nothing, but he won't let me go back to work for two more weeks."

Connie Robolo let out a disapproving hmmph. "If I had my way, you wouldn't be going back to the *Globe* at all. Ever."

Here it comes, Kelly thought. The beginning of the why-don't-you-find-a-safer-job sermon. Kelly had heard it dozens of times before but never more so than since the shooting. Ignoring the comment, tempting though it was, would be pointless. "I know, Ma. You made that perfectly clear in the hospital."

"But are you listening?" Then, because a day wouldn't be complete without Connie making her point, she added, "I don't see why you can't find a nice safe job somewhere. A girl with your brains and your education should have no trouble at all. You could do anything you want."

"I *am* doing what I want, Ma. Of course," she teased, "I could always join the circus and fly a trapeze like Uncle Stefano."

"My daughter, the comedian." In the background, a familiar voice yelled something. "You heard that, Kelly?" Connie asked, talking above the clang of pots and pans. "Benny is making your favorite today—swordfish Calabrese. He says you should come for dinner."

For a moment, Kelly was tempted. She loved spending time at San Remo, the South Philly Italian restaurant the Robolos had owned for three generations. Her mother ran it alone now, with Benny, her longtime and devoted sous-chef. Sometimes, when the restaurant was very busy, Kelly would pitch in and wait tables, something she had done throughout high school. She knew how much her mother appreciated the help, especially now that her husband of thirty-seven years had passed away.

"Can I take a rain check, Ma? I have a pile of laundry to do tonight."

"Bring the laundry here. I'll do it."

Kelly laughed. Her mother never gave up. "Save me some swordfish," she said as she reached her street. "I'll stop by tomorrow."

"Wait a minute—"

"Got to go, Ma. I'm home. Love you." She dropped the phone back into her bag and concentrated on finding a parking space which, at this time of night, was just as frustrating as dealing with the traffic.

After circling the block twice and almost losing a tire to a mammoth pothole on Pine, Kelly finally spotted a space on Second Street and slid into it in the nick of time. Her tote bag slung over her shoulder, she locked the Beetle and headed for Delancey, a quiet, narrow cobblestone street in the heart of Philadelphia's historical district.

Kelly had bought the modest two-story Federal-style home two years ago, using every penny she could scrape together for the down payment and financing the rest. With the exception of a few thirty-somethings, her neighbors were older and all longtime residents. She had met most of them at a block party shortly after she moved in. She felt good here, safe—until the vandalism had started.

Trying to stay upbeat, she reminded herself that except for that patrol car following her earlier, not much had happened in the last few days, not even a ticket. Maybe her tormentors had grown tired of the game after all.

But before that thought had even sunk in, her town house came into view and she stopped dead in her tracks.

The miniature evergreen her mother had given her as a housewarming present had been pulled out by the roots and lay limply across the rim of the terra-cotta pot outside her front door.

"Damn." Kelly ran the short distance to her front porch and stared helplessly at the torn roots and mangled branches. Tears pricked her eyes. Who would do something so cruel? Who would take a beautiful living thing and destroy it without a second thought?

From her crouched position, Kelly let her gaze sweep over the deserted street. In the mood she was in, she wished the bastard would show himself. But he was too much of a coward to do that. He was probably hiding in the shadows, watching her, enjoying her reaction.

"Whoever you are," she muttered between clenched teeth, "don't let me catch you."

The evergreen in one hand, her keys in the other, Kelly let herself in and flipped on the foyer light. For once, the mess that had been so intrusive these past few months of renovation—ladders, cans of paint and white cloths spread out everywhere—was instantly reassuring, even soothing. With a small sigh, she shut the door with the heel of her boot and gave a quick click of the dead bolt before heading for the back of the house.

As in all town houses of that period, a hallway led to the living area and a small garden that was filled with impatiens and geraniums in the summer and yellow mums in the fall. On the other side of a breakfast counter was a galley kitchen she used mostly to make coffee and reheat the food her mother brought her.

The living room, with its honey-colored walls and polished hardwood floor, was her sanctuary. She had furnished it with a chintz sofa and chairs, and oak tables crowded with old family photographs. Facing the seating area was a brick fireplace flanked by floor-to-ceiling bookcases. A television set and an antique rug matted down by time and traffic completed the decor.

She didn't realize she still held the tree until she sank onto the sofa and looked down. Tears welled up again and this time she didn't try to stop them. It was silly to cry, she knew. It was only a tree, a dwarf tree at that, but dammit, it was hers and someone had killed it. Letting go of the evergreen, she covered her face with her hands and wept hopelessly.

Maybe her mother was right, she thought, indulging in a rare moment of self-pity. Maybe this job had finally become too much for her. But what else could she do? From the moment she had been elected editor of her college paper, she had known that investigative reporting was her true passion. She loved chasing a story, searching for clues, putting them all together. Her gutsy, well-researched articles had eventually brought her to the attention of the editor of the *Philadelphia Globe,* Lou Ventura, a crusty newspaperman with a nose for a story and a heart of gold.

Those first few years at the *Globe* had been the most exhilarating of her young life. She had honed her craft the way all rookie reporters did, by covering city news, attending boring council meetings and rushing in the middle of the night to cover a fire.

The hard work had paid off. Four years later, when

one of the *Globe*'s two investigative reporters had retired, Lou had told Kelly the job was hers—if she wanted it. Too happy to even talk, she had stood there with her mouth open while Lou chuckled.

"I won't let you down," she had blurted out once she could talk. "You'll see. I'll be the best investigative reporter you've ever had."

She had kept her word, working night and day, taking any kind of assignment that was handed to her, digging deep into her stories and even making a pest of herself at times. Hard work didn't scare her, nor the risks she took occasionally. She loved her job, and the Pulitzer had been icing on the cake.

Then, five weeks ago, her life had been dramatically altered. While attending her weekly martial arts lesson in Chinatown, Randy Chen, who owned the laundry next door, had interrupted her session with Dr. Ho. In an obvious state of panic, Randy Chen had asked to talk to the instructor in private.

Because Kelly had heard earlier rumors that a protection racket was terrorizing the neighborhood, she had eavesdropped on their conversation, hoping to learn who was behind the extortion scheme. Fortunately, after ten years of studying martial arts with Dr. Ho, her knowledge of the Chinese language, though basic, was good enough for her to understand that someone was waiting at a warehouse on Tenth Street.

"You have to pay, Grandmaster," Randy Chen had

told Dr. Ho in an urgent whisper. "If you don't they will kill you."

Dr. Ho's quick, angry reply had caused Randy to wring his hands in anguish. He had reminded the older man of what "they" would do, not only to the local merchants, but to their wives and children as well.

To Randy's great relief, Dr. Ho had finally agreed to pay. Muttering under his breath, the old man had walked over to a safe, retrieved a bundle of money and stuffed it into a paper bag.

Kelly was stunned. When she had first heard that someone was squeezing money out of Chinatown merchants, she had questioned Dr. Ho, hoping that the warm, trusting relationship they had enjoyed all these years would incite him to confide in her. Dr. Ho had remained stubbornly silent, claiming not to know what she was talking about.

No wonder he hadn't wanted to talk. He was afraid of what the racketeers would do to him and the rest of the neighborhood. Seeing a chance to help her old friend, Kelly had followed Randy Chen to the warehouse where the Chinese New Year Committee stored their floats every year. The cavernous room had been dimly lit and thick with the smell of sandalwood, a fragrance used to repel moths.

Moving silently, Kelly wove her way around dragon heads, beaded costumes and feathered head-dresses. But when she reached the far corner of the room, she stopped, frozen in shock. Under a single lightbulb, three men stood waiting. Two were unknown to her, but the third was not. Matt Kolvic was a detective with the Philadelphia Police Department.

With hands that shook, Kelly took her cell phone out of her bag and dialed police headquarters, not to call for help, but to talk to homicide detective Nick McBride, with whom she often worked. As Matt Kolvic's best friend, Nick would know what to do. In her haste to make the call, however, Kelly tripped against a float and dropped her phone.

The three men spun around at the same time, guns drawn. The last thing Kelly remembered after that was the intense pain as one of the bullets hit her in the chest, and the fading smell of sandalwood.

She had hung between life and death for twenty-four hours. The doctor who had operated on her hadn't been very optimistic.

"The bullet hit a pulmonary vein and she's lost a lot of blood," Dr. Brady had explained to her family. "Her vital signs are down and her heartbeat erratic. The next twenty-four hours will be critical."

By the second day she was out of danger, and by the third she was well enough to have visitors and give a statement to the police. She was told that a patrol car had been cruising the area when they heard the shots. The two men she hadn't recognized were part of an organized ring the police had been trying to break for months. The third one, Detective Matt Kolvic, had been doing undercover work for the department.

He had been killed in the crossfire.

The story had dominated the headlines for days, and while Kelly's editor had praised her openly for her courage, the Philadelphia Police Department hadn't felt the same way. In a press conference Kelly had watched from her hospital bed, the police commissioner had expressed his anger with the press, stating that because of an overzealous reporter, a good cop was dead.

The phone rang, putting an end to Kelly's thoughts. In no mood to talk, she kept her head pressed against the sofa cushion and ignored it.

At the fourth ring, the answering machine came on. Seconds after that, her friend Victoria's distraught voice filled the room. "Kelly, if you're there, please pick up. It's Jonathan. He...he's missing."

Kelly pounced on the phone. "I'm here. What do you mean missing?"

"He was supposed to meet me at LaFarge dance studio for Phoebe's dance recital this evening and he never showed up."

Knowing how forgetful Victoria's husband could be when he was working, Kelly tried to sound reassuring. "He must have been detained at the office. You know how he is when he gets busy—"

"He's not at the office!" Victoria's voice had turned shrill. "He left for Miami this morning and never came back!"

The panic in Victoria's voice was enough to snap Kelly to attention. Her own problems momentarily forgotten, she glanced at her watch. "Where are you?"

"At the shop."

"Stay there. I'll be right over."

Two

Kelly parked the VW in a small lot on Manning
Street, took the ticket from the attendant and walked
briskly toward Rittenhouse Square. Named after the
president of the American Philosophical Society and
designed more than a hundred years ago, the famous
square at Eighteenth and Walnut had long been one
of the city's swankiest addresses. Luxury condomin-
iums, hotels and elegant boutiques surrounded a small
park, creating an exclusive enclave that attracted
thousands of sight-seers every year.

Victoria's antiques shop, aptly named All My Yesterdays, was on the west side of the square, nestled
between a branch of the Philadelphia library and a tea
salon. Although her wealthy aunt, Cecily Sanders,
owned the shop, it was Victoria's exquisite taste and
knowledge of art that had made All My Yesterdays
the success it was today. The small space was
crammed with unique, carefully chosen items, from
antique clocks to delicate stemware and accessories
Victoria brought back from all over the world.

Victoria sat at her desk, her hands clasped in front
of her mouth, her eyes closed. Her long blond hair

was coiled into an elegant knot at the back of her neck, a style that emphasized her great bone structure. She wore a cranberry pantsuit that accentuated her small frame and a white blouse with a hint of lace at the collar. Other than a modest diamond engagement ring, she wore no jewelry.

At the tinkling sound of the bell, Victoria looked up, her beautiful green eyes heavy with worry. "Oh, Kelly." She sprang from her chair and waited for Kelly to close the door before coming forward to give her a warm hug. "I'm so glad you're here."

"Jonathan hasn't called?"

"No." Her friend's voice was tight and controlled and Kelly knew she was making a supreme effort to stay calm.

Taking Victoria's cold hand in hers, Kelly drew her toward the twin Queen Anne chairs that faced the desk. "All right," she said when both had sat down. "First things first. What was Jonathan doing in Miami?"

"I don't know. And neither does Syd."

Syd Webber was the owner of the Chenonceau Hotel and Casino in Atlantic City, where Jonathan was a vice president. A controversial man with a somewhat shady past, Syd had been the major reason Victoria's aunt had been so against her niece marrying Jonathan.

"You talked to Syd?"

"Yes. He's as puzzled as I am. He said that Jonathan called in sick this morning and he assumed he was home.''

Calling in sick didn't sound like Jonathan at all. He practically had to be at death's door before he missed a day's work. "How do you know he went to Miami?"

"He called me from his cell phone this morning. At least I assumed it was his cell phone because it kept cutting out on him. He said that Syd was sending him to Miami on business and he'd be back that same afternoon."

"Did he say anything about missing Phoebe's dance recital?"

"We were disconnected before we could even discuss it. I tried to call him back to remind him, but he must have been in a dead zone because I couldn't reach him."

"Did you keep trying?"

"Every five minutes for the last two and a half hours."

Victoria's voice broke and she pressed her fists against her mouth as if to keep from crying. A superb businesswoman with a reputation for remaining cool under the heat of tough bidding, Victoria was worthless in a family crisis.

"What airline does he normally use?" Kelly asked, reaching for her phone.

"American and I've already called them. They confirmed that Jonathan boarded Flight 2399 to Miami at 9:02 this morning. He was scheduled to return on the 2:58 p.m. flight, but never showed up.''

''Did you verify the ticket purchase through his credit card?''

''He paid cash.''

Kelly was silent for a moment, trying to understand what she had just heard. No one paid cash for an airline ticket anymore—unless they had something to hide. But that wasn't the case with Jonathan, since he had told Victoria about the trip. ''Does he know anyone in Miami?'' She would have known if he did, but Kelly asked the question anyway.

''Not a soul. We've only been to Florida once, when we took Phoebe to Walt Disney World and that was Orlando, not Miami.''

''Are you sure Jonathan doesn't have a relative there, a business acquaintance, an army buddy?''

''No one that I know of. Jonathan's only family consists of an elderly uncle who lives in San Diego and some distant cousins we haven't heard from since our wedding.'' On her lap, Victoria's hands clasped even tighter. ''I keep thinking of the crime wave in Miami in recent weeks and I imagine Jonathan lying in the street, the victim of a mugging or carjacking.'' She closed her eyes. ''Or worse.''

Kelly shook her head. ''Someone would have found him and reported the incident to the police. In fact...'' She flipped her cell phone open and pulled out the short antenna.

''Who are you calling?'' Victoria asked.

"The Miami police. They're the only ones who can put your fears to rest." She dialed the long-distance operator, asked for the number of Miami police headquarters and wrote down the information on a pad she had taken from her bag. "What was Jonathan wearing?" she asked as she dialed again.

Victoria spoke without hesitation. "A navy pin-striped suit, a white shirt, a red and navy-blue tie in a geometric design and black wingtips."

An officer named Barry Brown took Kelly's call. After identifying herself, she gave him what little information she had, along with a description of Jonathan. She also gave him her cell phone number.

"All right, ma'am,' the officer said. "I'll check and see what we come up with."

"Now," Kelly said, turning to face Victoria. "Let's try to figure out what could have happened while we wait. Is everything all right between you and Jonathan? Did you have an argument?"

"No."

"Did he seem different in any way lately? Preoccupied, perhaps?"

Victoria pressed a rolled-up handkerchief to one eye. "Well…now that you mention it, he did seem a little…moody the last few days."

"Did you ask him what was wrong?"

"No." She looked away, as if feeling guilty. "My mind was on that auction I had to attend this morning. I'm afraid I wasn't paying much attention to anything else."

"Did he talk about something in particular? A problem at work?"

"No." Victoria stood up and walked over to her desk where she started to straighten a stack of catalogs that didn't need straightening. "It was a morning like all the others, or so I thought at the time. We had breakfast and we talked about the week ahead. I reminded him of the recital and how much Phoebe was looking forward to it. He said he'd meet me at the studio at six this evening. Then he kissed me goodbye and left."

"What time was that?"

"A little after seven." She turned to face Kelly. "At eight-thirty he called to tell me he was on his way to Miami."

"Did he call from the car? Or from the airport?"

"The airport. The connection was terrible. There was a lot of static and I could barely hear him."

The connection shouldn't have been that bad. Not from the airport.

Her arms folded across her chest, Victoria walked over to the window and gazed at the lit-up square. "Earlier you asked me if anything out of the ordinary had happened."

Kelly was instantly alert. "Yes?"

"Something did, though I'm not sure it has anything to do with Jonathan."

"Tell me anyway."

Turning around, Victoria let her gaze drift toward a wall-mounted glass cabinet where a collection of antique Chinese snuff bottles were displayed. They ranged from carved and hollowed hard stone to molded and inscribed coconut shells. All were collector's items and very expensive. "One of my bottles is missing."

Kelly, who knew nothing about Oriental art except what she had learned from Victoria over the years, followed her friend's gaze. "Which one?"

"The blue enamel. It was part of the Chinese Whisper collection. It was gone when I opened the shop this morning."

"Are you sure you didn't misplace it?" The question was unnecessary. Victoria was as well organized as Jonathan was reliable, and misplacing an object of such value was simply unthinkable.

"I'm sure."

"Could a customer have taken it?"

"That's possible but unlikely. I rarely leave the showroom when someone is in the shop. In fact, most of the time I'm by their side, helping them select something or answering their questions. Friday was busy, though. And I did have to go in the back a couple of times." She shook her head. "I can't imagine any of the people who patronize my shop stealing from me."

"Did you report the theft to the police? Or the insurance company?"

"No. I wanted a chance to talk to my aunt first." She continued to gaze at the cabinet. "Now I don't know what to do."

Kelly heard the uncertainty in her voice. "You think Jonathan took it?"

"No!" Victoria ran a weary hand along her smooth hair. "I don't know what to think anymore, Kel. I'm so confused." She pressed her index fingers against her temples. "I don't give a damn about the snuff bottle. I just want my husband to come home."

Kelly pushed the up sleeve of her leather jacket to check her watch. Nine o'clock. "I tell you what. It could be a while until we hear from Officer Brown. What do you say we close the shop and go home? We'll search through Jonathan's clothes once we get there. He may have left a clue about the Miami trip."

Victoria was already reaching for the phone. "Give me a minute to make sure Lucy put Phoebe to bed. I don't want to have to explain to my little girl why her daddy not only missed her recital but isn't home."

Three

The Bowmans lived in Bryn Mawr, a pleasant, upper-class neighborhood that was less than a twenty-minute drive from downtown Philadelphia.

Shortly after Jonathan was promoted to vice president, Victoria had suggested moving out of their little Cape Cod in Haverford, and buying a house in New Jersey so Jonathan wouldn't have such a long daily commute. Knowing how much his wife enjoyed being close to her aunt and uncle, however, Jonathan had taken her to see the Bryn Mawr house instead, knowing she would fall in love with it.

Such generous gestures on Jonathan's part were commonplace. He loved to shower Victoria with attention, and whenever possible, with presents. The gifts, expensive at times, were his way of showing not only Victoria but her aunt as well that he was quite capable of giving his wife the kind of lifestyle she had enjoyed all her life. To Victoria, those attestations were unnecessary, but she understood why Jonathan did what he did and she loved him for it.

The baby-sitter, an attractive teenager with waist-long brown hair, sat in the living room with the tele-

vision on when Kelly and Victoria arrived. As per
Victoria's instructions, Lucy had already put Phoebe
to bed. Doing her best not to show her anxieties, Victoria paid her, escorted her to the door and waited
until the high-school senior had reached her front
door, two houses down, before going back inside.

"I'll go and check on Phoebe," she said, rubbing
her arms to ward off the night chill.

"I'll come with you."

At the sight of her little goddaughter sleeping
peacefully, her arms wrapped around her redheaded
Cabbage Patch doll, Kelly felt the same wave of affection she always did when she saw Phoebe. With
her long, lustrous blond hair, her flawless complexion
and her heart-shaped mouth, the five-year old was a
tiny replica of her mother. Only her eyes, a light hazel
like her father's, identified her as a Bowman.

After she and Victoria had kissed Phoebe on the
forehead, both tiptoed out and walked soundlessly to
the master bedroom at the end of the hall. They
started searching Jonathan's closet, which was as neat
and orderly as the person himself. All his suit pockets
were empty and Kelly and Victoria soon turned their
attention to his bedside table. The single drawer was
filled with neatly stacked parking receipts, credit card
charges, little reminders hastily jotted down on scraps
of paper and an E-Z pass voucher from the Delaware
Port Authority.

After a half hour of fruitless searching, Kelly shook
her head and both women headed back downstairs. In

the cozy yellow kitchen, Victoria immediately busied herself with the mundane task of preparing coffee.

"Would you like me to do that?" Kelly offered

Victoria shook her head. "I need something to do." With movements that were stiff and controlled she opened the refrigerator, took out a small white bag and spooned some of the contents into the basket of the coffeemaker. Moments later, the carafe began filling and Victoria came to sit at the round maple table across from Kelly.

"How long do you think it will be until we hear from that officer?"

"It's hard to say. Miami is a big city. They need time to check with the hospitals, and the jails." Kelly didn't say the morgue, but the look in Victoria's eyes told her that she, too, had thought of it.

A lazy Susan made of the same dark maple as the table stood in the center. Almost absentmindedly, Victoria began to spin it. "This is so unlike Jonathan." Her gaze followed the spinning tray. "He doesn't take one step out of his office without letting me know exactly where he'll be. And he's never out of touch."

That was true. Jonathan was one of the most reliable men Kelly knew. He was also well aware of Victoria's worrying nature and how quickly her anxieties could turn into raw panic. He would never do anything to aggravate that condition.

The possibility that he was having an affair and had somehow lost track of time was too absurd to consider. Jonathan and Victoria adored each other and showed it in every possible way.

As though aware of the direction Kelly's thoughts had taken, Victoria searched her face. "You've known him almost as long as I have. Do you think he's doing this intentionally? Because he's angry about something?"

"The thought crossed my mind," Kelly admitted. "That's why I asked if you'd had an argument. But even if you had, I can't imagine Jonathan being so spiteful. It's not his nature."

As the red light on the coffeemaker came on, Victoria stood up and went to fill two mugs before sitting down again. Kelly sipped, half listening for the sound of Jonathan's key in the front door, his cheerful voice as he called out his wife's name. But the house remained silent, with only the gentle bong of the grandfather clock in the living room breaking the silence every fifteen minutes.

During the next few hours, which passed like years, Kelly called Officer Brown two more times, but he had nothing to report. They were still checking.

At 4:00 a.m., Kelly's cell phone rang. This time it was a Detective Quinn of the Miami police. At the official tone of his voice, Kelly's earlier confidence deserted her. "Did you find Jonathan?" she asked.

"May I speak to Mrs. Bowman, please."

Kelly handed the phone to Victoria. "Detective Quinn of the Miami police. He wants to speak with you."

Her face ashen, her eyes full of fear, Victoria only shook her head.

"I'm Kelly Robolo, Victoria Bowman's best friend, Detective," Kelly said quickly. "I'm afraid she's in no condition to talk to you right now. Can you tell me what you found out?"

The detective hesitated but only for a moment. "Very well. At 1:52 this morning, a bomb exploded at the Encantado, a motel just off I-95." He paused. "Mr. Bowman's name was in the logbook, next to his check-in time—11:45 a.m. on Monday."

As Kelly realized the terrible implication, her hand went to her throat. "Is Jonathan hurt?"

"All the injured have been accounted for, but your friend's husband was not one of them." The detective cleared his throat. "The bomb, however, was set in room 116—Mr. Bowman's room—"

"Oh my God!" Kelly gave herself a mental kick for not controlling her reaction. Across the table, Victoria looked as though she was about to faint.

"The explosion destroyed half the building," Detective Quinn went on, "scattering debris over a two-hundred-foot radius. It's a miracle more people weren't killed."

"Are you saying that...Jonathan was killed?"

At those words, Victoria let out a moan and covered her face with her hands. Moving swiftly, Kelly walked around the table, grasped her friend's hand and held it.

"We can't be sure just yet—" the detective said in reply to the question.

"Did you recover a body?"

"Only parts of a body, badly burned and mixed with debris from several adjoining rooms. It could be days until we make a positive ID."

"You said Jonathan's name was in a logbook. Did he fill out a proper registration form? With his home address, phone number and so forth?"

"The Encantado is known as a drug drop, Miss Robolo, a place where drug dealers come to do business. All the management requires from its customers is a name—any name—to put down in the book, and the price of the room, in advance and in cash."

"You must know who checked him in."

"I do. Unfortunately, the desk clerk is in the hospital with third-degree burns and a fifty-fifty chance of making it. Until he's off the critical list, I can't talk to him." He cleared his throat. "Does Mr. Bowman come to Miami often?"

"Never. Why?"

"Because the major part of the Encantado's trade is from out-of-state visitors who come to Miami to buy drugs from a drug cartel we've been trying to apprehend for months."

Kelly let out a short laugh. "And you think that's why Jonathan was there? To buy drugs?"

"I have to investigate every possibility, Miss Robolo, especially since someone seems to have wanted him dead."

"But that's crazy!" Kelly cried, momentarily forgetting that Phoebe was upstairs sleeping. "Jonathan is a family man, a devoted husband and father. He would never associate himself, much less be involved with, drug dealers."

"I hope you're right, Miss Robolo. For his sake. And his family's."

He didn't believe her, Kelly realized with a mild jolt. In his eyes Jonathan was already guilty or dead—or both. "Is there anyone who can identify Jonathan?" she asked, refusing to accept Quinn's version of this insane story. "A maid? Or a maintenance man?"

"The motel employs three full-time maids, one maintenance man and one coffee-shop attendant. All make it a practice to mind their own business, which means they don't see who comes in or out. Or so they claim. We've already had three homicides at the Encantado over the last six weeks, all victims of drive-by shootings. And we don't have a single eyewitness."

"Maybe if I talked to them—"

Detective Quinn laughed. "Look, Miss Robolo. I don't know how they do things in Philadelphia, but down here, we keep material witnesses in a murder case away from reporters."

At the risk of annoying him even further, Kelly made one more attempt to gain some ground. "I've had experience questioning reluctant witnesses, Detective."

"So has the local press who's beating down my door right now. Believe me, the last thing I need is an out-of-town reporter complicating my investigation."

"I told you I'm not acting as a reporter."

"You're a close friend of the family, yes, I know. My witnesses are still off-limits, no matter what hat you're wearing. Tell Mrs. Bowman that as soon as I have something to report, she'll be the first to know. You want more information, you can contact the Philadelphia police, which I'll keep fully informed. Good day, Miss Robolo."

Kelly had no time to reply. He had hung up.

"What did he say?" Victoria asked as Kelly pushed the End button with an angry little jab. "Is Jonathan all right? Is he hurt?" Her fingernails dug in Kelly's arm as she finally willed herself to ask the dreaded question, "Is he dead?"

"They don't know." Her eyes gritty from lack of sleep, Kelly repeated what Detective Quinn had told her, word for word.

"How can he possibly think Jonathan is involved with drug traffickers?" Victoria asked, outraged. "He loathes drugs."

"The Encantado is a motel where drug dealers come to do business," Kelly explained. "Anyone staying there would be under suspicion. I'm sure Quinn put each guest through a long, merciless interrogation."

The anger in Victoria's voice slowly ebbed and

worry returned. "What was Jonathan doing in a place like that, Kelly? Whenever he travels, it's always first-class." When Kelly didn't answer, she frowned. "What? Why are you looking at me like that? You don't believe that garbage Detective Quinn fed you, do you? You can't possibly believe that Jonathan went to Miami to buy drugs."

"No," Kelly replied, carefully choosing her words. "I don't believe it, but we have to be fair and look at Quinn's side. At the moment all evidence *seems* to point to the possibility that Jonathan was staying at the Encantado. If he was, we need to know why, and if he was set up, we need to know by whom."

Victoria closed her eyes. She looked exhausted. "I'm sorry. I shouldn't have snapped at you."

Kelly smiled. "Now we're even, for all the times I've snapped at you."

Instead of returning the smile, Victoria watched her intently. "Kelly, I want you to find Jonathan."

Kelly fell back against her chair. "Oh, Victoria, I can't."

"Why?"

"I'm the wrong person for the job. I'm too close."

"That's why it has to be you," Victoria said earnestly. "You know Jonathan and you've looked for missing persons before. Remember the Bonner kidnapping?"

Did she remember? It had taken Kelly three months to locate the trail of the eighteen-year-old Philadelphia debutante. The FBI, who was even less patient than Quinn when it came to reporters, had come down hard on Kelly. During a particularly unpleasant confrontation, they had even arrested her, claiming she was sabotaging their investigation. Lou had bailed her out within an hour, but she had learned to stay out of the feds' way.

"Please, Kel," Victoria pleaded as tears threatened to erupt again. "Help me."

Kelly's own eyes began filling up. She and Victoria had been friends since their first year at the University of Pennsylvania. Throughout the years they had been there for each other, dropping whatever they were doing to fly to the rescue of the one in need. How could Kelly turn her back on her friend now, in the worst moment of her life?

"Kel?"

Kelly felt a tug in her chest and nodded. "Yes, of course, I'll...do what I can."

"Thank you." Victoria smiled, a sad, tentative smile that was filled with uncertainty. Then, rising again, she walked over to the phone. "I have to call my aunt and uncle and tell them what happened before they hear it from the police, or worse, from the newspapers."

Four

Ward and Cecily Sanders arrived twenty minutes later, looking as elegant in their casual clothes as if they had come from one of the many social functions they attended throughout the year.

A reporter had once dubbed them Philadelphia's charmed couple, a label they wore with grace. Cecily's blond, sophisticated looks were the perfect foil for Ward's tall stature and patrician features. Both were successful in their own right. As CEO and president of one of the nation's largest charitable trusts, Cecily wielded a tremendous amount of clout not only in the Philadelphia community, which was certainly indebted to her, but with the Washington elite as well.

More low-key than his flamboyant wife, Ward was nonetheless a successful businessman who had managed to keep the small bank founded by his grandfather in the early 1920s not only private but thriving. In a world of mergers and hostile takeovers, that task hadn't been easy. The only one of the Sanders children to show an interest in banking, he was also the least appreciated by Monroe Sanders, his formidable, irascible father.

Victoria adored her aunt and uncle, with good reason. When her parents died in a Chesapeake Bay boating accident twenty-eight years ago, the couple had opened their arms to the grieving child and raised her as if she were their own.

Becoming a father hadn't been difficult for Ward, who came from a large family and had always longed for a child. Cecily, on the other hand, had been filled with doubts and anxieties at the thought of raising her sister's eight-year-old daughter. Childless by choice, she had worried that she wouldn't be able to meet the demands of her high-powered job as vice president of the Norton Charitable Trust and be a devoted mother at the same time.

She had surprised everyone, including herself. Within a few weeks, she had assumed the role so perfectly and effortlessly that Ward had fondly nicknamed her June Cleaver, after the ultimate TV mom of the fifties.

Six years ago, impressed by Victoria's extensive knowledge of art, Cecily had bought the antiques shop on Rittenhouse Square and put her niece in charge, a decision neither had ever regretted.

The only clash between the two women had occurred when Victoria had announced she was in love with Jonathan Bowman, then the general manager of the Chenonceau Hotel and Casino in Atlantic City, and that she intended to marry him.

Ward, practical to a fault, had immediately investigated Jonathan's background. When the Wilmington, Delaware, native turned out to be a decent, hard-working young man who was very much in love with Victoria, Ward had given his unconditional blessings.

Not Cecily. Though she herself had come from modest beginnings, she had lofty ambitions for her beautiful niece and those ambitions did not include marrying a man whose boss was suspected of having ties to the mob.

It had taken Ward weeks to convince his wife not only that the charges against Syd Webber had been dropped for insufficient evidence, but that Jonathan's job as a casino executive in no way reflected on his integrity or his ability to make Victoria happy.

Watching Cecily now, as Victoria told her about Jonathan's disappearance, Kelly was forced to admit that in spite of Cecily's occasional shortsightedness, her only goal had always been to make Victoria happy.

When Victoria was finished, Ward turned to Kelly. His attractive features were tight with concern and confusion. "Kelly, is that true? You don't believe Jonathan is dead?"

Kelly shook her head. "I'd rather say that I find it difficult to believe. The whole thing is just too bizarre."

"But what about the burned body in room 116?" Cecily asked.

Kelly shrugged. "It could be anyone's—maybe even a plant."

"So you do suspect some kind of foul play?" Ward asked.

"Frankly, Ward, I don't know what to think at this time. According to Detective Quinn, most people who stay at the Encantado don't use their real names. The fact that Jonathan did, not only proves to me that he wasn't there to buy drugs, but that he may have been set up."

"For what reason?"

"I don't know. Yet."

Cecily let out an impatient sigh. "Finding out if Jonathan was involved in drug trafficking could take a long time. The news could also leak to the press, which is why I intend to talk to Detective Quinn myself, right away. Kelly, you have his number?"

"No, Aunt Cecily." Victoria's voice was just as firm. If there was one thing she had learned over the years, it was to stand up to her strong-willed aunt. "I don't want you to do anything that will antagonize Detective Quinn. We're going to need him."

"But darling, we have to protect ourselves."

"That's the last of my worries. My first priority is to find Jonathan."

"What about Phoebe? Shouldn't *she* be your first priority? Can you imagine what the publicity will do to her?"

"Don't worry about Phoebe," Victoria said. "I'll take care of her."

Cecily turned to her husband. "Ward, say something."

Ward gave a helpless shrug. "What do you want me to say? I don't relish dealing with the press any more than you do. But this isn't about us. It's about Jonathan. Victoria is right. Finding him should be our number-one priority."

Cecily was too smart not to know when she was outnumbered. She gave a short nod and turned to Victoria. "All right, darling. What do you want me to do?"

"Stand by me," Victoria said simply. "And above all, keep an open mind about Jonathan."

That last request seemed to take Cecily by surprise. "Don't I always?"

Ward smiled but made no comment. Instead, he directed his next question to Victoria. "How do you propose to find Jonathan, dear? If you need the services of a private detective—"

"No private detective," Victoria cut in.

"Then how will you find your husband?"

"I've asked Kelly."

"Kelly?" Her name was spoken in unison as two sets of eyes turned toward her. "I thought Detective Quinn had made it clear you should stay out of his way," Cecily pointed out.

Kelly smiled. "That doesn't mean I have to listen."

This time it was Ward who sounded skeptical. "I don't mean to sound ungrateful," he said, sugarcoating his words with perfected diplomacy. "You're a top-notch journalist, and it's very generous of you to offer your time and expertise, but you're still recuperating from a very serious injury. Are you sure you're up to this?''

"I wouldn't have agreed if I thought I wasn't.''

"Still, I would never forgive myself if something happened to you.''

"Neither would I,'' Cecily echoed.

Kelly looked from one to the other. Why did she have the feeling they didn't want her involved? And not for the reason they had stated. "Nothing will happen to me,'' she assured them.

"Very well then. Just be careful, will you? And let me know if there's anything Cecily and I can do to help.'' Ward stood up and looked at his niece. "Why don't you go pack a few things and come home with us, Victoria? You shouldn't stay here alone.''

"That's sweet of you to offer, Uncle Ward, but I'd rather be home in case Jonathan calls. And I don't want to alert Phoebe that something is wrong.''

Ward, too practical to argue, nodded. "I hadn't thought of that.''

As he went to kiss Victoria goodbye, Cecily, her coat on her shoulders, approached Kelly. "Please don't do anything,'' she whispered. "And don't talk to anyone until you talk to me.''

Startled by the intensity in Cecily's voice, Kelly raised an eyebrow. "Why can't you talk to me now?''

"I'll explain everything when I see you. Can you be at my office at eight o'clock?''

Kelly thought of the eight hours of sleep she so

desperately needed. Now she'd have to settle for just a couple. "Yes, of course."

"I'll see you then."

At exactly eight o'clock that same morning, Kelly was ushered into Cecily's office, high above the Ben Franklin Parkway. Looking elegant and businesslike, Cecily pointed at a chair across from her desk. "Forgive me for asking you to come here so early, Kelly. I know you were up all night with Victoria, but this is important."

The phone rang, interrupting their conversation. With an impatient sigh, Cecily picked it up. "Debra, I thought I told you I didn't want to be— Oh. All right. Put him through." She covered the mouthpiece with her hand. "I have to take this. It's the mayor. I'll only be a moment."

"Do you want me to leave?" Kelly asked, half rising from her chair.

Cecily shook her head no, and removed her hand. "Mr. Mayor. What a pleasant surprise."

Tuning out the conversation, Kelly looked around her at the spacious, tastefully appointed office, so much a reflection of its occupant. A rosewood desk stood in the center of the room, and in front of a large window, overlooking the Parkway, deep chairs and antique tables formed an attractive, informal grouping. Expensive reproductions of old masters paintings dotted the walls, mingling beautifully with the polished wood and the deeply carved molding.

Kelly's gaze drifted back to Cecily, who was still on the phone, laughing at something the mayor had said and rolling her eyes at the same time.

What a diplomat, Kelly thought with a fond smile. And what an extraordinary woman. She had come from nothing, fought for everything and got where she was through sheer guts and hard work. Ambitious and driven, she had been the first in her family to finish college, earning a B.A. in business management from Penn State and an M.B.A. in finance from Wharton. Two weeks after graduating from the famous business school, Cecily had landed a job at a prestigious investment banking firm where the owner, a philanthropist by the name of H. B. Norton, had taken her under his wing and taught her everything he knew.

In 1985, thanks to her mentor, Cecily became the first woman to be offered a seat on the board of the Norton Charitable Trust, the foundation H.B.'s father had established four decades earlier. It wasn't long until Cecily's intelligence, fairness and impeccable work ethic singled her out from the rest of the board. But when H.B. retired as CEO and president of the Norton Trust twelve years later and named Cecily as his successor, the decision had taken everyone, including Cecily, by surprise. Cecily herself had told Kelly about the outcry of protest from several board members, many of whom were related to H.B. One member, a nephew, had even claimed that a woman

CEO would undermine the foundation. At that remark, H.B. had laughed and told him to grow up.

At last Cecily's conversation was over. "I'm sorry about that," she said as she hung up. "We won't be bothered again." She propped her elbows on the gleaming desk surface and steepled her fingers into a pyramid. "You must wonder why I asked you to come here at such an ungodly hour."

"Quite frankly," Kelly replied, "I'm more concerned about the secrecy of this meeting than the early hour. I don't like to keep things from Victoria."

Cecily's gaze, though direct, seemed a little tentative. "I'm sorry if I've put you in a delicate situation, Kelly. It's just that I didn't want to upset Victoria any more than she already is."

"What could upset her more than to have her husband missing?"

"Touché." Her eyes met Kelly's head-on. "Let me come straight to the point, then. I think the search for Jonathan should be left to the Miami police."

So that was it. Cecily wanted her to back off. Though surprised at the conviction in Cecily's voice, Kelly didn't show it. She had made a promise to Victoria, and nothing, no pleading, no amount of coaxing would convince her to do otherwise. "May I ask why you feel that way?" Kelly kept her tone even and calm.

"I didn't want to alarm Victoria last night, but I'm going to be completely honest with you. You're a high-profile journalist, Kelly. No matter how discreet you are, if you get involved in the search for Jonathan, someone is bound to find out. And once they do, the news of his disappearance and his connection with a drug cartel will be all over the papers.''

Kelly stared. ''You actually believe Jonathan is a drug dealer?''

''What other reason would he have for staying at that dreadful motel?''

''We don't know that he was!''

Cecily made a face as if she had suddenly smelled something foul. ''He works for a man who has ties to organized crime, Kelly. What does that tell you?''

''Those ties were never proven,'' Kelly pointed out, ''or the Casino Control Commission wouldn't have granted Syd Webber his license. But even if he did have such ties, secretly, why would you assume that Jonathan does?''

Cecily brought her hands down and gazed at them. For the first time since Kelly had arrived, she noticed the woman's unhealthy pallor. Was she really that concerned about a possible scandal? About the Sanders name being tarnished? It was true that her position as CEO of the Norton Trust demanded an impeccable background and not the slightest hint of scandal, but would the board of directors actually blame her for the actions of a relative? Kelly didn't think so. There had to be another reason why Cecily was so overwrought.

Kelly wanted to reach out to her. She wanted to tell her that whatever was troubling her, Kelly would listen. Maybe together they could find a solution to this puzzling problem. Kelly owed her that much. During those difficult twenty-four hours while she had so desperately clung to life, Cecily had sat outside the ICU with Connie and Kelly's brother, Ronny, for hours at a time, bringing them food, coffee and moral support. Kelly hadn't forgotten that.

"What is it, Cecily?" she asked gently. "What aren't you telling me?"

Clearly irritated, Cecily gave her an exasperated look. "Why are you assuming that I'm hiding some deep dark secret? I'm not. I asked you here because you have a lot of influence on Victoria and I was hoping you'd help me get her to see things my way."

"What exactly is your way, Cecily?"

"Logical." She leaned forward as if ready to explain a difficult problem to a child. "There are three possible explanations why Jonathan disappeared. One is that he did something stupid, will realize it in time and will come home before the press has time to find out about it. I won't be happy about his return, but if that's what Victoria wants, fine. The second possible explanation is that Jonathan did something stupid and has no intention of coming back. To that I say good riddance. I never wanted him married to Victoria in the first place, and by his actions, he's proven that I had good reason to feel that way. If he chooses not to come back, a brief statement will be issued to the press regarding Jonathan and Victoria's separation and that will be the end of it."

She sighed. "The third possibility isn't so pleasant, for Victoria or for the Sanders family. Jonathan did something stupid and paid for it with his life. In the event this proves to be true, we'll need to keep the circumstances of his death quiet—at least from the Philadelphia papers. That won't happen if you insist on investigating his disappearance and eventually his death." She gave Kelly a long, level look. "Are we in agreement?"

Everything had been thought out in minute detail, Kelly realized. Every possibility Cecily had mentioned had been carefully analyzed and weighed in relation to potential damage, not to Victoria, but to the Sanders name.

"Kelly?" Cecily raised a thin, well-arched brow. "Do you agree with me?"

"Only as far as the three possibilities regarding Jonathan's fate. I don't agree with anything else you said and I certainly don't intend to back down from my commitment to Victoria."

"Not even if it's in Victoria's best interest?"

"Victoria wants her husband back. We all know that."

"My niece is a hopeless romantic. Someday she'll pay heavily for that weakness."

Kelly stood up. There was nothing more to say. She wasn't getting through to Cecily, any more than Cecily was getting through to her. "I still think there's something you're not telling me." She picked up her purse. "When you're ready to tell me what that is, give me a call. And if it's something that could expedite the search for Jonathan, I urge you to tell me very quickly. Or the police if you'd prefer."

Cecily rose as well and walked her to the door. "I suppose deep down I already knew what your answer would be, but I had to try." A good sport, she smiled. "What will you do first? Talk to Syd Webber?"

"He's at the top on my list."

"Beware of him, Kelly. He may be rich, charming and successful, and he may rub elbows with all the right people, but underneath that pretty veneer is a corrupt man who will stop at nothing to get what he wants. Remember that when you talk to him."

Knowing how Cecily felt about Syd Webber, Kelly took the advice with a grain of salt. Her disapproval of the man, however, wasn't entirely unjustified. Earlier this morning, Kelly had logged on to Nexis, the newspaper database, and retrieved every bit of information she could gather on the casino tycoon. He was no saint. In Las Vegas, where he had made his fortune, Webber had befriended notorious crime boss Tony Marquese and had been implicated in a scam involving Chinese refugees. He was later exonerated, but a cloud of suspicion had hung over his head for a long time after that.

"I'll remember. Thanks for the advice."

"Will you keep me abreast of how your investigation goes?"

Kelly wasn't in the habit of giving day-to-day accounts of her activities to anyone, but Cecily was almost family. "I'll let Victoria know," she replied diplomatically. "I'm sure she'll fill you in."

Five

Every time Kelly came to Atlantic City she was astounded by the changes that had occurred to the small seaside town in the last couple of years. Once a playground for the elite, Atlantic City's reign as the queen of resorts had ended in the mid-sixties when airplane travel began to make other destinations more attractive. Before long, the town had decayed and the luxurious hotels that were once grand became old and tired. As a result, the crowds stopped coming and families who had lived there for decades moved away, leaving behind crime-ridden streets and ailing neighborhoods.

The advent of legalized casino gambling in the late seventies was supposed to have helped return the city to its former grandeur, but somewhere along the way politicians had lost track of their good intentions. While casinos prospered and developers made tons of money, behind the glitz and glamour of the boardwalk poverty remained untouched.

It wasn't until a new mayor was elected that the long-overdue renovation plans for Atlantic City began to take shape. Streets were repaired, unhabitable homes were torn down and replaced, and employment rose. The transformation wasn't happening overnight, but little by little, Atlantic City was coming back.

The ocean-front Chenonceau was a twenty-three-story glass-and-concrete structure that surpassed even Donald Trump's Taj Mahal in glamour and opulence. The vast lobby was a study in gold, with a huge marble fountain in the center and swank boutiques all around, where high rollers spent their winnings without bothering to look at the price tags.

From the busy casino floor, Kelly could hear the continuous clang of slot machines and an occasional shout of triumph as a gambler hit the jackpot.

Although she had made an appointment to see Syd Webber, it took the receptionist nearly fifteen minutes to locate him. When he finally showed up, he recognized Kelly right away, even from a distance. He hadn't changed at all since she'd last seen him, at Jonathan and Victoria's fourth wedding anniversary party. Of medium height and build, he walked with the quick, long stride of a man sure of himself. His eyes were dark, his mouth wide and well-defined. Thick black hair, touched with gray and cut longer in the back, curled around his collar, giving him the kind of bad-boy appeal women loved.

He assessed her quickly, with an appraising head-to-toe glance, and smiled, exposing perfect white teeth. "Miss Robolo," he said, taking her hand into his. "How good to see you again. And I'm so sorry to have kept you waiting. We had a crisis in the theater. Pavarotti is scheduled to perform in exactly eight hours and the sound system has chosen this very moment to break down.''

"I'm sorry, too. I seem to have caught you at a bad time.'' Kelly allowed him to hold her hand a second longer before withdrawing it. "If this visit could wait, I'd leave right now, but it can't.''

"What made you think I'd let you leave?'' Before she could think of an appropriate answer, he took her arm and led her toward a bank of elevators behind the lobby. "Still no news of Jonathan?''

"Not the kind we wanted to hear.'' She told him what she knew but made no reference to Detective Quinn's drug-trafficking suspicions.

He pushed a button labeled Executive And Administrative Floor. "Do you have any idea what Jonathan was doing in Miami?'' he asked.

"Not yet. I was hoping you could help me with that.''

"I don't see how, but I'll do my best.''

On the eighteenth floor, the doors slid open and he led the way toward a door with a simple brass plaque bearing his name. There were other offices on this floor and Kelly assumed one of them belonged to Jonathan.

Webber's office was a surprise. There was no flash here and not a speck of gold. Elegant and masculine, the room was furnished with teal chairs upholstered in a nubby fabric, a large mahogany desk, an Oriental rug that didn't look like a reproduction and large wraparound windows that offered an unobstructed view of the Atlantic City skyline and its famous boardwalk. The ocean, murky gray at the moment, stretched out as far as the eye could see.

"Great view, isn't it?" He stood in front of a well-stocked liquor cabinet and poured sparkling water into two crystal tumblers.

"Fabulous."

"The view is the reason I put the executive offices on the eighteenth floor." He handed her one of the glasses. "Please sit down, Kelly. It's all right if I call you Kelly, isn't it? It's such a pretty name." He gave her another of his dazzling smiles. "Though not very Italian."

"My father's choice. My mother won the other round, with my middle name."

He took a sip of his water. "Which is?"

"Very Italian. Noemi." She chuckled as she said it. "After my grandmother."

"It's lovely, too."

"And you're very flattering, Mr. Web—"

"Uh-uh." Holding up his glass, he raised his index finger and shook it. "Syd. Please."

Deep inside her mind, Kelly heard the sound of a warning bell. Her host was much too charming, almost to the point of being distracting. She might even have enjoyed flirting with him a little if the circumstances of her visit were different.

She uncrossed her legs and assumed a more professional pose. "Syd it is." She put her glass down.

"I know you're busy so I'll try to make my questions brief. First of all, I'd be a hypocrite if I pretended to have never heard of your…alleged mob connections."

The remark brought an amused twinkle to his eyes. "As long as you remember they're alleged."

"Did that bother Jonathan? Did he question you about the problem you'd had with the Casino Control Commission prior to opening the Chenonceau?" She already knew the answer to that question but she wanted to hear it from him.

"We discussed it. Those rumors, as it turned out, were manufactured by another casino developer eager to bury the competition. But to answer your question, no, the allegations did not bother Jonathan and they did not stop him from coming to work with me. He's a bright young man. He knows a winning hand when he sees one."

She smiled at that. "Yes, I'm sure he does." She looked into her drink for a second before asking, "Are you surprised that he went to Miami?"

"Very. I don't recall him ever mentioning Florida before except when he went there with Victoria and Phoebe."

"What about you?" she asked casually. "Do you ever go to Florida?"

"Only to visit my father. He retired to Key West some years ago and I try to get down every chance I get." His eyes bored into hers with such intensity that she almost looked away. "And if I'm correctly guessing your next question, no, Jonathan has never met my father. I don't even believe he'd know how to get in touch with him.''

He *was* smart. And quick. ''Would you say that you know Jonathan well?''

Syd shrugged. ''As well as could be expected under the circumstances.''

''What does that mean?''

He took another sip of water before replying. ''Jonathan is a very private man, as I'm sure you know. Being a private man myself, I respect his wishes to keep his personal life separate from the Chenonceau. Frankly, that's not very difficult. Except for casino-related matters and Monday-night football, Jonathan and I didn't have many things in common. He plays golf and tennis, I don't. I like deep-sea fishing, he won't go near a boat. He's married, I'm a confirmed bachelor.''

A confirmed bachelor with an eye for beautiful women and a new one by his side every couple of months. ''But surely you would have known if he was in some kind of trouble.''

''I'm not a mind reader, but yes, I suppose I would have noticed.''

''Victoria said he had been moody the last few days. Would you have any idea why?''

''None.'' He glanced at her glass, which was still full, and walked over to the cabinet to refill his. ''To my recollection, Jonathan was his normal self that entire week. I didn't even notice he was getting sick.''

Syd came back to his seat. "But then I guess he wasn't, was he?"

"Apparently not. Are you the one who took his call yesterday morning?"

"No, his secretary did."

That would be Martha Grimwald. Jonathan always spoke highly of her. "Would you mind if I spoke with her?" Kelly asked.

"Not at all." Syd picked up an extension on a side table and pressed a button. "Martha, could you come in for a minute? Thank you."

Martha Grimwald was a pleasant, middle-aged woman with graying brown hair and a look of quiet efficiency about her. As if sensing that the summons may have confidential overtones, she quickly closed the door.

"Martha, this is Kelly Robolo," Syd said, rising from his chair to meet her halfway. "She's a reporter for the *Philadelphia Globe,* but more important, she is a close friend of the Bowmans'. She's here to try to make some sense out of Jonathan's disappearance."

At Syd's silent invitation, Martha sat down. "I'll do whatever I can to help, Miss Robolo."

"Thank you, Mrs. Grimwald." Kelly waited until Syd had taken his seat again before continuing. "I need to know if Jonathan did anything unusual in the past week or so. Did anyone you didn't know come to see him? Or perhaps you overheard a phone conversation?"

Martha's shoulders stiffened slightly. "I don't eavesdrop, Miss Robolo."

"I didn't mean to imply that you did." Trying to amend herself, Kelly smiled. "I was being hopeful."

Kelly's candor brought a smile to Martha's lips. "I don't recall anything out of the ordinary, Miss Robolo. Jonathan is a creature of habit, you see. He loves his routine and seldom varies from it."

"Can you tell me what a typical day is like for him?"

"Surely. He's vice president in charge of marketing, and as such, one of his first duties each morning is to meet with his marketing staff. They go over promotional brochures, special hotel packages and other ways of promoting the casino. After that he goes back to his office, catches up with his mail, makes phone calls and meets with Mr. Webber."

Syd concurred with a short nod.

"Does he go out to lunch or does he eat in the casino?" Kelly asked.

"Neither. Mr. Bowman always orders a sandwich from the cafeteria and eats at his desk while he works." She shook her head in disapproval. "I keep telling him that's not healthy, but he won't listen."

"Do you screen all his calls?"

"Only if they come through the main switchboard."

"Why wouldn't they?"

"Mr. Bowman and the other VPs have private lines. So does Mr. Webber."

"I see." The phone records could be requisitioned, but only by the police.

"Does he have a palm pilot?" she asked suddenly. "You know, one of those electronic wonders that keeps track of your appointments?"

"He keeps one with him at all times, but he backs everything up on his computer so I know where he is if I need to contact him."

Kelly glanced at Syd, who again bowed his head. "I'll be happy to take you to Jonathan's office. Right now, if you're finished with Martha."

Kelly rose. She was very anxious to see Jonathan's office. "Right now would be fine, thank you."

Six

Kelly's visit to the Chenonceau had been disappointing. While Syd Webber and Martha Grimwald had seemed eager to help, both had failed to provide a single clue as to Jonathan's disappearance.

Confirming what Martha had told her, Jonathan's appointments for the week had been entered in his computer and were available at the click of a mouse. With Syd's permission, Kelly had sat in front of the monitor and quickly scrolled up and down the screen. Jonathan's work week was pretty much as his secretary had described. Meticulous to a fault, he had outlined the subject of his various meetings, who he meant to call that day and why. The entry for February 7 showed a meeting with his marketing staff and Phoebe's dance recital, both of which he had missed. There was no mention of a trip to Miami.

As Kelly merged onto the Atlantic City Expressway, she thought of some of the more complex stories she had investigated over the years. In many instances, time had been on her side. She didn't have that luxury with Jonathan. As in a kidnapping, each hour that passed made the search more difficult, the trail colder, the hopes more desperate.

Not to mention that this time she didn't have the cooperation of the police.

Her thoughts turned to Detective Quinn. Maybe she hadn't played her cards right with him and should try a new approach. A little groveling, perhaps. Such tactics weren't exactly her style, but in a pinch, she could grovel with the best of them.

As her right hand rummaged through her bag in search of the detective's phone number, she kept her eyes on the road, looking for a place to stop. Five minutes later she was pulling into a rest area, Quinn's number in her hand.

"Let me see if he's in," the desk sergeant said when she identified herself.

When Quinn came on the line, he sounded just as cranky as he had before. "Yes, Miss Robolo?" He made no effort to disguise the irritation in his voice.

"Good morning, Detective," she said in her most affable voice. "I was wondering if you could give me an update on the desk clerk's condition."

"Unchanged."

"What about the identification of the body?"

"I've requested dental records to be sent from Philadelphia. Correct me if I'm wrong," he said before she could fire another question, "but didn't we agree that from now on you'd be directing your questions to the Philadelphia PD?"

"If you don't mind, I'd rather deal directly with you."

"Now, I wonder why that is?" She guessed from his sarcastic tone that he had already spoken with someone at the PPD and had been thoroughly briefed on her unpopularity with the city force.

"Could it be," he continued in that same mocking tone, "that you're *persona non grata* with your own police department? I believe one person I talked to referred to you as Typhoid Kelly."

Great. Terrific. How could she expect his cooperation with such negative publicity? "This isn't about me, Detective," she replied as sweetly as she could manage. "It's about a missing man."

"It's also about an open investigation, which means I can't discuss it."

"Can you at least—"

"Am I speaking Esperanto here? I can't talk about the case. I've told you too much already, considering you're not even a member of the Bowmans' family."

It took a tremendous effort on her part not to snap back at him. "I'm just trying to help out a friend, Detective. You could make my job so much easier if—"

"No." Just as rudely as he had earlier today, he hung up.

She stared at her phone. So much for groveling.

She merged back onto the highway, wondering what other resources she had at her disposal. The list was meager. Practically non-existent.

Except for one possibility.

She gave a mental shake of her head. No, no way. Too crazy. But the thought kept coming back, taking shape, gaining momentum. So what if it was crazy? When had that ever stopped her?

By the time she reached the toll plaza, she knew what she had to do.

The last time Kelly had talked to Nick McBride was in her hospital room. Unlike her other visitors, however, he hadn't come bearing flowers or to wish her a speedy recovery, but to give her hell on what had gone down in Chinatown.

She had deserved every bit of his anger. Weeks earlier, when she had told him about the extortion rumors, Nick had warned her, gently, to back off, explaining the police were investigating.

Because she and Nick were friends, Kelly had left the story alone. Until that fateful night when Randy Chen had run into Dr. Ho's *dojo.*

Four days later, Nick stood in her hospital room, no longer the Nick McBride she knew. Each time she tried to defend herself, he cut her off.

"You're as bad as those rag reporters that call themselves journalists," he had told her in one last parting shot. "Just because you write for a big newspaper and have a Pulitzer doesn't make you any better than the rest of them." And then the words that had hurt the most. "Why I ever trusted you, I'll never know."

And now here she was, outside the Walnut Street Training Center, considering asking him for help. Had she lost her mind? Or did she just enjoy being humiliated? Neither, she decided, gathering her courage. She just believed in hunches, and this one was too strong to ignore.

Last year at this time, Nick's father, the chief of security at the Chenonceau, had been killed in the casino parking lot, the victim of a robbery gone wrong. It was widely known that Nick hadn't been satisfied with the police's theory. Nor was it a secret that he and Syd Webber had hated each other at first sight. On the surface, the chance that Patrick's death and Jonathan's disappearance were related was slim. The two men had nothing in common except for their connection to the Chenonceau. Yet the possibility of a connection had crossed Kelly's mind. If Nick came to the same conclusion, he might be curious enough to want to help her.

Taking a chance he'd be inside, working out, she pushed the door open and walked into the building.

The building was an old boxing arena an enterprising businessman had saved from destruction by buying the landmark and turning it into a training center for aspiring young boxers. At any other time, it would have been jam-packed with teenagers and instructors, even a scout or two, but at noon on a school day the place was practically empty.

Kelly's gaze swept over the large room where a boxing ring held center stage. Off to the side, a man in gray sweats jumped rope while another ran on a treadmill. Nick McBride was on the other side of the ring, beating a punching bag.

Kelly stood under the archway and observed him for a moment, hoping he wouldn't notice her until she felt confident enough to approach him. He was an attractive man, with reddish-blond hair, deep blue eyes and a physique any man would envy. His neck was thick, his bare chest broad and solid, and at the moment, covered with a thin sheen of perspiration.

Shamelessly, she let her gaze linger on the powerful thighs as he bounced around the punching bag with the grace of a dancer. Each punch sank into the heavy bag with a solid thud and was quickly followed by another. He was strong and fast, but Kelly wasn't surprised. He had been an amateur boxer once and on the verge of turning professional when he had changed his plans and entered the police academy instead.

Though it didn't show now, there was an edgy quality about him that instantly made him stand out from the rest of his colleagues. Even the criminals and witnesses he questioned sensed it and knew better than to play games with him. Maybe that's why his arrest/conviction ratio was one of the best in the department. No one dared bullshit Nick McBride.

She would be lying if she said she had never thought of him in a sexual way. It was difficult to be in the presence of a man like Nick and not feel a little weak in the knees. But she had never acted on those feelings. After two disastrous relationships, Kelly had sworn off men, at least for the moment.

Besides, he didn't have a stellar track record himself in the romance department. Rumor had it he was too passionate about his work, almost to the point of being fanatical about it. Coming in second to a job wasn't something many women could put up with. His ex-wife certainly hadn't, and to Kelly's knowledge, neither had anyone after her.

She waited until he had sunk the last punch and was reaching for a towel from a nearby bench before pulling away from the door.

Seven

At the sound of quick, sharp footsteps hitting the concrete floor, Nick looked up and slowly wrapped his towel around his neck as Kelly Robolo made her way across the room.

Considering that only five weeks ago she had been close to dying, she looked remarkably well. Her black hair, longer than he remembered, was cut in practical layers and framed a face his sister thought belonged on a cover model. Her eyes were by far her best feature. They were large and dark and in constant motion, as though afraid they'd miss something.

As she walked toward him in that quick, purposeful stride, he took in the rest of her, the lean tweed skirt that reached midcalf, and the bulky Irish fisherman sweater that kept her figure from becoming a distraction. Having seen her with a lot less on, he knew that could be a problem.

He had met her three years ago when she had needed information on a swindling scheme she was investigating. Though Nick didn't work with reporters as a rule, he had made an exception for Kelly—partly because her reputation preceded her and partly because he had liked her right away. She didn't act cute or flirtatious like some reporters he knew. And she wasn't afraid to follow a lead no matter how risky it might be. In Philadelphia, her name alone could evoke admiration or fear, depending on who stood at the receiving end of those four dreaded little words: "Kelly Robolo is here."

Maybe the respect he had felt toward her was the reason he had broken his golden rule about working with reporters. And he had lived to regret it. He had trusted her and now his best friend was dead.

She stopped in front of him. "Hello, Nick."

Nick wiped his face with the towel. He had no idea what she could possibly want with him, but it had to be serious for her to come here. The last time they had spoken to each other was in the hospital, four days or so after the shooting. And he had been the one doing all the talking then.

He gave a short nod. "Kelly."

The chilly greeting didn't seem to faze her, or if it did, she didn't show it. "Do you have a minute?" she asked.

"No." He started unrolling the hand wrap around his knuckles.

"Look, Nick. I know I'm not your favorite person right now, but when you lashed out at me that day at the hospital, you didn't give me much of a chance to defend myself."

"Defend yourself how?" He had been trying to put that damn night behind him for weeks and now here it was, shoved down his throat once again. "You were interested in only one thing—breaking that story."

A light flush rushed to her cheeks. "That's not true! I didn't give a damn about the story. All I wanted was to help a friend in trouble. I never thought for one moment that an undercover cop would be there. If I had..." She looked away, as if the memories of that night were too painful to think about.

Nick tossed the hand wrap on the bench and started removing the other. "You should have called me when Dr. Ho gave the paper bag to Randy Chen."

"You wouldn't have made it to the warehouse in time."

"I could have questioned your instructor."

"He wouldn't have told you a thing. He was too scared."

Nick said nothing. What was there to say? All the accusations in the world wouldn't bring Matt back.

In spite of the uncomfortable silence, Kelly showed no sign of leaving. Instead, she came to stand in front of him, so close he could smell that perfume she used all the time. He remembered its name. Magie Noire. Black magic. Once he had wondered what it would feel like to fall under the spell of Kelly Robolo.

She looked at him without flinching. "I need your help, Nick."

He hadn't expected that, not after their last conversation. "Then you've come to the wrong guy." He started to turn around, but she stopped him by touching his arm. Almost immediately she pulled her hand back.

"Victoria's husband is missing."

The sentence, spoken in one fast breath, took him aback. He waited a moment, absorbing the news. Although he had never met Jonathan Bowman, he knew he was a vice president at the Chenonceau, where Nick's late father had worked as chief of security.

Nick's antennae popped up. They always did when Syd Webber was involved, even indirectly. "How long?"

"Twenty-four hours."

"What does Webber say?"

"He is as baffled as we are. Yesterday morning, Jonathan called his secretary and told her he wouldn't be coming in because he was sick. Moments later, he called Victoria and told her Syd was sending him to Miami on business and he wouldn't be back until late afternoon, in time for his young daughter's dance recital."

Nick remembered his own marriage and how badly he had wanted to get away at times. "Men need space."

"At four o'clock this morning," Kelly continued, "a Detective Quinn from the Miami police called to say that a bomb had exploded in some seedy motel off Interstate 95. Jonathan was not among the injured but a charred body was found in room 116, where he was supposed to have been staying. I don't believe that body is his. I don't even believe Jonathan was ever in that motel."

Nick couldn't help it, he was curious. "Is that what Detective Quinn thinks?"

"He's not saying anything yet, but he has sent for Jonathan's dental records."

That would make sense. Nowadays, sophisticated forensic dentistry and special X rays made it possible to identify victims no matter how badly they were burned. "I still don't understand why you came to me," he said. He did, but a perverse part of him wanted her to spell it out.

"The desk clerk at the motel is the only one who can identify the occupant of room 116. Unfortunately he's in the hospital with severe burns. He won't be able to talk to the police until he's off the critical list. There are other motel employees but Detective Quinn is playing hardball. He won't let me speak to them."

"That's his right."

"I realize that." She kept her expression neutral. "That's why I'm here. I'd like you to call him, Nick. I need to talk to those people."

"Cops don't like other cops butting in."

"You wouldn't be butting in. Quinn plans to notify the PPD. He may already have."

"So why not check with Mariani at the Roundhouse? Or any other detective?"

"Oh, come on, Nick." Her smile was sarcastic. "Do you really think that anyone at police headquarters will want to help me?"

Before he had a chance to reply, Kelly reached inside her bag and pulled out a piece of paper. "Here," she said, handing it to him. "Quinn's phone number."

Nick glanced at it but didn't touch it. "I can't help you."

She stiffened. "Can't or won't?"

He shrugged, aware that his questions had misled her into believing he would help. He hadn't meant to play games with her but he had been interested. "Take your pick. Either way the answer is no." What else did she expect him to say? Because of her, his best friend was dead, leaving behind a grieving widow and two fatherless little girls.

She held his gaze for a moment, then, with the candor she was known for, she asked, "Do you have any idea how difficult it was for me to come here today? How many times I talked myself out of it, only to change my mind again?"

Honesty on her part demanded the same from him. "I do know, Kelly. It doesn't change anything."

She stood there for several seconds, her expression unreadable. She was good at that—keeping her emotions under control. Most Italians he knew blew their corks at the slightest provocation. Not Robolo.

After a while, she gave a short nod, as if she had finally accepted his decision, then, her back rigid as a board, she walked away. She had just reached the ring when she turned around. "This conversation is strictly between us," she said. "Can I at least have your word that you won't mention it to anyone?"

Nick nodded and watched her until she had disappeared. As badly as he wanted to erase her visit from his mind, he couldn't, not so much because of Kelly, but because of the memories her request had brought back.

Next month would mark the first anniversary of his father's death. The senseless killing had taken place in the back parking lot of the Chenonceau, where employees kept their cars. Plagued by more than two dozens murders a year, the overworked Atlantic City police had been quick to blame the killing on one of the city's many homeless. Nick hadn't bought it. His father was an ex-Philadelphia cop, a tough one. He would have never allowed some two-bit robber to surprise him from behind, not even after a double shift at the casino.

Nick had investigated the murder himself, on his own time, questioning casino employees and of course Syd Webber. At first, the casino tycoon had been civil, even helpful, but his affability had flown out the window the moment Nick had mentioned Patrick McBride's recent mood shifts. At the suggestion that he may have discovered something suspicious at the casino, Webber had turned hostile.

"I run a clean establishment here, McBride," the man had snapped. "And I can tell you there's no connection whatsoever between your father's unfortunate death and my casino. So don't you come in here with accusations you can't substantiate."

Far from being intimidated, Nick had continued his investigation even though he had no jurisdiction in Atlantic City. That's when Webber had called the police.

The news had reached Captain Cross's office within the hour and his boss had given Nick a stern warning—stay away from Syd Webber or get suspended.

Even Nick's sister, Kathleen, had urged him to give up the investigation. "I don't like what it's doing to you," she had told him that same evening. "Please let it go, Nicky. Even if Webber did have something to do with Dad's death, he's too clever to be caught. And he'll only get you in deeper trouble."

In the end he'd had no choice.

But now another Chenonceau employee had met with foul play. Coincidence? Nick wondered as he walked toward the shower room. Or was a sinister pattern emerging?

Eight

Outside the training center, Kelly leaned against the wall and let out a long, frustrated breath. "Damn you, Nick," she muttered to herself. "You're as insensitive and bullheaded as your colleagues."

What a fool she had been to believe that he would let bygones be bygones and agree to help her. Men like Nick McBride didn't forgive. They got even, just as the rest of the Philadelphia force had been doing. Today had been Nick's turn.

Now what? she wondered. Kiss up to Quinn and get him to cooperate? She had already tried that. And now that he knew how much the Philadelphia Police Department hated her, he would be even less helpful.

Her thought process in high gear, she started walking down Walnut Street. Her first impulse after she had agreed to help Victoria had been to fly to Miami. So why not do that? Maybe a face-to-face meeting with Big Bad Quinn would give her an idea, some little thread to follow. Who needed Nick McBride?

Her mind made up, she fished in her purse for her cell phone and dialed Victoria's shop. "Heard anything?" she asked.

"No." Her friend's voice was flat. "What about you? Did you talk to Syd?"

"I did. I'm afraid I struck out. Twice, as a matter of fact." She told Victoria about her not-so-terrific idea of asking Nick McBride for help.

"You went to *Nick?*" For the first time in twenty-four hours, Victoria showed signs of life. "I can't believe it. The last time the two of you were in the same room together he almost took your head off. I had to physically shove him out the door."

"What can I tell you? I'm not getting any smarter in my old age."

"Was he nasty to you?"

"No, he just told me to go to hell. Well, not in so many words, but I got the drift."

"So what happens now?"

"I'm going to Miami. That way Quinn can't hang up on me."

"I don't know, Kelly." Victoria's voice was once again filled with uncertainty. "Your mother will kill me when she finds out what you're up to. You're still recuperating."

"My mother won't even know I'm gone. I'll take an early-morning plane and come back the same day." That would be the same flight Jonathan had taken. She hoped there wasn't some sort of negative karma about duplicating that doomed trip.

"All right." Victoria sounded only mildly reassured. "But I'll ride to the airport with you, if you don't mind. I finally located Jonathan's car in one of the garages and I want to bring it back to the house."

The first thing Kelly saw as she approached her front door was a sheet of yellow paper sticking out of her mailbox. She pulled it out almost absentmind-edly, assuming it was a flyer advertising some kind of service. It wasn't. Letters in various colors, sizes and shapes had been cut out and pasted on the paper to form words—not just words, she realized, but some sort of nursery rhyme.

Mary, Mary, quite contrary
Wouldn't stop prying
And soon our little Mary
Was no longer breathing.

Kelly looked up and scanned the street, just as she had the night she had found her mangled tree. A few feet away, George Cromwell and his young daughter were getting into the family car.

Kelly waved and started walking toward him. "How are you, George?" She smiled at the little girl. "Aren't you pretty today, Brittany. Going somewhere special?"

"My daddy is taking me to see *Barney on Ice*," Brittany said in a high-pitched voice.

"How wonderful." Still smiling, Kelly turned to her neighbor. "George, you didn't happen to see who was distributing these, did you?'' She waved the sheet of yellow paper in the air.

Her neighbor pursed his lips and shook his head. ''No, I didn't. What is it?'' He craned his neck, trying to see the writing but Kelly had already refolded the note.

''Just an ad for a carpet-cleaning service. Unfortunately there's no phone number.'' She shrugged. ''Oh well, maybe they'll come back.'' She flashed a quick smile. ''Thanks anyway, George. Have a good time today.'' She waved to the child, already in her car seat. ''You too, Brittany.''

Inside her house, Kelly read the chilling message again, wondering if it was the work of her old tormentor? For some reason she didn't think so. The previous incidents—the torn mailbox, uprooted tree and slashed tires—had been acts of revenge. This was different. This note was a direct threat.

Calling the police was useless. Kelly's neighbor, Mrs. Sheridan, had done just that the night she had noticed suspicious activity around Kelly's car. When the police found out who the car belonged to, no one had bothered to come.

She was on her own. And that was fine. She would just have to be a little more careful from now on, a little more aware of what went on around her.

With that thought in mind, she walked inside to book her flight to Miami.

Nine

"Happy birthday to you, happy birthday to you, happy birthday, dear Ashley, happy birthday to you!"

Nick felt a wrenching inside his chest as six little girls dressed in frilly dresses belted out the old song with all the gusto they could muster. Standing in front of the double-layered pink-and-white cake, four-year-old Ashley Kolvic inhaled deeply and then blew hard, her head circling wildly over the cake until all four candles had been extinguished.

Behind her, Matt's widow, a petite brunette with a gentle smile, did her best to put on a happy face but Nick knew the anguish she was experiencing, and would continue to experience, during this difficult first year without her husband.

Today's celebration was particularly painful because it was the first of its kind Nick's best friend would miss. For a while, Patti had considered not having a party at all, only a quiet gathering at home. But when her daughter had come home from preschool one afternoon and asked how many of her friends she could invite to her birthday party, Patti hadn't had the heart to disappoint her.

Aware that Patti would need some moral support, Nick had gone back to the station after his workout, cleared his desk and taken the rest of the afternoon off so he could attend Ashley's special day. He knew he was no replacement for the girls' father, but Ashley and her six-year-old sister, Tricia, had wanted him there. And so had Patti.

Looking at the older girl, Nick noted that she, too, was quiet, like her mother. Looking more like Matt every day, Tricia had taken the news of her father's death hard and wasn't rebounding from the tragedy as quickly as the four-year-old.

After Patti had served thick slices of chocolate cake and spooned out vanilla ice cream for everyone, she left her little guests in the care of a helpful neighbor and came to sit next to Nick on the living-room sofa, where she had a clear view of the balloon-strung dining room.

"Thanks for coming, Nick." Her voice was filled with misery.

"No need to thank me. I wouldn't miss Ashley's birthday for anything."

"Just the same, I'm not sure I would have gotten through those first few minutes without you here."

He touched her hand. "You're doing fine, Patti. One day at a time, remember?"

She nodded, her eyes on her girls. "I started to go through Matt's things yesterday."

He knew from experience how heart-wrenching

that task could be. "You should have called me. I would have done that for you."

"I couldn't. I've imposed on you too much already."

"Nonsense." He studied her profile for a moment. She seemed upset, more so than usual. "Something wrong, Patti?"

Her gaze followed one of the little girls as she paraded around the room with her balloon, making faces that made the other girls laugh. "I found something," she said, her voice barely audible.

He didn't immediately grasp the meaning of her words. "Found something?"

Her teeth clamped over her lower lip and he didn't press her. She appeared to be having a difficult time holding herself together and he was afraid that the slightest nudge would break her. After a moment, she rose. "Come with me."

Nick followed her into the kitchen, then to the laundry room, where a door led to the garage. On the threshold, Nick stopped. He and Matt had spent hours together in this garage, working on Matt's old jalopy, building shelves for the girls' rooms, repairing bikes or just drinking beer and shooting the bull.

Matt's workbench had been pulled away from the wall. Behind it was a sheet of plywood Matt often used as an extension for his dining-room table at holiday time. Nick watched as Patti slid the plywood out of the way, revealing a safe with a combination lock on it. Nick approached it slowly. "I didn't know Matt had a safe in here."

"Neither did I. Until yesterday." She moved away. "Go ahead, open it."

"Why?"

"Open it. The combination is left nineteen, right twenty-two and left ninety-six. Nineteen for my age when Matt and I met, twenty-two for the number on his football jersey in high school and ninety-six for the year he made detective. It took me a while to figure it out, but I finally did."

With a foreboding he couldn't explain, Nick crouched in front of the safe and spun the wheel from left to right until he heard a soft click. He held his breath as he turned the handle. Inside the safe were stacks upon stacks of twenty-dollar bills, all neatly bundled and held together by rubber bands. He looked at the money for a long time, his mind spinning, before he looked up at Patti.

"Where did that come from?"

"I don't know, but I have a pretty good idea."

So did he, but he didn't want to believe it. Not Matt. There had to be another explanation, another reason for this money to be in here, hidden. But even as he tried desperately to make excuses for his old friend, he knew he was only kidding himself. Unexplained, unreported cash in a cop's house was never a good sign.

"I couldn't believe it either," Patti said as though reading his thoughts. She reached inside the safe and took out a small spiral notebook. She handed it to him. "Then I found this."

Nick opened the notebook. At the top of the first page, in Matt's familiar handwriting, were the names of the two men who had been arrested the night of the Chinatown shooting, along with their phone numbers. There was also a long list of names, presumably all Chinatown merchants. Beside each name was an amount, ranging from fifty to three hundred dollars, and a date. In another column marked "My Cut" was a smaller amount. The last column was entitled "Turned in to Capt. Cross." That would be the money Matt had handed out to his superior every week.

With a small difference. That amount was only a portion of what he had actually been paid.

The first notation was dated April 2. Two weeks after Matt had been assigned to the racketeering investigation.

"He was on the take, Nick," Patti murmured, wiping a tear from her face. "He wasn't investigating that protection racket as we all thought. He was part of it."

She leaned against the workbench and looked up at the exposed support beams in the ceiling as if seeking an answer from them. "How could I not have guessed what was going on? How could I not have seen the signs? They were right there, under my nose."

"You can't see what people don't want you to see."

"I was his wife, Nick. I should have known. He was always upset about not making enough money. He kept saying that if he earned more, we could take vacations, buy a new house, send the girls to a private school. I tried to tell him we were fine, that we didn't need money to be happy." She shook her head. "It didn't do any good. Then last spring, everything changed. He began to smile more and he stopped being so obsessed with money, or the lack of it." She let out a small, sad chuckle. "He even started singing in the shower."

"Don't blame yourself, Patti."

"Why not? If I had paid more attention, Matt might still..." Unable to continue, she covered her face with her hands and wept softly.

Nick let her cry. Tears were an outlet he had no right to deny her. When the sobs had subsided, she looked at him through a veil of tears. "I want you to be the one to tell the captain, Nick."

He nodded, already dreading it. "You realize this will put an unwanted spin on the story." Matt had died a hero. Once the money was turned in, his name would forever be a black cloud on his family and the department.

"I can handle it."

"What about the girls?"

"I called my parents earlier. We'll be staying with them in Dayton for a few months, until the publicity dies down. Tricia can finish the school year there. After that, I don't know. I can either come back here or stay there."

It was a healthy decision, Nick thought, the best she could make under the circumstances.

Without saying another word, Patti took an old battered suitcase from a shelf and started stuffing the money into it. She set the spiral notebook on top, then stood up. "I know how angry you were with Kelly Robolo for the part she played in Matt's death. Maybe now you can make peace with her. God knows she's going through enough as it is."

Kelly. Christ. For a moment, he had forgotten all about her. This turn of events didn't make Matt's death any less tragic, but it certainly put a different light on what had taken place that night in Chinatown.

"What do you mean, she's going through enough?"

Patti looked surprised. "You don't know?"

He shook his head.

"You didn't hear it from me, but Kelly is being harassed by the department."

"Harassed how?"

"I've heard that a couple of patrol officers have been giving her tickets, and that her house was vandalized a few times. The word *bitch* was spray-painted on her front door, her mailbox was torn out and the tires on her car were slashed."

"Did she report it?"

"No, but one of Kelly's neighbors did. I don't believe anyone bothered to investigate the complaints, though.''

Nick's adrenaline began to pump harder. If there was one thing he couldn't stomach, it was police officers abusing their power. "Do you know who's behind this?''

"No. And remember, you didn't hear it from me. I wouldn't have told you at all, but I know you and Kelly were friends once and I thought with Matt gone and me moving to Ohio, you could probably use—''

"Mommy, Uncle Nick!'' A beaming Ashley burst into the garage and threw herself in Nick's arms. As he scooped up the four-year-old from the floor, he saw Patti kick the safe door shut. "Look what I got!'' Ashley waved a brand-new Barbie dressed in a glittering silver gown.

"She's beautiful, pumpkin. Just like you.''

"Madeline gave her to me. And Cindy gave me the wardrobe case that goes with it.'' She looked at Nick. There was a smear of chocolate frosting on her round cheek and Nick wiped it off with his thumb. "But I like your present best of all, Uncle Nick.''

"What? That ugly red bike?''

She laughed. "It's not ugly! It's beautiful. Want to see me ride it? I don't need training wheels anymore.''

"Not in that dress, darling,'' Patti reminded her. "Later, when your friends leave, you can change and show Uncle Nick how well you can ride.''

Ashley nodded but her smile faded quickly. Nick

had seen a lot of those shifts of mood lately and knew they were part of the grieving process. "I wish Daddy was here to see me ride my new bike." She looked at Nick with sad, solemn eyes. "But my daddy is in heaven with the angels and he won't be coming back."

"I know, pumpkin." Nick's voice was thick with emotion. "But you remember what I told you the other day, right? Your daddy will always be with you."

She nodded vigorously and poked herself in the chest with her fat little finger. "Because Daddy is in my heart."

"That's right. And he'll always love you and watch over you. Which means," he added, tickling her stomach, "that you'd better eat all your vegetables."

She laughed. "I will, I will!" Then, still giggling, she said, "Stay for dinner, Uncle Nick, please."

He hadn't planned on that, but how could he refuse? "Well now," he said in a teasing tone, "that depends on what's for dinner."

Ashley thought for a moment, then grinned. "Cake and ice cream?"

Nick laughed. "In that case you've got yourself a deal." He put her down and watched her run out of the garage to rejoin her little friends.

"You're so good with children," Patti said softly. "You'll make a wonderful father someday."

He had thought so, too, but his wife, Nina— ex-wife now—had been dead set against the idea.

"Snotty noses and dirty diapers aren't my idea of fun," she had told him during one of their many discussions about starting a family. "When you make enough money to hire a full-time nanny, we'll talk."

He had never brought up the subject again.

Pushing his thoughts aside, he took the suitcase by the handle. "I'll be back in an hour or so. Is that all right?"

Patti nodded. "Take your time, Nick—and thank you."

"Let's go in."

Ten

Nick sat in his parked Ford Taurus, the suitcase on the passenger seat. Directly in front of him was the Roundhouse, a circular, six-story concrete structure that was home to the Philadelphia Police Department.

After telling himself over and over that the right thing to do—the *only* thing to do—was to turn the money in to his captain, Nick was still trying to figure out a way to spare Matt's family from needless embarrassment.

His first impulse had been to burn the damn thing and just forget about it. That way Patti and the girls wouldn't have to run away and leave behind the friends who loved them, the friends they so desperately needed right now.

He might have done it, too, if it hadn't been for Jake Matias and Miguel Santos, the two thugs who were awaiting trial. They hadn't ratted on Matt and Nick knew why. Soon the operation would need another cop on the inside. That would be possible only if the chosen man felt he could trust them. Matias and Santos knew that once Patti found the money, the first person she'd go to would be Matt's best friend. If the money wasn't turned in, the mob would know Nick had disposed of it, and that would give them a huge advantage. They would expect favors in exchange for their silence, which was something Nick couldn't allow. He had joined the force for one reason—to help rid this city of scum like Matias and Santos.

So far he hadn't done too badly. The police academy, from which he had graduated at the top of his class, had given him the solid foundation a cop needed to do his job. The rest he had learned from a master—his father.

For a while, Nick had toyed with the idea of becoming a professional boxer. After winning a string of titles in the middle-weight division and being approached by several high-level scouts, the thought of turning pro and making the kind of money a nineteen-year-old could only dream of had been almost overwhelming. But when Patrick McBride had been shot in the line of duty during a bank robbery, Nick's priorities had suddenly changed.

As he sat beside his father's hospital bed, waiting for him to regain consciousness, Nick realized that his values had been all wrong. Money wasn't what mattered, or boxing. What mattered was coming home at night with a sense of pride and accomplishment, the belief that what you had done that day had made a difference.

The risks for a man on the force were high, the monetary reward low and the glory nonexistent. But Nick had known at that very moment that being a cop was his destiny. When his father had opened his eyes and heard of Nick's decision, the look in the old man's eyes was all Nick had needed to know he'd made the right choice.

A knock on his window brought an end to his reverie. A rookie he knew waved to him. Nick waved back and watched him head toward the Roundhouse. The young man's jaunty walk and sharp uniform reminded Nick of himself when he had first joined the force nineteen years ago. He had been full of youthful spunk in those days. And he'd been impulsive. He still was. The captain called him a hothead, and only let him get away with it because Nick got the job done.

He threw one last look at the suitcase. "Sorry, Matt," he murmured. "Got to do it by the book."

Grabbing the handle, he opened the car door and got out.

"Aw, shit." Captain David Cross was a tall, muscular African-American with three commendations to his name and a reputation for being tough and demanding. He was also the kind of cop whose emotions ran deep, especially where his men were concerned.

He took one look at the contents of the suitcase Nick had placed on his desk, along with the notebook, and looked close to tears. "Not Matt. Christ, not Matt."

Fists on his hips, he walked around his office like

a caged lion. "How in hell did that happen?" He looked at Nick as though expecting him to know the answer, but Nick felt as helpless as his boss.

Cross stopped his pacing and came to stand in front of the open suitcase. "I was reluctant to put him on a sting operation at first, did you know that?" He didn't wait for an answer. "I thought he was too much like you, impulsive and a little crazy." Cross barked a laugh and shook his head. "He told me crazy was good, that it kept the bad guys on their toes. He was the last person I expected to give in to the temptation.

"The day before the shooting," Cross continued, "I asked him how the case was coming along. He said he was making progress, gaining the confidence of Matias and Santos and that it wouldn't be long until he found out who the head honcho was." He picked up one of the bundles. "You counted it?"

"No, but I'd say there's about twenty-five thousand dollars in there."

"Corruption in the department. The press is going to have a field day with that one." He glared at the money as if willing it to disappear. After a few more seconds, he asked, "How's Patti?"

"Better now that the money is out of her house. She'll be moving to Ohio for a while, so the girls won't be affected by the publicity. She's thinking of staying there permanently."

Cross nodded. "Good idea. I'll hold off making a

public statement as long as I can. That'll give Patti a little time.''

''She'll appreciate that.'' Nick started to leave. He couldn't stand looking at that money for another second.

''Nick, wait.'' From the mountain of paper work on his desk, Cross took a fax. ''A Detective Quinn from the Miami police called me earlier. You know Jonathan Bowman?''

Nick nodded. The news had spread fast. ''I know he's Cecily Sanders's nephew by marriage.''

''Detective Quinn says Bowman flew to Miami on Monday morning and now there seems to be evidence that he's either missing or dead.''

Nick listened to the details of Bowman's disappearance for the second time today without letting on that he already knew about the incident.

''I normally wouldn't get involved,'' Cross continued, ''but Cecily Sanders, as you know, has done a lot for Philadelphia and for our police force. We owe her.''

''Have you talked to her?''

Cross nodded. ''I told her about Quinn's call and assured her we would cooperate fully with the Miami PD. She wants to be kept informed.''

''What's the latest information on Bowman?''

''Quinn requested dental records and the family's complying.'' He closed the suitcase lid as if he, too, couldn't bear the sight of all that dirty money. ''I'm assigning you to the case, Nick, but only as a liaison between Quinn and this department. And for God's sake, don't breathe a word of this to the press. Cecily Sanders was adamant about that.''

''A bomb explosion isn't something you can shove under the rug,'' Nick pointed out.

''I know. Let's just try to keep the story under wrap as long as we can.''

Because the police department was one big party line, it didn't take Nick long to find out which two patrol officers had been harassing Kelly. Officers Demaro and Swan were young, full of self-importance and eager to right the perceived wrong their way.

Both were in the locker room, changing from their uniforms into their civvies and looking forward to a night on the town when Nick caught up with them. Faced with Nick's fury, they had quickly admitted following Kelly's bright blue Beetle and writing her up with phony violations whenever they thought they could get away with it. But no matter how much Nick pushed, they vehemently denied vandalizing her town house.

''We just wanted to shake her up a little,'' Swan said with a bitter edge in his voice. ''Believe me, she deserved a lot more than a couple of tickets, but that's all we did. I swear.''

''So do I,'' Demaro said.

''You two clowns didn't spray-paint her front door?'' Nick demanded. ''Or slash her tires?''

"Hell, no! You think we're crazy? You think that's worth losing our jobs over?"

Nick had been around enough liars in his life to recognize them a mile away. These two men weren't lying. They were telling the truth.

Which meant only one thing. Someone else had an ax to grind with Kelly Robolo.

Eleven

The sky was a cloudless blue and the temperature already a sweltering ninety-two degrees when Kelly arrived in Miami the following morning. Because this was the high season for Florida vacationers, the 6:22 to Miami had been fully booked and she'd had to settle for the next flight, which touched down at Miami Airport a little before ten.

Outside the terminal, travelers were already lined up, waiting for taxis and hotel shuttles, but thanks to an enterprising young man who kept moving the crowd along, Kelly was inside a cab within minutes and on her way to the Miami Police Department.

To her surprise, Detective Quinn was not nearly as irritated to see her as she had expected. In fact, he was almost civil, a transformation she couldn't explain but didn't question. In his late fifties, he was a beefy man with a ruddy complexion, a bulbous nose and the tired look of a man with not enough hours in the day. On his desk was a half-eaten cinnamon roll and a can of Pepsi.

"Why can't reporters ever take no for an answer?"

he muttered as he took Kelly's offered hand and shook it.

"If we did, we wouldn't be reporters for long." Kelly sat down in a gray metal chair across from his desk and set her purse on the floor. "Besides, I wanted to meet you, you know, face-to-face."

He took a bite of his roll. "Why?" he asked as he chewed.

He was still a grouch but with a softer edge. "Because," she replied, "I was afraid I had made a bad impression on the phone the other night and I wanted a chance to correct that."

"And then you'll leave?"

Kelly smiled. Big Bad Quinn had a sense of humor. "Not exactly."

"I was afraid of that."

"I only have a couple of questions and then I'll be out of your hair."

"I'll save you the trouble, at least with the first question." He took a paper napkin and wiped the crumbs from his mouth. "You want to know if the lab has ID'ed the body in room 116. The answer is no. Bowman's dental records were delivered to us less than an hour ago, but the lab is backed up at the moment. I don't expect to hear anything for another couple of days."

"You'll call me with the results?"

Two bushy eyebrows went up. "Do I have a choice?"

She was starting to like the man. "What about the motel clerk? Is he conscious yet?"

Quinn's expression turned regretful. "Domingo Nardis died early this morning. I never had a chance to talk to him."

"Oh no." Kelly fell back against her seat. The clerk had been the one person who could have identified the occupant of room 116. Now they would have to wait for the lab report.

"What about the rest of the staff? They might feel differently now."

"Already tried them. They're gone."

"What do you mean gone?"

"Gone, vanished, left without a forwarding address."

Kelly couldn't believe it. What was it with this city that people kept disappearing? "They can't just vanish. Don't they have families? Bills to pay?"

Quinn laughed, though he didn't seem amused. "Most of the people who work in places like the Encantado are illegal immigrants who enter the United States with phony papers or no papers at all. The last thing they want is to be questioned by the police."

"So we're back to square one."

"Not exactly." He drained the last of his Pepsi and tossed the can in the wastebasket beside his desk where it landed with a loud *clang*.

Kelly sat up, waiting for him to continue.

"Here's proof that your friend's husband was in Miami on Monday." Quinn pushed a three-by-five index card toward her, turning it around so she could read what was scrawled on it. There was a name and an address—Magdalena Montoya, 412 Ocean Drive, Miami Beach.

Kelly looked up, puzzled. "Who is Magdalena Montoya?"

"A friend of Mr. Bowman's. We found her phone number in the motel phone records and tracked her down."

Kelly gained a new respect for the detective. He might not have much in the congeniality department, but he was getting things done. "Did you talk to her?"

He nodded. "That was my first priority. Not only did she confirm that Mr. Bowman had called her on Monday morning, but she told me they had lunch together."

"That doesn't make any sense," Kelly said, remembering how long she had questioned Victoria the other night. "Jonathan doesn't know anyone in Miami. And he certainly never mentioned anyone named Magdalena Montoya."

"I don't suppose he would."

Kelly didn't miss the little smirk on Quinn's face. "What does that mean?"

Quinn cleared his throat. "Mr. Bowman and Miss Montoya were lovers."

Kelly's mouth opened in shock and it was some time until she could close it. "And you believed her?" she asked when she could talk.

"She had no reason to lie."

"But she must have. The idea alone, that Jonathan would even look at another woman, much less sleep with her, is ludicrous." She looked at him defensively, expecting a roadblock to her next request. "I want to talk to her."

To her surprise, Quinn nodded at the index card. "I figured you'd say that. Go ahead, go talk to her, provided she agrees to see you."

"You don't mind?"

"Not if it gets you off my back." He pointed a warning finger at her. "But I want no funny stuff, you hear? By that I mean no threats, no pressure, and none of those heavy-handed tactics some of you reporters are famous for."

"That's not how I work."

"Good, because if you so much as sneeze on her, I'll throw the book at you. And I promise you, you won't like our jails."

For drama, diversity and quirkiness, no place on earth could compare to the nonstop spectacle on Miami's South Beach. The famous promenade, with its art deco hotels and trendy boutiques, was a constant parade of in-line skaters in skimpy shorts, drag queens in glittering boas, tanned young men flexing their impressive muscles and senior citizens taking it all in with a mixture of awe and delight.

Magdalena Montoya's beachfront condo was on the sixth floor of a pastel-pink building that had an unrestricted view of the ocean. A uniformed maid let Kelly in and politely asked her to wait in the foyer.

From where she stood, Kelly could see a large, breezy living room with white wall-to-wall carpeting, white sofas and a white baby grand in the center of the room. White lilies in huge terra-cotta urns flanked the French windows.

The maid was back in an instant. "Señorita Montoya is waiting for you on the terrace."

Señorita Montoya lay on a blue chaise, her face half hidden behind large Jackie O sunglasses. She appeared to be in her mid-thirties and was as spectacular-looking as her all-white living room. Snug white capri pants and a black tube top skimmed her perfect body like a second skin. Her long, cascading black hair and peekaboo hairstyle reminded Kelly of those seductive femmes fatales of the forties—the kind that always got men in trouble. A tall glass half filled with a thick creamy drink stood on a small table.

Dipping her chin a little, the woman pulled her sunglasses down her nose and surveyed Kelly above the rims. "Good morning, Miss Robolo." Though she looked as Latin as her name implied, she didn't have the slightest trace of an accent. "Could I interest you in a Puerto Rican milk shake? It's made with papayas, bananas and pineapples. Marisol whips them up fresh daily."

"Nothing for me, thank you."

Magdalena waved to another lounge chair across from her. "Don't just stand there. Sit down."

"Thank you." Kelly sat on the edge of the chair and glanced at the beach six floors below. A lively game of volleyball was in progress, men against women. All were young, deeply tanned and spectacularly built. Whoever had told her that Florida was for old people was seriously misinformed.

Already warm, Kelly unbuttoned the jacket of her white linen suit but did not remove it. "You don't seem surprised to see me."

"Detective Quinn just called. He told me you would be stopping by."

Kelly wondered what else he had told her. Nothing too bad, apparently, or Magdalena wouldn't be so friendly.

"You wanted to question me about Jonathan?" She picked up her glass and started sipping through the straw.

To hear Jonathan's name spoken by this strange woman was more of a shock than Kelly had expected. "Yes. Yes, I do." She cleared her throat. "Have you...known him long?"

"A year this month." She turned the straw into the thick milk shake, lifted it and licked the end with the tip of her tongue. It was a very sensual gesture, yet totally uncalculated.

"I understand that the two of you are...uh...close friends?"

This time, the attractive Latina removed her sunglasses and pushed them into her hair. Her eyes were enormous, and very black, with long, silky lashes that couldn't possibly be real but probably were. "We are more than close friends, Miss Robolo. Jonathan and I are very much in love. I know this must come as a shock to you, but it's the truth. That's what you came here for, isn't it? The truth?"

"I did, but you can't blame me for being a little skeptical. I've known Jonathan for many years. He's a happily married man. He would never betray his wife."

"How can you really be sure of that, Miss Robolo?"

Her logic couldn't be dismissed. Thrown off for a moment, Kelly made a helpless gesture. "I can't even believe we're talking about the same man."

Magdalena swung her legs to the side and rose, graceful as a swan. "Come with me."

She walked back inside, her hips undulating with each step. From a glass mantel above the fireplace, she took a framed photograph and brought it back.

"Here," she said, handing it to Kelly. "Maybe this will convince you."

Kelly took the photo from her and had another jolt. The smiling couple in the picture looked radiantly happy. They sat at a table, cheek to cheek, in what appeared to be a nightclub. The woman in the white strapless dress was Magdalena. The handsome, beaming man beside her, was unquestionably Jonathan.

"That was taken last December," Magdalena said. "Right here in South Beach."

Kelly remembered an overnight trip to Las Vegas

Jonathan was supposed to have taken a couple of weeks before Christmas. It would have been easy enough for him to cut the trip short and come to Miami before returning to Philadelphia. "Did he come down often?"

"About once a month. He would get in early, spend a couple of hours with me, then fly back home."

It could be done. As a vice president, Jonathan wasn't required to punch a time clock. Nor did he have to account for his whereabouts every minute of the day.

"I'm sorry about all the heartache my relationship with Jonathan is going to cause his wife and the rest of his family. Believe me, I hadn't planned on the truth ever coming out, but when Detective Quinn showed up yesterday with the news that Jonathan was either dead or missing—"

"We have no proof that he is dead."

"I know, and I want to believe with all my heart that my Jonathan is alive. But if it's true that he was staying at the Encantado..." She shook her head. "That's a terrible place. The police should have shut it down long ago."

For a woman who claimed to love Jonathan so much, she wasn't exactly overcome with grief, Kelly thought. Or maybe she knew Jonathan was alive and wasn't saying anything.

"Do you have any idea why he would stay in such a place?"

"No. As for Detective Quinn's suspicions that Jonathan might be involved with a drug cartel, I can't comment on that because I don't know."

"You never asked what kind of business brought him to Miami month after month?"

"No."

A mistress who didn't ask questions. How convenient. Kelly walked over to the mantel and put the photograph back on the glass shelf. "Would you mind telling me where and how you met Jonathan?" She turned back to face Magdalena and looked for a flicker in the woman's eyes, a nervousness in her voice that would signal she was lying. Magdalena remained the picture of poise and self-control.

"We met at Salamander," she said without hesitation. "It's a nightclub in the western part of town." She flipped her long hair behind her shoulder. "I used to work there as an exotic dancer."

The thought that Jonathan had fallen for a stripper was even more ridiculous. The night before his wedding, rather than accompany his wedding party to a strip club, Jonathan had spent his last night as a bachelor in his apartment, playing gin rummy with his upstairs neighbor.

Magdalena's expression turned wistful. "The moment he walked in, I knew immediately he was different from any of the other men. He didn't make snide remarks as I danced, he didn't talk dirty and he didn't grope. He just smiled. At the end of my act, he invited me to sit and have a drink with him. We spent half the night talking and by the time we said goodbye the following morning, I was totally infatuated with him." Her eyes glistened. "He was so sweet and so handsome."

Kelly's intuitions about people had never failed her. Whether the subject was male or female, she could form an opinion within the first few minutes of an encounter. Magdalena Montoya, however, was an enigma. Kelly wanted to dislike her and couldn't. As for her story about her affair with Jonathan, as improbable as it seemed, it had the cold ring of truth.

The barrette in Kelly's hair had come loose and she clipped it back. "If we could get back to yesterday for a moment," she said. "I understand that Jonathan called you as soon as his plane landed?"

"That's right. We went out for an early lunch, then we came back here for a couple of hours."

"What time was it when he left?"

"A little before two."

More than enough time to get to the airport for his flight back to Philadelphia. Except he had never boarded it. Somewhere between South Beach and Miami International, something had happened. "Did you know Jonathan was married when you first met him?" Kelly asked casually.

"Yes." Magdalena walked over to a table, opened a silver box and extracted a cigarette. "I also knew he was unhappy. His wife was always working."

Kelly couldn't imagine Jonathan saying something so cruel and so untrue to anyone, even a mistress.

Admittedly, Victoria was busy and had to travel abroad a couple of times a year, but she had never neglected her family. If anything, Jonathan was the one who worked long hours, often coming home too late to put his daughter to bed.

Kelly looked around the lavish surroundings. Magdalena didn't look as though she punched a time clock either. "You said earlier that you used to be an exotic dancer. Does that mean you're no longer working?"

Magdalena let out a rich, throaty laugh. "Heavens, no. Jonathan wouldn't allow it, even though my boss was very unhappy about my leaving." She gave her long tresses another flip. "I was his best dancer. I brought in more customers than all the other girls put together."

That part wasn't difficult to believe. Magdalena exuded sex from every pore and wasn't shy about flaunting it. "Pardon me for asking, Miss Montoya, but, if you're not working, how do you afford a place like this?"

"Jonathan pays my rent." She said it without the least bit of embarrassment. "And all my other expenses as well."

Kelly was speechless. How could Jonathan afford such an expensive mistress? Granted, he earned a good salary, and so did Victoria, but between the mortgage on the new house, Phoebe's private school, the membership at an exclusive golf club and a couple of vacations each year, there wasn't much left of their monthly budget.

Where had the money come from if not from drugs?

"Miss Robolo? Are you all right?"

At the concerned question, Kelly quickly nodded. "Yes, I...I was just thinking. Don't mind me."

As she started to turn, an object on the other side of the mantel caught her eye. Startled, she stared at the small, delicately carved bottle in a brilliant shade of blue and recognized it immediately. It was the snuff bottle Victoria had described—the one that had disappeared from her shop.

"May I ask you where this bottle comes from?" she asked.

Magdalena blew her cigarette smoke toward the ceiling. "Jonathan gave it to me to add to my collection." She nodded toward a white lacquered cabinet across the room. Inside was an assortment of miniature bottles of every shape and color. "Why do you ask?"

"Because a very valuable snuff bottle identical to this one disappeared from Victoria Bowman's antiques shop two days ago."

Magdalena's face registered instant shock. "Oh, my God! And you think this is it?"

"It certainly fits the description."

"But—" Magdalena crushed her cigarette in a silver ashtray. "The bottles in my collection are very inexpensive, no more than a hundred dollars at the most. Jonathan knew that." She took the bottle from the shelf. "Could you be mistaken?"

"I could be. I'm not an expert, but Victoria would know."

Magdalena looked clearly uncomfortable. "Look, I don't want to get in trouble." Her hand shook as she handed the bottle to Kelly. "Take it," she said. "Give it back to Mrs. Bowman. And please tell her I had no idea this was a valuable collectible, or that Jonathan had taken it from her shop. I would have never accepted it otherwise."

Kelly hesitated. Taking such an expensive object with her was a huge responsibility, but it was the only proof she had that Jonathan had been here on Monday. "I'll need something to wrap it in," she said.

"Of course."

Magdalena disappeared into another room and came back a few moments later with a small sheet of bubble wrap. Afraid the plastic would destroy the fingerprints already on the bottle, Kelly first wrapped the object in her handkerchief, then in the bubble wrap. As she worked, Kelly's thoughts remained on Jonathan. How could she have so totally misjudged him? How could he have seemed such a perfect husband on the surface, and have had this secret life in Miami? Other men might be capable of such deception, but Jonathan?

When the bottle was safely tucked away inside her bag, Kelly handed Magdalena her business card. "Will you let me know if you remember anything else?"

Magdalena glanced at it. "Remember what? I told you everything."

"Jonathan may try to contact you. If he does, will you let me know?"

Magdalena raised her chin. "Would you betray the man you love, Miss Robolo?"

In other words, Kelly thought, the answer was no. In spite of her disappointment, Kelly couldn't help admiring Magdalena for standing by her man. Or maybe it wasn't that at all. Maybe her true concern was that if Jonathan was found and returned to his wife, or in the worst-case scenario, arrested, she would lose her meal ticket.

Kelly kept those thoughts to herself. "Thanks for being so candid with me," she said as they walked to the door. "All that prying into your private life couldn't have been easy for you."

Magdalena gave a small shrug. "That's okay. You were a lot nicer to talk to than Detective Quinn." Her smile turned teasing. "But not nearly as sexy as that other detective."

The words brought Kelly to a halt. "*Other* detective?"

"The good-looking one. Tall, with red hair and blue eyes. His name was Nick McBride."

Twelve

"*McBride* was here?" Kelly almost choked on the words. "When?"

"This morning. As a matter of fact, he left just a few minutes before you arrived."

Kelly thought of Nick's sudden interest when she had told him about Jonathan's disappearance and how his questions and comments had led her to believe he would help her. Then he had turned her down at the last moment making her feel like an idiot.

"Was he here on official police business?" she asked.

"He showed me his badge, so I assumed he was. What other reason would he have for being here?"

What other reason indeed? "I was just curious."

Kelly forced herself to think rationally. Okay. So Nick, on official business or not, had gotten to Magdalena first. What harm was there in that? He hadn't learned any more than she had, unless Magdalena, with her obvious affinity for handsome men, had been more forthcoming with him than she had been with Kelly.

"Don't take this wrong, Miss Montoya, but did you

by any chance tell Detective McBride anything you didn't tell me?" Kelly tried not to sound accusing but must have done a poor job because Magdalena looked hurt.

"Why would I do that? I have nothing to hide from either one of you."

"I'm sorry, I had to ask. The man has a million tricks up his sleeve. You want to be careful with him."

Magdalena's eyes twinkled with amusement. "He didn't look so dangerous to me."

"He works at it."

The temperature and humidity had risen a few more degrees by the time Kelly stepped out of the air-conditioned building and into the brilliant South Florida sunshine. The beach volleyball game was over and instead a juggler in swimming trunks and an alligator headdress entertained a small crowd, bowing every now and then as delighted children laughed and clapped. An elderly woman with blue hair and lime-green slacks walked by, licking an ice-cream cone. She smiled at Kelly, who smiled back.

How different yet uncomplicated life seemed here, Kelly mused. Was that why Jonathan kept coming to South Beach time after time? Or was there another, more lucrative reason for those monthly visits? She didn't want to believe he was involved in something as sordid as drug trafficking, but how else could he afford to pay the rent on Magdalena's condo?

And what other reason could he have had for staying at a place like the Encantado?

Glancing at her watch, she saw that she had another three hours before her flight back to Philadelphia. Maybe instead of waiting at the airport, she could put the time to good use and try to find out a little more about the lovely Señorita Montoya.

She was in luck. Salamander, the nightclub where Magdalena had worked, was open from noon to 4:00 a.m. and was located just off Thirty-seventh Street.

It took her cabdriver only fifteen minutes to get there, but what a difference the short drive made. Leaving the glitz of South Beach behind, the cabbie drove west, past the downtown area, then through several neighborhoods that ranged from run-down to downright scary. Kelly held her bag against her chest, praying she hadn't made a mistake in taking Victoria's snuff bottle with her.

Before she could dwell too long on her fear of being robbed, the driver pulled into a long, dingy alley off the main thoroughfare and stopped. "Here you are." He glanced up at the sign above the battered wooden door, looking nervous.

Kelly followed his gaze and understood his uneasiness. Whoever had chosen the location for Salamander hadn't done it for the view. Two high walls covered with graffiti bordered the alley, shutting out all sunlight. A nearby apartment building with a crumbling facade and most of its windows boarded up made the place even more of an eyesore.

Kelly almost told the driver to turn around and take her to the airport, but then chided herself. She had been in worse places than this, and Thirty-seventh Street, though not heavily traveled, was only fifty feet away. All she had to do was make sure her cab was there when she came out.

Trying not to show her own apprehension, Kelly took twenty dollars out of her purse. "I have to get to the airport after I'm finished here," she said, holding the bill just out of his reach. "If you wait for me, I'll let you keep the change from this twenty and I'll double your fare to the airport."

The cabbie's eyes darted right and left. "Okay," he said, snatching the bill. "But you gotta make it quick, lady. This is a bad area. I don't want no trouble."

"I'll only be a few minutes."

The interior of the tavern was dim, and Kelly had to wait several seconds for her eyes to adjust to the darkness. Once they did, she saw a plump, heavily made-up woman with bleached blond hair sitting at the bar, nursing a drink. In a far corner, close to a small stage, two large men with their arms tattooed from one end to another played a pinball machine and drank beer from the bottle.

At a call from the blonde, a surly bartender with a two-day stubble, a dirty T-shirt and a toothpick in the corner of his mouth appeared from a back door and watched Kelly approach, while the two pinball players made suggestive remarks. Kelly ignored them and walked straight to the bar. "May I have a club soda, please?" As the bartender filled a glass, she once again dug into her bag for money, this time two twenties and a ten. She also took out a photograph of Jonathan she had borrowed from Victoria. "Is the owner around?"

"I'm the owner." The man put the glass in front of her with a bang.

"In that case, I'd like some information." She put the money on the counter, along with Jonathan's photograph.

The bartender eyed the bills, then the photograph. "What kind of information?"

"Have you ever seen this man?"

The toothpick was switched from one end of his mouth to the other. "Yeah, I seen him." His voice was heavy with resentment.

"When was that?"

"'bout a year ago. Son of a bitch took my best dancer away."

So that much was true. "Did he ever come back?"

"No. Or Magdalena. I still owed the bitch a week's pay but she never bothered to come and pick it up."

Of course not. She had latched onto a very generous sugar daddy. "Tell me about that night," Kelly said, wondering how much more her fifty dollars would buy. "Did he come in alone?"

"Came alone, sat alone and only had eyes for Maggy. That's 'bout it."

"Had you ever seen him before that?"

"No." His mouth pulled into what could have passed for a smile. "We don't get too many of his kind 'round this joint."

His thick fingers grabbed the money and made it disappear. The blonde at the end of the bar yelled something, and he walked away to pour his customer another drink. The conversation was over.

Seeing no reason to hang around the place a moment longer, Kelly slid down from her stool, her club soda untouched, and hurried out, glad to see that the two gorillas were no longer playing pinball. Out in the alley, she stopped and looked around in dismay. Her cab was gone.

She thought about going back inside and asking the bartender to call another taxi, but the prospect of waiting for a driver to come to this part of town did not thrill her. She was better off taking her chances on the main thoroughfare.

"Hey, beautiful!"

Kelly's heart did a little flip as she recognized the raspy voice of one of the men in Salamander. Had they been waiting for her? Once again, she ignored them and quickened her step, telling herself not to panic. She knew martial arts. Once they realized that, they'd leave her alone.

A cry of alarm rose from her throat as both men suddenly jumped in front of her and started walking backward, grinning from ear to ear.

Up close, they looked even larger and more ominous than they had inside the bar. The one who had addressed her had long brown hair held back in a ponytail and a gold upper front tooth. Dangling from his right ear was an earring in the shape of a skull. His companion was no less frightening. An inch or two shorter, he wore a red bandanna around his shaved head and stared directly at her chest, leaving little doubt about his intentions.

"Where you going so fast, baby?" Gold Tooth asked.

Kelly kept on walking, remembering Dr. Ho's instructions when faced with imminent danger. Stay calm. Breathe deeply. Consider all options. The only option she could think of at the moment was to run, but considering the obstacles, that was impossible. "I'm meeting some friends at the corner," she said.

The man laughed. "You hear that, Paulie? She's meeting some friends at the corner. You see anyone at the corner?"

The man he had addressed as Paulie glanced over his shoulder and laughed. "I see shit, man."

They stopped walking, blocking her path. A cold fear lodged in Kelly's throat. "Look," she said as calmly as she could manage. "I don't know who you are or what you want, but I wouldn't try anything if I were you. I know karate."

At that remark, both men laughed. "Did you hear that, Paulie? The girl knows karate."

Paulie scratched his crotch. "I heard."

"Show her what *you* know, Paulie."

Obviously glad to have been asked, Paulie executed

a series of quick hands-and-knees movements Kelly immediately recognized as wing chun kung-fu with some Thai kickboxing thrown into it.

It was clear she was no match for him and would have to think of some other way to escape. Her thoughts never went farther as Gold Tooth, still laughing, wrapped an arm around her waist, lifting her off the ground and carrying her inside the dark, dank doorway.

Kelly screamed and pounded his head with her fists, but he didn't appear to feel the blows. If anything, her efforts seemed to excite him more.

"You keep this up, and I'm gonna be too hot for foreplay." He pinned her against the wall, crushing his body against hers. "You like foreplay, don't you, baby?" He ran the back of his finger down her throat.

Kelly did some quick thinking. What did they want most—sex or money? Probably both, but if she enticed them with the money first, they might forget about raping her long enough for her to escape.

"Look," she said, praying the lure of cold hard cash would win. "I have money. Two hundred dollars. You can have it. Just let me go."

Gold Tooth laughed. "Oh, we'll get the money. But first, me and my bud, we want a little action. Know what I mean?"

Her only answer was to duck under his arm. She was immediately slammed back against the wall. "My, my, you're a slippery one, ain't you?"

Behind him, Paulie chuckled. "I like 'em slippery."

Seemingly unconcerned about her lack of response, Gold Tooth started rubbing Kelly's thigh. His hand was rough as sandpaper and sweaty, his breath foul as he breathed heavily into her face. "You feel good, doll. Real good."

She had to get out of here. She had to put this brute out of commission and take her chances with Paulie. Not an easy task considering their size and strength.

There was one method of self-defense, however, that didn't require a lot of power, just accuracy. After she was nearly abducted three years ago, Dr. Ho had made her practice that technique over and over until she could do it in her sleep. She had never put it to use but knew it worked. At the moment, it was her only chance. But first she had to stop struggling and pretend she was enjoying what her aggressor was doing to her.

Trying hard not to gag, Kelly began moving her own body in a slow, suggestive way that brought out a moan from the man's throat.

"Oh, baby, what are you doing to me?"

"Give me a little more room and I'll do more."

Thank God he was too stupid to realize she was setting him up. His lower body still glued to hers, he pulled his torso back an inch or two, then took her hand and pressed it to his crotch. "Yeah, baby. Do it."

Behind him, Paulie was getting excited as well. "Hey, I want some fun, too."

His friend gave him a vicious swat. "Wait your turn, man."

That was all the distraction Kelly needed. In one fast motion, she yanked her arm out, put the heel of her hand under the man's chin and pushed up with all the force she could manage within the confined space. It was enough. The man's head snapped back and he let out a long, agonizing growl. The fact that he couldn't scream told her she had achieved her objective. She had broken his jaw. A harder push would have broken his nose as well.

He fell to his knees, the lower part of his face cupped between his hands. Blood seeped through his fingers and his eyes were closed as he rocked back and forth in obvious pain. It was a wonder he hadn't passed out.

"You *bitch*." Kelly heard a click and before she could identify what it was, Paulie's powerful arm was around her, the point of a blade pressed against her carotid artery. "You're gonna pay for hurting my friend."

Kelly held her breath. One wrong move on her part, and the blade would sink in.

"Let her go!" a male voice shouted.

The command took Paulie by surprise. Instinctively, he let go of Kelly and whipped around, his expression mean, his voice low and threatening. In the darkness, the other man was only a shadow. "Beat it, asshole, if you know what's good for—"

The rest of his sentence caught in his throat. In a split second, Kelly's rescuer, who seemed to have come from nowhere, landed a hard punch to the man's jaw.

The knife flew out of Paulie's hand, but almost immediately his leg shot out in a roundhouse kick. The other man quickly blocked it with his elbow before delivering a heel-kick to the groin. A grunt that sounded like rolling thunder rose from Paulie's throat. His head low, he charged and went down, taking the other man with him.

Fearing his advantage over the stranger, Kelly ran toward the wrestling bodies and gave Paulie a hard kick to the ribs, jumping back before he could grab her leg. It was enough to give the newcomer the break he needed. With the agility of a cat, he bolted up and yanked his opponent to his feet. He finished him off with a right hook that would have made Mohammed Ali proud.

Kelly heard the sickening crack of bones breaking. Before Paulie could decide whether or not he was up for another round, his friend was back on his feet. Still unable to speak, he slapped Paulie on the arm and thumbed him out.

In an instant they were gone. "Thank you." As she spoke, Kelly bent to retrieve her purse from the ground and was relieved to see it hadn't been trampled on during the tussle. "I don't know what I would have done if you hadn't come along."

Holding a handkerchief, the man looked around, found the switchblade and went to pick it up. "You should know better than to venture into such a neighborhood all alone."

Kelly took a step back. The man who had just saved her from being raped, and possibly killed, was none other than Nick McBride. Like a punctured balloon, her gratitude quickly deflated. "What are you doing here?"

Nick brushed the dust from the sleeve of this tan sports jacket. "A simple thank-you will do."

"Thank you? You think I'm stupid? You probably staged this little ambush."

He looked amused, which infuriated her even more. "Now why would I do that?"

"God only knows. I've stopped trying to figure you out."

"You're upset because I scooped you."

"You didn't scoop me," she snapped, her face suddenly hot. "You wouldn't know how. And I wouldn't be bragging if I were you. What you did was low and deceitful."

"You've got it all wrong, Kelly."

"Do I? You pretended not to be interested in Jonathan's disappearance, then you sneaked behind my back, came down to Miami and made sure you were one step ahead of me the entire time. What would you call that?"

"Lucky—for you that is. Just think where you'd be right now if I hadn't shown up." He took out his cell phone from his breast pocket and punched in a number.

"Don't try to make yourself into a hero, McBride. I can take care of myself."

"Your gratitude is touching. Maybe I should have left you in the hands of those two thugs. The experience would have taught you a little humility." His voice rose. "Detective Quinn, please," he said into the phone. "Tell him it's Detective McBride. And it's urgent."

Within seconds, he was speaking again. "Hi, Carl. No, nothing helpful. She told me the same thing she told you, but I didn't call about Magdalena. I need to report an aggravated assault. Kelly Robolo. No, she's all right." He winked at Kelly. "I got here just in time." There was a slight pause. "Two of them. Caucasian, late twenties. Big, six-three to six-four, about two hundred and forty pounds each, tattoos on both arms. One wears a ponytail. He's the one with the broken jaw." He laughed. "No, Kelly did. I'm only responsible for a broken nose on the other guy, who by the way has a shaved head and wears a red bandanna."

As he talked, Nick walked out of the doorway and into the alley. Kelly followed him. Though she hated to appear interested, she didn't want to miss one single morsel of the conversation.

"The incident took place outside Salamander,"

Nick continued. "It's a strip club at night and a tavern... You know it? Good. Check with the owner. He may know the perps. They were playing the pinball machine when I was there. Oh, and one of them dropped his switchblade. Yes, I have it." He looked at Kelly. "Can you add anything to the description I just gave?"

The thought of teaming up with him brought Kelly's irritation to a new level, but she didn't let it show. She had as much stake in wanting those two men apprehended as he did, especially if they had anything to do with Jonathan's disappearance. "The one with the ponytail had a gold front tooth and an earring in the shape of a skull. The other was named Paulie."

"Did you get that, Carl?" Nick said into the phone. He nodded. "Sure. Give us about twenty minutes or so."

He hung up and slid the phone back in his pocket. "He wants us to stop by the station to look at some mug shots."

She had figured that much. "I'll miss my plane."

"I'll make sure it waits for you." He took her hand and started walking rapidly toward the main thoroughfare, forcing her to run to keep up with him. "Hurry up. My cab is waiting."

His cab was waiting? He had to be kidding.

At the curb, Nick put two fingers in his mouth and let out a shrill whistle. To her astonishment, a cab pulled out from across the street, made a fast U-turn and came to a screeching stop in front of them. Nick opened the back door and motioned Kelly in.

After what had just happened in that back alley, she would have been stupid to turn down the ride, but no way was she going to cozy up in the back with him. Instead, she opened the front door on the passenger side and sat down, grateful for the blast of cold air coming from the air conditioner.

The driver turned to Nick. "To the airport, *amigo?*" he asked.

"The police station first, Luis. On Second Street." He closed the door. "Then the airport." He leaned forward, his head almost touching Kelly's, and handed her the sunglasses she thought she had lost in the shuffle. "Here. You dropped these earlier."

"Thank you," she said curtly.

As the cab wound its way through traffic, Nick, apparently in a talkative mood, told Kelly about his first trip to Florida when he was ten—a father-and-son fishing expedition that had begun in Fort Lauderdale and ended up in Key West, where Nick had caught a five-foot swordfish. Nick's relationship with his father must have been very special, just like hers had been with her own dad. It was a funny, if one-sided, conversation. From time to time the cabdriver glanced at her, as if waiting for Kelly to answer, or to make a comment. She remained silent during the entire trip to the police station.

Thirteen

"**K**elly, here!"

Kelly raised herself on tiptoe and peered over the stream of travelers exiting from the jetway until she spotted Victoria.

Nick, she knew, was right behind her. Though they had taken separate cabs from the police station to the airport, they had come back to Philadelphia on the same plane. Kelly had barely made it, while Nick, who had called ahead, had boarded late. A female flight attendant had greeted him warmly, calling him by name and pointing to his seat before pulling the cabin door shut.

"What is Nick McBride doing on your flight?" Victoria handed Kelly her black London Fog coat.

"Long story. I'll tell you later."

"What about Jonathan? Did you find him?"

"Let's get out of here first."

Victoria's features tightened but she said nothing as she followed Kelly toward the garage elevators. Moments later, in the quiet comfort of her black Ford Explorer, Victoria turned around in her seat. "It's bad, isn't it? Or you would have reassured me right away." Her eyes took on a haunted look. "Is Jonathan dead?"

"They don't know. His dental records arrived today but they haven't done any tests yet. To complicate matters, the motel clerk who could have identified Jonathan died this morning as a result of his burns."

"What about the other employees? You said there were maids, and a maintenance man."

"They've all vanished." She repeated what Detective Quinn had told her about illegal immigrants.

"Kelly, tell me the truth. Do you believe Jonathan is alive?"

"I don't know. I'm getting mixed signals and until I've sorted them all out, I can't even make an educated guess as to what happened." She watched a couple with two young boys, both wearing Mickey Mouse ears, make their way toward a station wagon. "One possibility is that he may be hiding," she said softly.

"Hiding from what?"

"I don't know. Maybe he's in some kind of trouble."

"He would call me if he was."

"Not if he was afraid of putting you and Phoebe in danger."

"Danger from what?" Victoria searched Kelly's face. "There's something you haven't told me. What is it?"

Kelly forced herself to meet her friend's worried gaze. "This is going to hurt, Victoria."

"The only thing that would hurt me unbearably right now is if I found out that my husband was dead. Anything else I can handle."

Kelly studied Victoria's lovely face for a moment. For once her eyes were free of panic, her chin set, her hands steady on the steering wheel. The last two days had toughened her up, but she couldn't possibly be prepared for what she would hear next. Kelly took a breath and released it. "Jonathan is having an affair."

Victoria's hands slipped to her lap, and anger rose to her cheeks in a burst of red. "You're crazy!"

"I have proof—"

"Fuck your proof!" Victoria shouted, pounding the steering wheel with her fist. "You don't know what you're talking about. Why are you doing this?"

"I met her," Kelly said gently.

"Oh, God." Victoria pressed her head against the headrest and closed her eyes.

"Maybe we should wait until we're home," Kelly suggested.

"No." Victoria opened her eyes. "Tell me now. Tell me everything."

As gently as she knew how, Kelly told her about Magdalena and the relationship she and Jonathan had been having for almost a year. She left nothing out. She told her about the beachfront condo, the photograph on the mantel, and about Jonathan's frequent trips to Miami over the last twelve months. She even brought up her run-in with Paulie and his friend, and how Nick had rescued her.

Victoria listened quietly and when Kelly was finished, all sign of hysteria had vanished. "I don't believe any of it," she said, meeting Kelly's eyes. "Jonathan would never cheat on me. He loves me. Phoebe and I are his entire life."

"That's what I kept telling myself over and over. I was so sure the whole thing was a case of mistaken identity. Or a scam of some sort."

"And that's exactly what it is. A scam, engineered by that...tramp."

"Magdalena never came forward with the information, Victoria. Quinn tracked her down and went to question her. She had no reason to lie."

"I don't care! I know my husband. He would never get involved with another woman, a stripper no less. She's making all this up."

Without a word, Kelly reached inside her purse, pulled out the package and began to unwrap it. As the last layer of bubble wrap was removed, Victoria gasped.

"My snuff bottle."

She reached for it, but Kelly held it away. "Don't touch it. We have to preserve the fingerprints."

"Where did you find it?"

"At Magdalena's condo. Jonathan gave it to her on Monday. She collects miniature bottles but had no idea this one was so valuable, or that it was missing from your shop."

"Are you saying…" Victoria swallowed as though she had difficulty getting the words past her throat. "That Jonathan *stole* the bottle from me to give to her?"

"I'm sorry."

Overwhelmed, Victoria rested her forehead against the steering wheel and began to sob. The last time Kelly had felt this helpless in front of such raw grief was when her father died and she had been unable to console her mother.

It took a while for the sobs to subside. When they finally did, Victoria looked up. "I'm sorry." She wiped her wet cheeks with the palm of her hands. "I didn't mean to break down like this."

"Don't apologize." Kelly lay a hand on her friend's arm. "I'll drive if you want."

Victoria shook her head. "I'm all right now." She turned on the ignition and backed out of the parking space. At the ticket booth, she gave the attendant a ten-dollar bill, took her change and headed toward the Penrose Avenue Bridge.

"If it's any consolation," Kelly said as Victoria drove the SUV with an expert hand, "Detective Quinn put out APBs up and down the Florida coast, at all airports, seaports and bus terminals."

"I know."

Kelly looked at her, surprised. "How?"

"A Captain Cross at the Roundhouse has been in

constant communication with my aunt. He's even promised to try to keep the story out of the papers."

"Didn't he mention Magdalena?"

Victoria shook her head. "Cecily would have told me if he had. Maybe he doesn't know."

Quinn must have kept the information quiet, assuming Kelly would want to tell Victoria herself. It was a nice gesture and Kelly made a mental note to thank him later.

Inside her bag, her cell phone rang. She answered it, half expecting to hear her mother's voice. Instead, she was greeted by Martha Grimwald, Jonathan's secretary.

"Miss Robolo," the woman said excitedly. "I did remember something after all. I don't know how it slipped my mind in the first place. I'm so sorry."

"That's all right, Mrs. Grimwald. Why don't you tell me what it is you remembered." As Victoria threw her a quick, questioning glance, Kelly gave her the thumbs-up sign.

"Jonathan broke his routine this past Friday, though I can't verify it because he didn't write it down."

"How did he break his routine?"

"He went out for lunch instead of eating at his desk."

Kelly felt a ripple of excitement. At last, a break. "Did he go alone?"

"I don't know, but Mr. Webber was in Las Vegas that day so I know he wasn't with him."

"What about another board member?"

"I've already asked," the efficient secretary replied. "Only two board members were in town that day and neither saw Jonathan."

"Did Jonathan tell you the name of the restaurant?"

"No, but it had to be somewhere in Atlantic City, or close by, because he was back at his desk within the hour."

"Thank you, Mrs. Grimwald. You've been a big help."

"What did she want?" Victoria asked.

"Jonathan went out to lunch last Friday, but she doesn't know where or with whom." Kelly dropped her phone back in her purse. "It wasn't with Syd Webber or any of the board members."

"We may be able to find out the name of that restaurant." The color was slowly returning to Victoria's cheeks and her eyes had lost some of their dullness.

"How?"

"I found an American Express receipt in Jonathan's nightstand drawer the other night when we were looking through his things. I didn't pay attention to it at the time because we were focusing on the Miami trip, but I think it was from a restaurant."

Kelly gripped her friend's arm and squeezed it. "Victoria, you're a genius!"

"No. Just a woman desperate to find her husband."

Fourteen

"**Y**o, Kelly!"

At the typical Philadelphia greeting, Kelly looked up and waved at Vince Gambone. The old man and his meat shop on Ninth Street had been a part of the Italian neighborhood ever since Kelly could remember. Vince's grandfather had been one of the first Italian immigrants to start a business here, and Kelly's great-grandfather had followed suit by opening a restaurant two blocks down the street.

"How's it going, Vince?"

"Pretty good now that I have a new knee." He bent his leg a few times to show off his returned flexibility. He laughed. "Maybe I'll even enter the Boston Marathon this year."

Other area merchants were coming out, closing shop, waving at Kelly and shouting from across the street.

Kelly loved it. This was home. This is where she had grown up, attending school at St. Maria Goretti and playing street hockey with the boys in front of her parents' restaurant. If she closed her eyes she could almost hear the old Mario Lanza records her father used to play every night as he served his customers. Her mother had been more into the Golden Boys of South Philly—Frankie Avalon, Fabian, Jimmy Darren and Bobby Rydell. Framed photographs of the famous singers were prominently displayed throughout the restaurant, each lovingly signed to Connie.

San Remo was brightly lit when Kelly arrived. A few early diners were already there, munching on marinated eggplant and thin slices of mozzarella.

Kelly waved at a couple she knew and made her way to the kitchen, inhaling her mother's fragrant tomato sauce. Quick to respond, her stomach gave an angry growl, reminding her she hadn't eaten a thing since that cinnamon bun at the Philadelphia airport early this morning.

"Well, what do you know?" Connie Robolo said when Kelly came through the swinging doors. "I do have a daughter after all."

She was a short, round woman with Italian good looks and the same Eydie Gorme hairdo she'd had for thirty years. A white apron splattered with tomato sauce was wrapped around her waist.

"Where were you?" she asked as Kelly kissed her cheek. "I've been trying to reach you all day."

Instead of answering, Kelly tore a piece of bread from a crusty loaf on the counter and dipped it into a simmering pot.

"I even called Victoria. She said she didn't know where you were, but she sounded funny." Connie gave Kelly her you-can't-fool-me look. "Like she was lying to me."

"Ma, I'm thirty-five years old. I don't have to tell you where I am every minute of the day."

"Sure you do. I'm your mother." She watched as Kelly chewed. "How's the sauce?"

Kelly made a circle with her thumb and forefinger.

"You think it needs more basil? Benny says I never put enough basil."

Kelly had no idea. She could never taste the basil anyway. "It's fine the way it is, Ma. I love it."

"You tell Benny." Connie took a bowl of home-made pasta from the refrigerator and set it on the gleaming stainless-steel counter. "You going to answer my question or are you going to ignore me all night?"

Kelly thought about lying, maybe inventing an old friend she hadn't seen since college. At the last minute, guilt enveloped her like a bad aura and she couldn't do it.

"I was in Miami."

Connie put the pasta down. "In Miami? Where they shoot *Miami Vice?*"

The popular series had been off the air for years, but Connie still watched it on cable. Kelly and her brother often teased her about having a crush on Don Johnson. "Yes, Ma, that Miami."

"You went out of town without telling me?"

"I left early. You weren't up yet."

"What were you doing in Miami?"

"Looking for Jonathan. He's missing."

Connie's hand went to her breast. "Victoria's Jonathan?"

Kelly nodded and brought her mother up to date. She didn't mention the attack outside Salamander, or Nick's rescue. The first would have freaked her out and the second would have put romantic thoughts in her matchmaker head. Connie and Nick had met only once, when Kelly had invited him to San Remo for dinner, in repayment for Nick's help with an investigation. Upon leaving, Connie had kissed him on both cheeks and loaded his arms with lasagna and cheesecake. Then, to Kelly's horror, she had told him that he and Kelly made a very handsome couple and they should go out more. Mortified, Kelly had avoided Nick for weeks afterward and never asked him back to the restaurant.

When Kelly was finished, Connie wagged her spoon at her. "You're doing it again, Kelly. You're putting yourself in danger. I don't like it. Let the police find Jonathan."

"Missing persons don't rank very high with police departments, Ma. Miami is no exception. They'll look for him for a few days then they'll move on to something else."

"Then tell Victoria to hire a private detective."

Kelly dunked another piece of bread into the sauce. "Maybe I shouldn't have told you, Ma. I thought about it, you know."

Connie looked hurt. She was good at that. Even

better than Kelly's grandmother, who had mastered the art. "You would lie to your mother?"

Her and her big mouth. "I didn't lie, Ma. I just thought about it."

This time the spoon came within an inch of Kelly's nose. "That job of yours will be my death. You know that, don't you?"

"Ma, come here." In spite of her mother's protests, Kelly took the spoon away and pulled her to the counter. "Do you remember when Pop had his first heart attack?"

Connie gave an unladylike snort. "How can I forget? I almost lost him that day."

"We all thought that, including Dr. Catelli. I was only a little girl at the time but I remember him telling Pop he should slow down, maybe sell the restaurant."

"But would he listen? Of course not. He was just like you—stubborn as a mule."

"Pop was right not to sell, because in the end, the restaurant was his best therapy. Even you were amazed at how fast his health improved afterward." Her voice turned husky as she remembered the old days. "He went on to live a wonderful, productive life for twenty-eight long years, doing what he loved most—working side by side with you every day, the way his parents and grandparents had done before him."

"Your father wasn't running around town getting shot all the time."

"Once, Ma. I got shot once. I could live a hundred years and I'll never get shot again."

Connie's frown slowly faded. "All right. You're off the hook this time." She walked over to a large hutch. "But it will cost you."

"Ah, Ma, you're not going to make me wait tables again, are you?" Kelly teased.

Connie set a dinner plate on the counter and pointed to the stool in front of it. "I'm going to feed you. Sit."

Kelly laughed. "I thought you'd never ask."

Half an hour later as Kelly was trying, unsuccessfully, to turn down a thick slice of Benny's tiramisu, Victoria called.

"I found it, Kel. The restaurant where Jonathan had lunch on Friday is called the Pink Seagull. It's in Absecon."

"Bingo," Kelly whispered.

The Pink Seagull was tucked away in a small shopping center off the beaten track and was close enough to Atlantic City to make it popular with casino workers.

Kelly had made a point to arrive a little after two, as the lunch hour was winding down and the staff wasn't so busy. A gum-chewing cashier sat behind her desk, reading *Brides* magazine and not paying much attention to anything else. When Kelly told her she was doing a story on area restaurants and wanted to talk to the waiters, the girl pointed at two young men in black pants and white shirts before returning to her magazine.

Kelly took her position in front of the kitchen door, and stopped one of the waiters as he came toward her. "Excuse me," she said politely. "I'd like to talk to someone who worked the lunch shift this past Friday."

"Rick and I work every day, every shift, lunch and dinner." He did not look happy about it and didn't return Kelly's smile. "What do you want to know?"

Kelly produced Jonathan's picture and held it in front of him. "Did you wait on that man?"

He glanced at the photograph before gazing back at Kelly. "You're a cop or something?"

Kelly decided to drop the Miss Nice Girl act. It wasn't getting her anywhere. "Or something. Did you? Wait on him?"

He shook his head. "Nope." He shouldered his way through the double doors and disappeared into the kitchen.

Unfazed, Kelly waited for the other waiter to come her way. When he did, she asked him the same question, calling him Brad, which was inscribed on his name tag. Brad was better-looking and friendlier.

He nodded as he looked at the photograph. "Yeah, I waited on Mr. Bowman."

"You know him?"

"I know all the casino execs."

"So he comes here often?"

"No, but when he does, he tips well. You remember good tippers." His smile faded. "I heard Mr. Bowman is missing. Is that true?"

So the news was already out. Cecily wouldn't be happy. "Yes. That's why I'm here. I'm a close friend of the family and I'm trying to track him down." She slid the photo back into her bag. "Did he come here with someone?"

"Yeah. No one I knew." From the kitchen, someone called Brad's name. He started to leave but Kelly held him back. "Could you describe him?"

Brad pursed his lips for a long second. "He was in his late fifties with gray hair. Well-dressed and good-looking. I remember him because he reminded me of Cary Grant. Except that he had a red birthmark." He touched the right side of his forehead. "Right here."

Kelly leaned against the wall.

The waiter had just described Ward Sanders.

Fifteen

The Sanders' three-story colonial in Villanova, with its perfectly manicured lawns and stately old oaks, was one of the most magnificent properties on the entire Philadelphia Main Line. Several generations of Sanders had occupied the house over the last century, and though Ward and Cecily had lived in it for more than thirty years, the deed was still in Monroe Sanders' name. And he never let them forget it.

Kelly had spent many wonderful moments here. At first, the luxury and grandeur of the place had put her off, but in time she had come to regard the house as her second home, and the Sanders as her surrogate family. From the beginning, Ward and Cecily had made her feel welcome, taking an interest in her aspirations and encouraging her with the same passion they encouraged Victoria.

From the parking lot of the Pink Seagull, Kelly had called Ward at the bank and told him she needed to talk to him in private. Puzzled but agreeable, he had told her to meet him at the house. He was on his way to Baltimore on business, and would be stopping in Villanova first.

The butler opened the door and gave one of his stiff, courteous bows. "Good afternoon, Miss Robolo."

Adrian had joined the household in the mid-nineties when another Main Line couple had moved into a retirement home and no longer had any use for him. In spite of Ward's protests that they did not need another servant, Cecily had coaxed and cajoled, insisting that a man in the house would take some of the burden off their aging housekeeper, Nela. Of Rumanian heritage, Adrian spoke with a light middle-European accent and greeted each guest with an old-fashioned deference Kelly had never gotten used to. He was totally devoted to the Sanders, especially Cecily, whose intervention had allowed him to remain on the Main Line.

"How are you, Adrian?" Kelly allowed him to help her out of her coat.

He bowed. "Very well, Miss Robolo. Thank you."

"Mr. Sanders in?"

"He's waiting for you in the drawing room." His back rigid as a board, Adrian led the way and announced her before proceeding down the hall, carrying Kelly's coat.

Ward was already walking toward her, hands extended, when she entered the well-appointed room. "Kelly. Come in, my dear. I've been worried ever since you called. It's not Victoria, is it?" Concern shadowed his face. "The news of Jonathan's infidelity left her devastated and I'm worried about her."

"So you know."

"She stopped here last night after dropping you off." He led Kelly to a sitting arrangement of sofas and chairs upholstered in rich green brocade. "Cecily and I could hardly believe it. What a terrible thing for Jonathan to do to Victoria. She adored that man."

"She still does."

Ward sighed. "Yes. I suppose that's not going to change overnight."

"Ward." Kelly folded her hands on her lap. "I didn't come here to discuss Jonathan's affair."

"Oh?" He looked surprised.

Knowing he appreciated directness as much as she did, she came straight to the point. "Why didn't you tell me, or Victoria, that you had lunch with Jonathan on Friday?"

Ward's complexion turned pasty. "How did you find out?"

"I'm an investigative reporter. Didn't you think I would?"

He didn't reply.

"My God, Ward, how could you keep something like that from the rest of us?"

"I couldn't tell you. I couldn't tell anyone."

"Why not?"

"Because I gave Jonathan my word that I wouldn't!" He was immediately apologetic. "I'm sorry, Kelly. I didn't mean to shout. I—"

She cut him off with a wave. "Don't worry about that." She waited until he had regained his composure before saying, "Look, Ward, I understand your reluctance to betray a friend's confidence, but we're talking about high stakes here. Jonathan's life could be at risk."

Ward kept staring at his hands. As the silence stretched to a full minute, Kelly felt more and more uncomfortable. "Ward. Say something."

He nodded. "Yes. All right. I suppose it doesn't matter now."

"What doesn't?"

"Jonathan wanted to borrow money."

Kelly let out a sigh of relief. After all the possible wrongdoings on Ward's part she had imagined, finding out that Jonathan had wanted to borrow money was a huge weight off her chest. "What did he want the money for?" she asked.

"He wouldn't tell me."

"Did you ask him?"

"Of course, several times during the course of our lunch. He refused to discuss it with me."

"How much money did he ask for?"

"A hundred thousand dollars."

"Dear God!"

"I know. I was shocked, too. At first I thought he was gambling and needed to repay a loan shark. It wouldn't be the first time a casino employee—even a high-ranking executive—got suckered into the game. Then I wondered if he was being blackmailed."

"By whom?"

"My first guess was a woman, but Jonathan emphatically denied being involved with anyone." His mouth dropped at the corners in a bitter, downward smile. "Knowing what we now know about Magdalena Montoya, I wasn't so far from the truth, was I?"

"Did you give him the money?"

Ward let out a short laugh. "Oh, Kelly, where would I get that kind of cash without my father finding out? I may run the Eastland Bank, but Dad is still CEO, a very hands-on CEO."

"What about Cecily?"

"Yes, Cecily certainly had the means to help Jonathan, and she would have, if only to spare the family a scandal. But Jonathan made me swear I wouldn't say a word to anyone, most of all Cecily."

"What happened then?"

"We finished our lunch, though Jonathan barely touched his. I kept trying to get him to confide in me. He and I have always enjoyed a good relationship and I was hoping that whatever the problem was, I'd be able to help him—if not with money, then at least with advice or moral support."

When he looked back at her, there were tears in his eyes and Kelly knew they were genuine. "In hindsight, I wish I had done things differently, gone to my father perhaps."

Kelly couldn't quite picture Monroe Sanders handing out a hundred thousand dollars and not expect something in return—like a huge profit. In financial circles, the old man was known as an astute businessman and a little bit of a bastard when the circumstances called for it. Kelly had seen that side of him often, especially with Ward, whom he ordered around as if he were a servant rather than the president of his bank.

"You realize you'll have to tell Victoria about this."

"Why? What purpose would it serve?"

"She's Jonathan's wife and she needs to know every detail of his disappearance, no matter how unpleasant. Besides, she knows I went to the Pink Seagull and is waiting to hear what I found out. I won't lie to her, Ward."

"I don't expect you to."

"Then tell her," she pressed. "Before you go to Baltimore."

He nodded, rising when she did, but instead of escorting her to the door, he held back. "Cecily told me she asked you to drop the investigation."

"Did she also tell you I refused?"

"Yes." He moistened his lips. "I was hoping you'd reconsider."

"Oh, Ward." Kelly made no attempt to hide her disappointment. "Not you, too."

"The situation has changed, Kelly." His voice was stronger now. "At first I agreed we should do everything possible to find Jonathan, but now, with the news of his sordid affair with a stripper and the threat of a drug charge still hanging over his head, I agree with Cecily. Trying to force Jonathan to come back could bring this family a great deal of ugly, unwanted publicity."

"What about Victoria?"

"Victoria needs time to sort out her feelings."

"She already has. She wants her husband back."

"She doesn't know what she wants!"

A deep, intuitive uneasiness swept through her. This was the second time Ward had yelled at her. For a man who never lost his temper this was totally out of character. What was wrong with him? Had Cecily totally convinced him Jonathan should not be found? Or was he hiding something else?

"I think I'd better go," she said sharply. "This conversation isn't getting us anywhere."

"You're angry."

"Damn right, I'm angry. I don't understand you, Ward. Or Cecily. You both claim to love Victoria, but you're conspiring behind her back to keep her separated from the man she loves. Why?"

"We don't want her hurt."

"And I do? Is that what you think?"

When he didn't answer, Kelly shook her head and walked out of the room and down the hallway. Adrian, whom Kelly had once teased about having radar, was already at the door, her coat over his arm. Before he could help her with it, she snatched the garment from the butler's arm, said a curt thank-you and walked out.

Twenty minutes later, Kelly was still thinking about her strange conversation with Ward when she stopped at a red light on Broad Street, beside a news-stand. Glancing at the stack of *Daily News* piled high on the sidewalk, she caught sight of the screaming headlines.

Atlantic City Casino Executive Vanishes Without A Trace.

Quickly, she rolled down her window. "Yo," she yelled, trying to catch the attention of the newsstand attendant. When he turned, she waved two dollar bills out the window. "The *Daily News*. Quick, please, before the light changes."

Moving with practiced speed, the man grabbed a paper, rushed to her window and made the exchange just as the light turned green. Behind her, impatient commuters were already honking their horns. "All right, I'm going," Kelly yelled.

She had to wait until the next light before she could read the short article.

Jonathan Bowman, a vice president at the Chenonceau Hotel and Casino in Atlantic City, has not been seen since leaving his Bryn Mawr home yesterday morning.

According to airport officials and the Miami police, Bowman boarded a Miami flight later that morning and checked into the Encantado, a local motel. Later that night, a bomb set in Bowman's room exploded, injuring six motel guests and killing two.

It is not yet known if the remains found in room 116 belong to Mr. Bowman.

Philadelphia police have been in constant contact with their Miami counterpart but will not elaborate any further on the matter. Jonathan Bowman, a Delaware native, is the nephew by marriage of Cecily Sanders, CEO and president of the Norton Trust, one of the largest charitable organizations in the country.

Neither Ms. Sanders nor Bowman's wife, Victoria, were available for comment.

Kelly tossed the newspaper on the passenger seat and said a silent thanks to Detective Quinn. True to his promise, he hadn't mentioned his earlier suspicion that Jonathan may have been involved in drug trafficking. Cecily's precious name would remain untarnished, her golden future secure, but more important, Victoria and Phoebe would be spared a painful scandal.

A quick call to Victoria quieted her fears. Not surprisingly, a mob of reporters had showed up on Victoria's front step half an hour ago and was met by Cecily. Calm and gracious, she had answered their questions, being careful to comment only on what they already knew, and had promised to keep them informed of any new developments.

Kelly smiled as she hung up. No one handled the press better than Cecily.

A block from her house, Kelly let out a groan. Her

editor, looking like a volcano about to erupt, was pacing up and down the sidewalk. A copy of the *Daily News* was tucked under his arm.

At sixty-six, Lou Ventura was a small but powerfully built man with an explosive temper and a voice loud enough to reduce the most intrepid reporter to mush. Kelly had learned how to handle him early on, having discovered that under that rough exterior was a pussycat. At the moment, however, the pussycat was more like a rabid lion.

"Hello, Lou." Smiling, Kelly climbed out of her car.

"Glad you finally decided to come home." Lou wasn't big on greetings, not with deadlines hanging over his head all day long. "You read the papers?" It was more an accusation than a question, but before she could comment he yanked the *News* from under his arm and held it under her nose.

"Let's go inside, Lou."

He stormed in after her, hardly missing a beat. "You want to tell me why my star reporter let a rival paper print an exclusive she should have turned in twenty-four hours ago?"

"Lou, in case you've forgotten, I'm on medical leave."

"Don't give me that shit. You think I'm stupid? You think I don't do my homework? You went to Miami. You're investigating this story, Kelly."

Kelly sighed. Why was she surprised? Lou was one

of the best newspapermen in the country. Nothing ever got past him.

"Come and sit down, Lou. How about a drink? I've got some of that good Irish whiskey you like."

"I don't want whiskey, dammit! I want answers."

"All right. You want answers, I'll give them to you." She took off her coat and threw it on the sofa. "I didn't give you an exclusive because I couldn't. In the first place, the family was trying to keep the story quiet."

"They did a great job."

"And in the second place, I wasn't about to take advantage of my best friend's situation so the *Globe* could sell more newspapers."

"It's news, Kelly. The people have a right to know what's happening in their city. That's why they buy our newspaper."

"Jonathan Bowman isn't news. No one even knows him, or cares about him, except his family."

"He's Cecily Sanders's nephew. *That* makes him news."

Kelly folded her arms and held his angry gaze. "If that's how you feel, then assign someone else to the story, because I'm not doing it."

His eyes narrowed. "What are you hiding, Kelly? What do you know and are not telling me? And don't say nothing because something is going on. I can smell it."

Of course he did. He hadn't earned the nickname of hound dog for nothing. "I don't know any more than what you've read in the *News*," she said, hoping he wouldn't see through her. She'd pay dearly for her lie later but for the time being, lying was the only way to protect Victoria. If Lou had the slightest suspicion that there was more to the story than what she claimed, he'd go after it himself.

"My trip to Miami was a complete waste of time," she continued. "I learned absolutely nothing."

"What was Bowman doing in Miami?"

She shrugged. "I have no idea. No one does."

He fixed her with a steely glare. "You'll do the story afterward? When you have all the facts?"

"No. And neither would you if you were in my place. You'd quit before you betrayed a friend."

His cheeks flared up again. "Are you threatening to quit now?"

"I'm just turning down an assignment, Lou. What's the big deal? It's been done before."

"Hughes could fire you over this. He wants this story."

She didn't doubt it. Orin Hughes, who had inherited the *Globe* from his father two years ago, was interested in only one thing—circulation. He didn't give a damn about loyalty or fairness, and certainly wasn't above embellishing the truth a little, as long as it sold newspapers.

"I know he could," she said, her voice a little more humble. "I'm counting on you to talk him out of it."

Shrewd eyes studied her for a while and though she couldn't be sure, she thought she saw his mouth twitch. The crisis was over. He would assign someone else to the story.

He pointed a finger at her. "You owe me, Kelly."

Before he could push her away, she planted a resonant kiss on his cheek. "Big time, Lou."

Sixteen

Holding a sponge dampened with terra-cotta glaze, Kelly stepped back from the bathroom wall to admire her handiwork.

In spite of her earlier doubts regarding her artistic abilities, she hadn't done too badly. The glaze had produced exactly the textured look she had hoped for. All she had to do now was wait for the wall to dry before starting on the faux window with the *trompel'oeil* garden view. She hated windowless rooms and until recently she hadn't been able to solve the problem. A photograph of a faux window in a magazine had put an end to her dilemma.

Contrary to her mother's opinion, the renovation work was good therapy. Most of the time she immersed herself in her task so totally that she blocked out everything else. Tonight, however, she hadn't been able to get Jonathan out of her mind. He and Victoria had everything a couple could possibly want—a beautiful home, a darling little daughter, good jobs, good health. So why had he risked it all for an ex-stripper? Sex? Maybe. But why Miami? Couldn't he have found the same kind of pleasure a little closer to home instead of going to that dingy nightclub?

Finished for the night, she dropped the sponge in a bucket and started peeling off her gloves. She was missing something. It was right there, on the edge of her mind, but what was it? Why couldn't she put it all together? Her speculations came to an abrupt end when her doorbell rang.

She walked down the stairs, but before opening the door she looked through the peephole, a habit she had picked up when the vandalism on her property had started. "Well, I'll be damned," she muttered under her breath.

Nick McBride stood on the front step, his hands behind his back, his head lowered as though he was reading her doormat, which, most inappropriately at this moment, spelled out Welcome.

For a moment she thought of pretending she wasn't home. It would serve him right for not calling first. Then she remembered that she had turned on the staircase light before coming down and he was bound to have seen it through the transom window. Not to mention that the VW, which every cop in town recognized, was parked in front for a change. Talk about bad luck.

"What do you want, McBride?" she asked through the door.

"To talk to you."

"Then you have a problem, because I don't want to talk to you."

"Come on, Kelly, open the door, before the old lady across the street starts spreading rumors about us."

Kelly rolled her eyes. Mrs. Sheridan, the neighborhood's most notorious gossip. "Damn you, Nick," she muttered as she swung the door open.

Nick's right hand came from behind his back, holding a bottle of wine. "As you see, I've come with my own version of an olive branch."

Kelly let out a sarcastic laugh. "You think I'm going to drink with you?"

"Why not? It's your favorite. I thought we could talk over dinner."

The man was not only arrogant, he was a lunatic. "Dinner? Here? In your dreams, McBride."

"Don't worry, I know you don't cook." His left hand came out, holding a paper bag. "I brought dinner."

That smile she had once thought so engaging failed to move her. In fact, if it hadn't been for Mrs. Sheridan, who was still watching them from behind her lacy white curtain, Kelly would have shoved him right back out. Instead, she waited until he was inside, then slammed the door shut.

He didn't seem to notice. "You've been painting." He ran his thumb over her cheekbone. "You have a little smudge here."

She jerked her head back. "You said you wanted to talk, so talk and talk fast. I'm busy." She led the way into the living room and wished she hadn't made a fire. The place looked much too cozy.

He must have thought so too. His gaze swept across the room, taking in every detail. "Very nice."

"I'm so glad you approve," she said dryly.

He held up the bottle. "All right if I open the wine?"

She made a grand gesture toward the kitchen. "By all means, make yourself at home."

She didn't follow him but watched through the wide opening over the breakfast counter. He had never set foot in her house before tonight and yet he looked as though he belonged here. Even searching for a corkscrew and glasses took him only seconds.

There were other sounds, a rattle or two, then he was back with their drinks. "I put the food in the oven on low." He handed her one of the glasses.

"You're a regular Betty Crocker."

"Thank you." He raised his glass in a salute and took a sip, nodding in appreciation. "Excellent."

With no snappy reply coming to mind, Kelly took a sip as well. It *was* her favorite wine—a California sangiovese she had discovered during a trip to her uncle's Napa Valley winery last year. It took all her willpower not to ask how he knew.

"Now." Nick leaned against the armrest of an easy chair. "About Miami. I owe you an explanation."

"And an apology, but you can start with the explanation."

He gave a gallant bow of his head. "You'll have

both." He met her gaze, his expression suddenly serious. "When I got back to the Roundhouse on Tuesday, Captain Cross had just heard from Detective Quinn."

"I told you he'd call."

"Yes, you did." He took another sip of his wine. "Cross immediately called Cecily Sanders and assured her the PPD would cooperate with the Miami police in every possible way. Then he assigned me to the case."

So he had gone to Miami on official business after all. "And that's why you came here tonight? To tell me Cross had assigned you to the case?"

"No. I wanted to tell you why I'm personally interested in Jonathan Bowman's disappearance."

Maybe it was the wine, but Kelly felt herself mellow, just a little. "I'm listening."

"I think Jonathan's disappearance is connected in some way to my father's death a year ago."

"Because both men worked at the Chenonceau."

He lowered his glass. "You made the connection, too?"

"The thought occurred to me." She sat on the edge of the other chair. "What else makes you think the two incidents are connected?"

"One of my father's greatest qualities—or greatest flaws, depending on how you look at it—was his curiosity. That's what made him such a good cop. When he latched onto something, he didn't let go until he had all the answers.

"The last few days before his death, his mood changed. He was quieter, and seemed preoccupied. He also started working overtime, even though he didn't have to. Between his policeman's pension and his salary, he had more money than he could ever spend. When I questioned him about it, he said that the extra work gave him something to do. I should have known something was wrong right there and then. Filling out his spare time had never been a problem before. On the contrary, he never seemed to have enough hours in the week for his hobbies—fishing, playing cards with his friends, tending to his garden."

"So why do you think he did it?"

"That's where I screwed up."

She couldn't imagine Nick McBride screwing up on anything. He was too good a cop for that. "What do you mean?"

"I was working around the clock, trying to crack the Patterson murder case and I didn't pay enough attention to the signals my father was sending me. If I had…"

He didn't finish the sentence, but Kelly knew what he had been about to say. Her heart filled with compassion. Assuming the blame for a loved one's death was a terrible cross to bear. Now she understood why he had tried so hard to solve his father's murder last year, and why he had jumped at the chance to investigate Jonathan's disappearance.

"You think your father had an ulterior motive for wanting to work the extra shifts?" she asked.

"The executive offices are empty at night, easy to access for an insider and easy to search."

She watched him closely. "Search for what?"

"I don't know, but something must have made him suspicious." He looked at the ceiling. "If only he had come right out and told me what was bothering him. I could have helped him. Now I'm fumbling in the dark, making guesses I can't back up."

"Maybe there was nothing to tell." She was offering him a lifeline, something that would ease the guilt.

Nick shook his head. "My gut feeling tells me differently."

"But even if your father was suspicious, he didn't find anything, did he? Surely if he had he would have told you."

"Or maybe he did find something and was killed before he had a chance to do anything about it."

Kelly was thoughtful. His theory had merit—so far. "What about Jonathan's disappearance? How do you connect it to your father's death?"

"As vice president, Jonathan has access to records and information he never had when he was general manager of the Chenonceau. He could have stumbled over some sensitive documents, something so incriminating it could have put Syd Webber behind bars."

"What are you saying? That Syd Webber killed Jonathan? Or had him killed?"

"I wouldn't put it past him."

Shaken, Kelly remained silent. She was well aware

of Nick's personal vendetta against Syd Webber and his belief that the casino owner knew more about Patrick McBride's death than he let on. Was it possible that his hatred for the man was affecting his judgment?

"All right," she conceded. "You have my attention. But even if you're right, how do you explain Jonathan's presence in Miami? If Syd Webber wanted to get rid of Jonathan, and I'm not saying he did, why would he do it in Miami?"

Nick stood up and walked over to the fireplace. After watching the flames for a moment, he turned around. "Maybe Jonathan was never in Miami."

Seventeen

Kelly stared at Nick, momentarily thrown off, then shook her head. "I had my doubts too when I flew down yesterday, but I don't anymore. You see, I have absolute proof that Jonathan was in Miami, and at Magdalena's condo."

Surprised, he pulled his head back a little. "You do?"

She told him about the Chinese snuff bottle that had been missing from Victoria's shop and where it had finally reappeared. This time he was quiet, lost in his thoughts. She could almost see that sharp mind of his analyzing what he had just heard, trying to make it fit with what he already knew and suspected. "Where is the snuff bottle now?" he asked after a while.

"I gave it back to Victoria."

"It'll have to be checked for fingerprints."

"I know. We handled it very carefully." She studied his face for a moment, not sure what to make of this sudden change in him, his friendliness, his willingness to share information. He hadn't really explained that, had he?

"Something wrong, Kelly?"

"No. Yes."

He smiled. "Which is it?"

"Why are you doing this? Why are you here?"

"I told you. Captain Cross assigned me to the case and I thought—"

"Being assigned to the case wouldn't have changed the way you felt about me. And we both know that you don't need me to conduct this investigation." She wanted to add, "And I don't need you to conduct mine," but she would have been lying. "So what gives, Nick? And don't tell me I'm wrong. I have gut feelings too. And they seldom let me down."

"In other words, you smell a rat."

"You could say that."

Still standing by the fire, he took the poker from its rack and gave one of the logs a little jab. There was a burst of orange flames and a hiss as the log collapsed, igniting the others. "I might as well tell you. It'll be out soon enough anyway."

"What will?"

"Matt Kolvic was part of that protection racket in Chinatown."

The words took a while to register. "I don't understand. I thought he was doing undercover work."

Nick turned around. "On the surface. In truth he was on the mob's payroll."

Kelly remembered Matt's funeral, which she had watched on TV. The police commissioner had been there. So had the mayor. Both had praised Detective Kolvic for his dedication to the force, his bravery and the ultimate price he had paid for trying to keep the city of Philadelphia safe. "My God, Nick, are you sure?"

"Patti found twenty-five thousand dollars in a safe she didn't know he had. There was also a notebook with names, dates and amounts."

Kelly was crestfallen as her thoughts turned to the widow and her two little girls. "Poor Patti. What will this do to her?"

"That kind of publicity is never pleasant. Fortunately, Patti is moving to Ohio to stay with her parents for a while. Maybe permanently."

"Does it have to come out? About Matt?"

He gave her an odd look as though he hadn't expected her to say that. "I'm afraid so. Captain Cross is trying to keep the whole thing as low-key as possible, but that won't be easy now that the case had been turned over to Internal Affairs."

He put the poker back. "I wish I had known what he was doing. I could have helped him."

"That's why I tried to call you that night," Kelly said softly. "I never intended to turn him in."

"I know that now. I was bullheaded and insensitive. I'm sorry."

She inclined her head but didn't say anything.

"Now it's your turn to come clean."

She gave him a blank look.

"I know about those two officers, Kelly, and how they've been harassing you."

"Oh, that." She waved her hand in dismissal. Her problems seemed so trivial compared to what Patti Kolvic was going through. "Don't worry about it."

"I won't have to. I talked to Officers Demaro and Swan and I can promise you you've received your last ticket. But I am worried about the vandalism to your house. The two officers swear they had nothing to do with that."

"How did you find out my house had been vandalized?"

"Apparently your neighbor across the street saw something suspicious one night and called the police."

She laughed. "For all the good that did."

"I know the call wasn't answered. I'm very sorry about that, Kelly. It won't happen again." He came to stand in front of her. "Who would want to vandalize your house?"

"I don't know." She had been so sure the PPD was behind those incidents. Now that they weren't, she didn't know what to think, or how to protect herself from a faceless enemy.

"Was there anything else besides the vandalism?"

Instinctively, she wrapped her arms around herself. "Yesterday I found a threatening note in my mailbox."

He stiffened. "Where is it?"

She went into the kitchen, took the folded sheet of

yellow paper from a drawer and came back. "I asked a neighbor if he had seen anyone around my house, but he hadn't."

She handed him the note and he read it, his expression blank. After a while, he slid it into his pocket. "We have a document unit at the department that specializes in analyzing paper, tracing its origin, testing it for fingerprints. I'll take it there myself first thing tomorrow morning."

"Thank you."

"You're welcome." He straightened up and flashed that smile again. "Now, what do you say we attack that Hunan beef I have in the oven? I'm starved."

As they ate, Kelly found out that Nick's presence in the alley in Miami hadn't been the result of luck alone. The owner of Salamander lived in that dilapidated building and after talking to him, Nick had wanted to take a look at his apartment, hoping to find some sort of incriminating evidence. He had been about to leave, empty-handed, when he'd heard the scuffle down below.

As they talked, Kelly was reminded of their earlier friendship, when she had depended on him for information, and vice versa. She could feel the trust between them building again, getting stronger.

Nick picked up a fortune cookie and cracked it open. "About those two men who attacked you," he said. "You'll be glad to know they've both been arrested."

"So soon?"

"Thanks to that broken jaw, Jimmy Higgins, known to his friends as 'Tiny,' had to seek medical attention. He and Paulie were arrested almost immediately."

"I hope they're both in pain."

"Excruciating, from what Quinn told me."

"Is there any chance they're connected to Jonathan's disappearance?"

Nick shook his head. "Quinn checked them out. They're just two thugs with a half-dozen priors. They won't be going anywhere for a while." He read the fortune cookie and handed it to her.

Kelly read it out loud. "'Your eloquence has a persuasive impact.'" She laughed. "I'll buy that."

"Open yours."

"Don't tell me you believe in that stuff."

"Of course I do. Open it."

She did, cracked the crisp cookie and pulled out the thin strip of paper. "'Love will set you free.' Now I know that's a crock."

Nick picked up a piece of cookie and ate it. "You're not a cynic, are you?"

"About love? A little."

An hour later, the food finished and the dishes cleaned, Kelly walked Nick to the door. "You talked to Quinn when you arrived in Miami, didn't you?"

she asked as they reached the door. "You're the reason he became so cooperative all of a sudden."

"You're giving me too much credit. The truth is, Quinn isn't as tough as he looks."

"He's a bear."

"Don't tell him that. He's got a big enough head already."

She waited until he was outside and had reached the last step before asking, "How did you know sangiovese is my favorite wine?"

"Don't you remember? That's what you drank the night you and I had dinner at San Remo. Later, your mother told me your uncle made it and you loved it."

"And you remembered?"

He smiled wickedly. "A man never forgets a matchmaking mom."

She watched him walk down the street. At the end of Delancey, he turned around and waved. She waved back, then, still smiling, she started up the few steps, and stopped abruptly. Something was in her mailbox. She could see yellow paper through the carved design on the front of the box.

With a sense of déjà vu, she pulled it out, unfolded it and held it under the yellow porch light.

A chill went down her spine as she read:

Tweedle-Dum, Tweedle-Dee.
One must die. Will it be thee?

Eighteen

As she had a few nights ago, Kelly searched the street with one long sweeping glance. All she saw were empty cars and the shadows they cast on the cobblestone surface. Even Mrs. Sheridan's window was dark, the lacy curtains motionless. And Nick was long gone.

Her heart hammering in her chest, Kelly hurried back inside and locked the door. In the four weeks since the harassment had begun, she had never received such direct threats as she had in the last twenty-four hours.

If the police weren't the culprits, then who?

She read the note again, this time out loud. "'Tweedle-Dum, Tweedle-Dee. One must die. Will it be thee?'" Maybe the fact that the message was written in the form of a well-known nursery rhyme had some kind of significance, but she was too tired right now to even guess what it could be. As she sank into her sofa, curling her legs under her, another thought hit home. Maybe the note had nothing to do with the Chinatown incident and everything to do with her recent decision to look for Jonathan.

Her pulse quickened. Who knew about her investigation? The list wasn't that long. There was her mother and Victoria, both of whom she dismissed immediately. Cecily and Ward, though above suspicion at first, had expressed strong feelings about her refusal to let the matter lie. Would either one resort to sending threatening notes? Hardly.

That left Syd Webber, Nick McBride, Detective Quinn, and of course, Magdalena Montoya.

She scratched out Nick and Quinn, but not Syd and Magdalena. Something about Jonathan's involvement with the former stripper bothered her, and until she had scrutinized every aspect of that relationship, she wouldn't leap to any conclusions.

She read the note a third time, studying it carefully. Suddenly, something she should have noticed before jumped out at her. *One must die,* the note read. *Will it be thee?* Did that mean that others were in danger as well?

She thought of her mother, all alone, and of Victoria and Phoebe, so vulnerable right now without Jonathan. Except for her brother who taught school in Atlanta, those were the three people Kelly cared about the most. Anyone who wanted to get back at her could do so by striking at any of them.

She had to get all three out of harm's way. Victoria wouldn't be a problem. She loved Phoebe and would do whatever was necessary to protect her daughter. Connie was another matter.

Unless... Kelly glanced at her watch. It was too

late to call her brother now, but first thing tomorrow, she'd give him a ring and tell him everything. Ronny had a clear, logical mind. He would know what to do.

Last night's threat was still very much on Kelly's mind when she woke up the following morning. Bleary-eyed from too little sleep, she padded down to the kitchen in her blue candy-striped nightshirt and the fuzzy Barney slippers Phoebe had given her last Christmas.

She had spent a restless night, tossing and turning for hours. When sleep had finally come, it had been filled with visions of huge dragon heads pursuing her and warehouses thick with the smell of sandalwood.

So it was no surprise that she was in a foul mood, a condition that would be vastly improved with a cup of strong black coffee.

She had barely reached the kitchen when the doorbell rang.

"Who is it?" she shouted, filling the carafe with tap water.

"Nick!"

She looked down at herself, thought of asking him to wait while she changed into something a little more presentable, then shrugged. As long as he insisted on dropping by unexpectedly, he would have to suffer the consequences.

She tried to ignore the look of amusement on his

face when she opened the door. "Rough night, Robolo?"

"Are you always this chipper in the morning?"

"It's my best time." He looked at her disheveled hair. "Not yours, obviously."

"What do you want?" she asked grumpily as she headed back down the hall.

"I've got good news. The security chief at Philadelphia Airport has agreed to let us look at their surveillance tape for February 7."

"Surveillance tape?"

"All major airports are now required to have them. They're placed at strategic points throughout the terminals—airline counters, security gates, the various concourses. If Jonathan boarded that plane on Monday, he'll be on that tape."

Kelly was impressed. And a little annoyed at herself for not having thought of the idea first. "Have you seen it?"

"He ran it for me, and I did see a man who answers Jonathan's description, but since I've never met him, I don't know if it's him or not." He looked at his watch. "How long will it take you to get ready?"

"First I'll need a cup of coffee—"

"We'll get some at the airport. I told Jack Templeton we'd be in his office by nine o'clock. And we still have to pick up Victoria."

Kelly gave him a dirty look. Her mother had been wrong to think she and Nick could ever hit it off romantically. He was much too bossy for her tastes, and the hours he kept were positively barbaric. "It's seven o'clock in the morning. Why couldn't you bring the tape here? Or to Victoria's house?"

"Because that would have required a court order." He shooed her with both hands. "Go get ready. Quickly. We don't have much time."

"You're a royal pain, you know that?"

"I'll grow on you." As she walked out of the room, he called after her, "Where do you keep Victoria's number? I'll call her and save us some time."

"In the kitchen, top drawer next to the stove."

In the kitchen that was becoming as familiar as his own, Nick found the small, leather-bound book and Victoria's number under the Bs. As he dialed, he heard the sound of the shower rumbling through the old pipes. It took all his willpower not to think of that steamy water running down Kelly's slick, soapy, naked body.

"Hello?"

The female voice at the other end of the line jolted him back. "Mrs. Bowman?"

"Yes."

"This is Nick McBride. I have arranged for you to look at an airport surveillance tape." He repeated what he had told Kelly a few moments earlier, explaining that he was at Kelly's house and they would pick her up shortly.

"Very well. Thank you." She paused. "May I ask where Kelly is?"

"Upstairs, taking a shower."

"I see." It was clear she didn't, but was too much of a lady to put him on the spot. "I'll be taking my daughter to school in about thirty minutes. If I'm not back by the time you get there, go in and wait. I won't be long and Kelly has a key."

Nick hung up and started to put the book back into the drawer when a yellow sheet of paper, identical to the one Kelly had given him the night before, caught his eye. It was another threatening note. This time, the colorful letters pasted onto the page spelled out a different message. *Tweedle-Dum, Tweedle-Dee. One must die. Will it be thee?*

"Son of a bitch."

Holding the note, he ran down the hallway and up the stairs, taking them two at a time. Why hadn't she told him about this second note? When had she received it? And what kind of sicko would keep send—

At the open bedroom door, he came to a dead stop. Kelly stood in front of a closet, her back to him, as she flipped through a half-dozen garments. She was stark naked.

Nick didn't realize he was holding his breath until he was forced to let it out. His mouth suddenly dry, he let his gaze move slowly over every inch of her, the slender back as it tapered to an incredibly small waist, the narrow hips, the round, perfectly shaped behind.

Unaware that she was being watched, she stepped back, holding two hangers. On one was a pair of tan

slacks, on the other a black silk blouse. Apparently
satisfied with her selection, she turned around and let
out a startled cry.

Like a shield, she brought both garments in front
of her. "Ever heard of knocking, McBride?"

"I'm sorry... I..." He caught a glimpse of her
scar, just over her right breast, where Santos's bullet
had hit. "I didn't think you—"

"You do that a lot, don't you? Act without thinking?"

"I..."

"Oh, for God's sake, Nick. Close your mouth and
turn around so I can get dressed."

He did as he was told. When he was certain he
could talk without stuttering, he said, "I found the
note in the drawer." He waved it in the air to show
he wasn't making up some lame excuse. "When did
you get it?"

"Last night after you left. It was in my mailbox."

He heard the sound of a drawer being opened then
shut, the rustle of soft fabric sliding over silky skin.

"All right, you can turn around now."

She looked more amused than angry as she weaved
a thin leather belt through the loops around her waist.
He forced the image of her gorgeous body out of his
mind. "Why didn't you tell me you had received another threat?"

"When did I have the time? You barge in here,
practically at the crack of dawn, demanding that I get
ready. I wasn't thinking about that note. I was trying

to stay awake. As you can guess, I didn't get much sleep last night."

"You should have called me. I couldn't have been far."

"You had already left. And what could you have done? Whoever delivered the note didn't stick around, not if he or she knew a detective was in the house."

"I'll have it tested along with the other." Nick put the yellow sheet in his pocket, but was under no delusion. People who went to the trouble of cutting out letters from different magazines and newspapers didn't suddenly screw up by leaving their fingerprints all over the evidence. As for the paper itself, it had probably come from some office supply warehouse and would be impossible to trace, especially since the buyer had probably paid cash. Like the airline ticket.

He caught her worried look. "I'll find out who's doing this, Kelly. I promise."

She hooked the strap of her leather purse over her shoulder. "It's not me I'm concerned about. It's my mother. And Victoria and Phoebe. What if that jerk goes after one of them?"

Nick shook his head. "He won't."

"How can you be sure?"

"Most killers don't waste their time sending threatening notes. They see an obstacle, they remove it. Period."

She didn't look convinced. "Maybe so, but I'm not taking any chances. I'm going to tell Victoria to move in with her aunt and uncle, just as a precaution."

He stayed behind her, smelling her perfume, admiring the gentle swing of her hips as she went down the stairs. "And your mother?"

"I thought I'd ask my brother to invite her to Atlanta for a week or two. The restaurant isn't all that busy at this time of year, and Ronny is on spring break." She took a black leather jacket from a hallway closet and put it on.

"Won't Connie be a tough sell?"

Kelly rolled her eyes. "Worse than tough, but Ronny is good at that kind of thing. He'll convince her."

And if he didn't, Nick thought, he would arrange for a squad car to patrol Connie's neighborhood every couple of hours. Demaro and Swan owed him a favor.

Jack Templeton was a former police commissioner who, at the age of sixty-four, had come out of retirement to take the job of security chief at Philadelphia International Airport. He was a handsome man with snow-white hair, piercing gray eyes and an iron grip.

After Nick had made the introductions, Kelly and Victoria sat side by side on a tan sofa while Templeton inserted the surveillance tape into a VCR.

"The first tape shows the activity around the airline counter," Templeton said, "where Mr. Bowman allegedly purchased his round-trip ticket to Miami." He pushed a button. "Since we already know that he called his wife at eight-thirty, I'll fast-forward the tape to a few minutes before that. Here we go."

Next to her, Kelly saw Victoria tense up. On the screen, travelers stood in line, waiting to purchase their tickets. Kelly leaned forward, furrowing her eyebrows as she studied one of the men on the grainy tape. He was second in line. The upper part of his features were hidden by a wide-brimmed fedora and the lower part was too indistinct for her to make an accurate guess.

Nick turned to Victoria. "Victoria?"

Victoria shook her head. "I don't know," she murmured. Kelly couldn't tell whether she was relieved or disappointed. "It's not a very good picture."

"No, it's not," Templeton agreed. "Let's see if I can improve it a little." He turned a knob but the picture was only marginally improved.

"I suppose it could be Jonathan." Victoria's eyes remained riveted to the screen. "I've never seen him wearing a hat before, though. Not that kind anyway. And the trench coat doesn't help because I can't see what he's wearing underneath."

"Did he have a trench coat that day?" Nick asked.

"No. His is at home, but he keeps a spare one in the car, for emergencies, and that's gone." She looked at the frozen image again. "The way he holds his hand...it's almost as if he was trying to hide his face."

Kelly nodded. "I was just thinking the same thing."

Nick gave Templeton a signal and the security chief fast-forwarded again. This time, Jonathan was at the counter, taking money out of his pocket. "How about this shot?"

Victoria shook her head. "I don't know. There are so many similarities and yet..." She inched closer and waved toward the screen. "Wait a minute! There at his feet. That's Jonathan's briefcase!"

Templeton froze the shot. "Are you sure?"

"Positive. I bought it for him when he was promoted to VP of the Chenonceau. He never goes anywhere without it."

"I recognize it, too," Kelly said. "Victoria and I were together when she bought it."

As if unable to watch the tape another second, Victoria stood up, and addressed Nick. "I just don't know. He looks like Jonathan, the briefcase is Jonathan's, but if you asked me to swear under oath that the man on that tape is my husband, I couldn't do it."

Victoria hardly said a word during the trip back to her Bryn Mawr house, but once inside, she fell apart. "Aunt Cecily is right," she said, collapsing into a living-room chair. "Jonathan meant to leave me all along and he didn't have the courage to tell me to my face."

Kelly was beside her in an instant. "Victoria, that's crazy. If he wanted to leave you he would never do it in such a despicable way. Not Jonathan."

"But what if it is him on that tape?"

"It still doesn't prove he left you. Why would he

do that?" She took Victoria's hands in hers. They were cold. "You and Phoebe are all he lives for."

Victoria snatched her hands away. "Don't forget Magdalena," she said bitterly.

Kelly didn't know what to say to that. She had run out of excuses for Jonathan and was relieved when the phone on the little console by the window rang.

Victoria sprung out of her chair to answer it. "Hello?" she said breathlessly.

Almost immediately the blood drained from her face. She gripped the phone with both hands. *"Jonathan?"*

Nineteen

Kelly's head shot up. Victoria's face was ashen, her knuckles white against the receiver.

"Jonathan!" she cried. "Is that you?" There was a short silence during which Victoria held her breath. Then came another anguished cry. "You can't mean that. Jonathan, wait! Please don't hang up. I love you."

But the conversation was over. Victoria sank into a chair and let the phone slip from her hands. "Oh, Jonathan." She covered her face with her hands and wept quietly.

While Kelly rushed to Victoria's side, Nick picked up the phone and spoke into it. "Bowman, are you there?" A short oath followed and he slammed the phone down.

"Was that really Jonathan?" Kelly crouched in front of Victoria.

Victoria nodded and continued to cry.

"Here." Nick handed her a folded white handkerchief. "I'll go find some water." He was back within seconds, holding a glass of water, which he placed between Victoria's hands. "Drink slowly."

Like an obedient child, Victoria drank, taking small sips. Every now and then a dry sob sent a tremor through her entire body.

When Kelly felt Victoria was sufficiently calmed down, she took the glass from her hands. "What did he say?" she asked.

"To stop looking for him. He said that...that he loved someone else and wasn't...coming back."

Kelly threw a questioning look at Nick but he was watching Victoria. "Is that it?"

Victoria nodded and pressed Nick's handkerchief to her eyes. "I heard what he said, every word, but I can't make myself believe it."

Nick sat on a tasseled hassock the same frosty blue as the rest of the room. "Are you absolutely sure it was him?" he asked.

Victoria gave a vigorous nod.

But Kelly was just as suspicious as Nick. "Think carefully, Victoria. Often, over the phone, a voice can sound—"

Victoria wrenched her arm free and sprang out of her chair. "Don't talk to me as if I were a child, Kelly! I know my own husband's voice." She ran out of the room, leaving Kelly momentarily stunned.

Mumbling a quick apology, she ran after her friend. She found Victoria sprawled on her bed, facedown, soaking the green satin spread with her tears. Kelly sat down beside her, stroking her hair, murmuring words she knew weren't helping.

After a while, the sobs subsided and Victoria sat

up. Her face was blotchy and her eyes filled with a misery that brought tears to Kelly's own eyes. "Why don't you try to get some rest," she suggested. "You're exhausted."

"I can't. I have to pick up Phoebe at noon. Today's only a half day."

"I'll pick her up, and take her to San Remo. She loves it there, with my mother and Benny. It'll be a nice change for her. What do you say?"

Victoria took a tissue from a silver box on the nightstand and blew her nose. "Yes, thank you. I guess it wouldn't be a good idea for her to see me like this."

"You promise you'll rest?"

"Yes." Victoria lay down without further argument.

Kelly sat at her friend's bedside until her deep, even breathing told her Victoria was asleep. Then, quietly, she returned to the living room.

"How's she doing?" Nick, who had been standing at the bay window, turned around.

"She's asleep, for now."

"Are you staying?"

"No. I'm picking up Phoebe at school and taking her to the restaurant. That should give Victoria a few hours to pull herself together."

She joined Nick at the window. "So what do you think?"

"You mean that phone call?" he asked.

Kelly nodded.

"I think it's phony as hell."

She wasn't surprised at his reaction. She had caught his skeptical expression the moment Victoria had hung up the phone. "Victoria didn't think so."

"Victoria is emotionally drained. And ready to believe anything."

"I don't know, Nick. She was rational enough in Templeton's office."

"Maybe the guy on the phone was more convincing. Personally, I'm not buying it, the tape or the phone call."

"You think this is some kind of setup?"

"Possibly." Nick walked around the room, stopping every now and then to look at various mementos. When he reached a framed photograph of Jonathan and his little family, he stopped, picked up the snapshot and looked at it for several seconds. "What did you think of that photograph on Magdalena's mantel?" he asked.

Kelly shrugged. "I was shocked by it. I never thought Jonathan could look that happy with anyone but Victoria."

Nick put the photograph back on the end table. "I think that picture was as phony as Jonathan's phone call a moment ago."

Kelly stared at him. "That's insane. You're implying that Magdalena made that story up. How could she? How could she even prepare when she had no idea Detective Quinn would track her down. The picture was already there. He saw it."

"It could have been placed there ahead of time."

"You mean someone anticipated all our moves before they happened?"

"Exactly."

"What about the owner of Salamander? He recognized Jonathan."

Nick shook his head. "That little scenario was just a little too pat for me, too...rehearsed, practically flawless."

"Even if that's true, there's still the mystery of the snuff bottle to explain."

"I don't have an answer for that yet. But I will, once I know who Magdalena Montoya really is."

"You ordered a background check on her."

He nodded. "I should have it in a day or two."

Kelly was silent for a moment, remembering her own conversation with Magdalena, the way she had believed her one moment and doubted her the next. If, as Nick believed, Jonathan's phone call was phony and the man on that surveillance tape was a plant, then why couldn't the picture on Magdalena's mantel be fictitious as well?

Nick smiled as if he had read her thoughts. "I see that my insane suspicions don't seem so insane anymore."

"Maybe, but you'll need to prove your theory before I totally embrace it."

"I'm working on doing just that. A private detective I know will be helping with some of the...more sensitive stuff I'm not authorized to do."

Translated, that meant illegal activities such as unlawful entry, wiretapping and stealing of evidence. "Do I know him?"

"I doubt it. His name is Alan Braden. He's a former NYPD detective who's now doing private work out of his Manhattan office."

"What exactly did you ask him to do?"

"Watch Magdalena's comings and goings for one thing. Keep track of who she meets or calls. Oh, and I've asked him to have that snapshot analyzed."

"Won't Magdalena notice the photo is gone?"

He grinned. "Not if it's still there."

"But how—"

"Alan is very good at what he does. Let's leave it at that."

It was almost time to pick up Phoebe. "You'll let me know what he finds out?"

He gave her one of his boyish grins. "Of course. We're partners, aren't we?" He didn't wait for an answer but walked briskly to his car. As he pulled away from the curb, he gave a quick honk of the horn and waved at her through the rearview mirror.

"Aunt Kelly!"

Kelly braced herself as forty pounds of sheer force and energy hurled toward her and into her open arms. "How's my sweetie?" She planted a loud kiss on Phoebe's plump cheek. "Did you have a good morning?"

Her gaze caught Mrs. Goddard standing at a distance and she waved. Phoebe's teacher responded with a short nod. When Victoria had enrolled her daughter at this exclusive Main Line school in September, she had taken Cecily and Kelly with her and introduced them to Mrs. Goddard so she would recognize them in the event that one of them had to pick up Phoebe.

"We made paper snowflakes." Phoebe started to unstrap her Pocahontas backpack. "You want to see them?"

"I sure do, but let's get you in the car first."

Her little hand cradled in Kelly's, Phoebe looked around her. "Where's Mommy?"

"She had a few errands to run." Kelly opened the VW's passenger door and waited until Phoebe had climbed in before securing the seat belt around her. "How would you like to go to San Remo and see Connie?"

Phoebe bounced up and down in her seat. "Can I have some of those Italian chocolates Connie always gives me?"

Kelly smiled. *Gianduias* had been her favorite candy, too. Connie still kept a supply in a big glass jar in her kitchen. "I'm sure she will. In exchange for a big fat kiss."

"Okay." Phoebe fell silent and watched the traffic for a while. "Aunt Kelly?"

Kelly kept her eyes on the road. "Yes, sweetie?"

"How come my daddy doesn't love me anymore?"

Kelly almost drove off the road. Alarmed, she

threw a quick glance at her little goddaughter, whose huge hazel eyes were filled with sadness. "Phoebe, why are you saying that? Your daddy loves you very much."

"But he hasn't called me. And he always calls when he's away."

"Oh, honey." Kelly swallowed past the lump in her throat, wondering how long Phoebe had lived with this belief that her father no longer loved her. "That's because your daddy is a very busy man. And if he doesn't call you, it's because he never gets back to his hotel room until very late, when you're already in bed."

She reached for the little girl's hand and held it. "Didn't Mommy explain all this to you?"

"Yes, but..." Tiny teeth clamped over her lower lip.

"But what, sweetie? Tell Aunt Kelly what's bothering you."

"Daddy doesn't love Mommy anymore either."

Oh, God. For a moment, Kelly was speechless, struggling to control her own emotions. Had Phoebe overheard one of their conversations? "Why do you think that, Phoebe?" she asked at last.

"Because Mommy is always sad. The other day I saw her crying."

"You did?"

Phoebe nodded. "She said she had something in her eyes, but I know she was crying."

"That's because grown-ups cry, too, for all sorts

of reasons. Sometimes we even cry when we're happy. Last week, in your mommy's shop, I saw a lady cry because she had finally found a vase she had wanted for a long time.''

''And she was happy?''

''Very happy, crying happy.''

Phoebe nodded again, as though she understood. ''Mommy takes me to her shop sometime, but I can't touch anything. You know why?''

Glad the conversation was moving in a more uplifting direction, Kelly shook her head. ''No, why?''

''One day?'' Phoebe said, ending her sentence like a question. ''I was there? And I broke something. A little green dog that cost a zillion dollars.''

Kelly smiled. This week, Phoebe only counted in zillions. The week before, it had been trillions. ''Oh, my.''

''I started to cry, but Mommy didn't get mad. She said it was an accident.''

Kelly laughed. ''I know what that feels like. When I was your age, I had lots of accidents.''

Curiosity burned bright in the child's eyes. ''What did you do?''

''Once I broke Connie's piano. The one she has in the restaurant's dining room?''

Phoebe gasped. ''Did Connie spank you?''

Kelly shook her head. ''No. Connie never spanked me.''

''But I bet you didn't get any Italian chocolates that day, did you?''

"*That* day? Are you kidding? I didn't get Italian chocolates for a whole *month!*"

Phoebe laughed and the sound of it warmed Kelly's heart. More than ever now, she was determined to find Jonathan and bring him back to his little girl—safe and sound.

Twenty

"Ronny, it's me." In the empty dining room of San Remo, Kelly glanced toward the kitchen where Connie was preparing Phoebe's favorite lunch—bow-tie pasta with Bolognese sauce—before continuing.

"Why are you whispering?" her brother asked.

"Because I'm at the restaurant and I don't want Ma to hear me."

He laughed. "What have you done now?"

"Nothing."

"Liar. I talked to Ma. She told me about Jonathan and what you're up to."

"I'm sure she made it sound worse than it is."

"I don't know, sis. Why don't *you* tell me how it is? That way I can judge for myself."

"For one thing, I have help. Detective McBride of the PPD."

"The guy you've got the hots for?"

A hot flush climbed to Kelly's cheeks. "I do not have the hots for Nick. What gave you that crazy idea?"

"You, actually, and the way you talked about him in the hospital."

"All I said was that Nick was justified in being angry with me." She wondered what Ronny would say if she told him that earlier today Nick had seen her naked.

"All right, so if Nick McBride is helping you find Victoria's husband, how did you manage to get yourself in trouble?"

He had always been like that, intuitive and direct, even as a kid. It was annoying as hell. "I need you to do me a favor."

"I figured that much. What kind of favor?"

"Invite Ma to come to Atlanta for a couple of weeks."

He was silent for several seconds. When he spoke again the light bantering tone was gone. "What's going on, Kelly? Why do you want her out of Philly?"

Kelly hesitated, but there was no way of escaping the truth. If she wanted Ronny's help, she had to level with him. "I've been receiving threatening notes. And I'm afraid that whoever is sending them might hurt Ma."

He didn't chastise her, and he didn't lecture. Instead, he said, "She won't come, Kelly."

"She will if she thinks you really want her there."

"We're in the middle of a snow blizzard. She knows I'd never ask her to fly in this weather."

"Tell her you need her. Tell her you're having problems with Angie and you need her advice." Nothing brought an Italian mother to the rescue faster than a son with marital problems.

"Are you crazy? Angie would kill me if she knew I used her that way."

"You think of something then."

"Christ." She could almost see him raking his fingers through his thick black hair—their father's hair. "Okay, give me a little time to come up with an idea."

"Thanks, Ronny. You're a doll."

When Nick arrived back at the Roundhouse, the first thing he saw on his desk was an envelope marked confidential and bearing the seal of the Miami Police Department. Quinn had come through for him and sent him that background check on Magdalena.

He tore the flap, pulled out three neatly typed sheets and started to read.

Magdalena Montoya, born Teresa Vasquez, had left her native Puerto Rico with her parents and her ten-year-old brother, Enrique, when she was four. While Teresa was still in high school, she and Enrique went into show business. Teresa sang and danced while her brother did impersonations of famous female celebrities. Apparently they were good enough to land a few gigs in local nightclubs on weekends and get favorably reviewed by one or two newspapers.

The partnership lasted two years. In 1981, brother and sister split up and went their separate ways. Teresa changed her name to Magdalena Montoya, began dating wealthy men and eventually married one of them, for a brief period. It wasn't until after her divorce that she returned to show business.

But in spite of her good looks, her career never

really took off. She tried acting for a while, appeared in a couple of shows and quit after scathing reviews. According to her landlord, she never missed a rent payment, not even when she was unemployed. Apparently money was not a problem, thanks perhaps to the many wealthy boyfriends she entertained throughout the year.

She was hired at Salamander as an exotic dancer in 1998 and left that job a year later.

As his sister struggled with her flagging career, Enrique was making quite a name for himself in Las Vegas. After several menial jobs in various casinos, he had returned to his first love, impersonating celebrities. In 1985, three years after arriving in the gambling town, the Lido signed Enrique for a six-week engagement. Practically overnight, Enrique Vasquez became a household name, with every casino in town fighting to have him appear on their stage.

Then in December 1991, at the peak of his career, Enrique stabbed and killed his live-in lover, a young attorney by the name of Steve Marquant, and skipped town before the police could stop him.

The report ended there, but Quinn had added a handwritten note:

I figured you might be interested in the brother, so I asked Sergeant Andy Harrison of the Las Vegas PD to send you a copy of the police report along with a tape of one of Enrique's Las Vegas performances. You can buy me a beer next time you're in town.

Nick dropped the file on his desk and leaned back in his chair. Quinn was right. Nick was interested in the brother, not only because he was wanted by the police, but because of the destination he had chosen after leaving Miami. Las Vegas. The town where Syd Webber had lived for many years before moving to Atlantic City.

More than mildly curious now, Nick walked over to the file cabinet and flipped through the folders until he found the one he wanted. At the time of his father's death, Nick had gathered enough information on Syd Webber to fill a book. If challenged, he probably could have recited the man's life in chronological order with his eyes closed, but it wouldn't hurt to refresh his memory.

The answer he was looking for was on the third page. Syd Webber had moved to Las Vegas from his hometown of Hoboken, New Jersey, in the spring of 1969. One of his first jobs had been at the Lido Hotel and Casino, where he had worked first as a bouncer, then as night clerk and finally as bookkeeper. It was during his stint as bookkeeper that Alister Graham, the owner of the casino, had noticed the young man's potential and quickly moved him up the ranks.

In 1990, when a Lake Tahoe skiing accident took Graham's life, Webber inherited not only the casino, but Graham's entire fortune as well.

The Lido. The same establishment where Enrique had first performed after arriving in Las Vegas. Well, well. Nick smiled. Wasn't that interesting?

His thoughts now on a single track, Nick picked

up a pencil and started writing down the names of the principal players in this exciting little drama—Enrique, Magdalena, Webber. Halfway down the page, he wrote Patrick McBride, Jonathan Bowman, Syd Webber. It didn't take a mathematical genius to see that both entries had one common denominator. Syd Webber.

He wondered if Webber and Enrique had kept in touch, or if Enrique had tried to get a booking at Syd's new casino, maybe under another name. No, too risky. Enrique was on the lam. He wouldn't be crazy enough to get on a stage when there was still an outstanding warrant against him.

But the thought had wormed its way into Nick's head and he couldn't let it go. He thought of going to Atlantic City and questioning Syd Webber, then talked himself out of it. That lying bastard would sell his own mother before he told one ounce of truth. But there was one person in Atlantic City Nick trusted implicitly—Joe Massino. As his father's best friend, Joe had been one of the first people to arrive on the murder scene. In spite of his heavy schedule following his immediate promotion to chief of security, Joe had found time to help Nick with his investigation. He'd be there for him again.

Twenty-One

Joe Massino hadn't changed much over the last twelve months. He still had that same thick, stocky figure, coarse gray hair and acne-marked face that had scared the daylights out of Nick when he was a kid.

As the Chenonceau's new chief of security crossed the lobby of the casino, Nick couldn't help noticing a few changes—an air of self-confidence that hadn't been there before, a certain ease of movement, and eyes that recaptured the old humor Joe was known for. Things had worked out well for his father's old friend, and Nick was glad. Joe was one of the world's truly good guys and he couldn't think of anyone who could have filled his father's shoes better than he.

"Hey, kid." In the same playful manner Nick remembered from the old days, Joe put up his two fists close to his face and feigned a couple of jabs before grabbing Nick and squeezing him into a huge bear hug. "How have you been?"

Nick returned the embrace. "Just fine, Joe."

"So, why don't you come down more often, huh?" He gave him a tap on the back before releasing him. "I can't even remember the last time I saw you."

"I'm sorry. I've been meaning to call." Together they started walking toward Joe's office in back of the lobby, the same one Nick's father had occupied for six years.

"You're a busy man, I know. I was just giving you a hard time." At the door, Joe stopped, his eyes misty. "Jesus, it's hard for me to look at you and not see your father. You look just like him when he was your age. Except you're bigger." He put up his fists again. "You still box?"

Nick laughed. "I'm getting too old for that."

"Ah, don't give me that." He opened the door and waved Nick inside. "Here, have a seat." He took a stack of newspapers from a chair and dropped it on the floor. "Don't mind the mess. I can't keep up with all the stuff I get every day. I don't know how your father did it. He was neat as a pin."

Nick looked around him, remembering his father behind that old wooden desk. Joe hadn't changed a thing. He had even kept the group picture of him and Patrick at their graduation from the police academy some forty years ago.

"You want something to drink?" Joe asked. "The coffee is still crummy, but there's a soda machine outside."

"Nothing for me, thanks."

Joe folded his arms across his massive chest and leaned his backside against the desk. "What's up, kid? Something bothering you?"

"You know me too well, Joe."

"That's because I've known you since you were a little tyke. You were terrified of my boxing gloves. You remember that?"

Nick didn't, though he had heard the story a million times from Joe and his father. Both had forgotten he had been too young to remember his legendary crying fits every time Joe put on his gloves. Nick always played along, just to make them happy. "Of course I do," he lied. "I ran out of your house screaming every time."

"You weren't scared for long, though, were you? You took to those gloves in no time." Joe's expression turned wistful. "I'll never forget the day you won the Golden Gloves for Eastern Pennsylvania. Your father went wild, yelling like a madman, 'That's my kid! That's my kid!'"

"And what about you?" Nick said with a laugh. "If I recall, you were yelling louder than he was."

"Ah." Joe sniffed, as if the memories were too much for him. "I was proud of you, kid. Still am." His face turned serious. "So what's up?"

Nick met his gaze. "I've decided to reinvestigate my father's death."

The change in the old cop was barely noticeable, but Nick didn't miss the slight tensing of his shoulders and the sudden wariness in his eyes. His reaction didn't come as a surprise. Like Nick's sister, Joe had been concerned that what had started as an investigation had turned into an obsession for Nick. In a way, it had.

"Why?" Joe asked after a few long seconds.

Nick answered with a question of his own. "What do you know about Jonathan Bowman's disappearance?"

"Not much except what I heard."

"And what's that?"

"Rumors mostly. At first, everyone thought Bowman had been abducted. Then, when they couldn't think of a reason for the abduction, they claimed he was involved with a woman, or had started messing around with some really bad characters. Me?" He shrugged. "I think the guy's going through some kind of midlife crisis. Give him a week or two, one month tops, and he'll be back, hopefully with his head screwed on right."

Nick leaned back in his chair and propped his ankle on one knee. "I have a different theory. I'm kind of surprised you didn't think of it."

Joe spread his arms wide. "What can I tell you? I'm getting old, and I'm not as sharp as I used to be."

Nick didn't believe that for a minute. "I think there's a connection between Bowman's disappearance and my father's death."

The wariness in those shrewd old eyes intensified. "That's crazy, Nick. Those two didn't even know each other. They said hello when they crossed paths, but that's about it. Patrick only answered to Syd Webber, just as I do now. He never had much to do with Bowman."

"Two unsolved incidents involving the Chenonceau's employees within twelve months. Doesn't that make you curious?''

"Your father's death was solved."

"Not to my satisfaction."

"And we both know you're too damn stubborn to listen to the advice of an old man, so I'll spare you the sermon. Just tell me what I can do."

That was what Nick had been waiting to hear. "Tell me what you know about Jonathan Bowman."

Joe scratched his head. "Jesus, there's not much to tell. I hardly know the guy. From what I see and hear, he's friendly, always has a pleasant word for the staff and he's a hard worker."

"Did you have a chance to run into him the last few days before he disappeared?"

"Sure. Once or twice."

"How did he seem to you?"

Joe shrugged. "Fine. In a hurry, but that's the way he is, always running to get somewhere." The older man gazed at Nick for another second. "I'm sorry, kid. I know I'm not helping, but I don't see the connection there. Not at all."

Nick focused on the photograph of the two best friends. They had been close, throughout their years on the force and afterward, when both had worked at the Chenonceau.

"Me and my buddy, we come as a package," Patrick had told Syd on the day of his interview. He had said it half-jokingly but Syd had liked them both and hired them on the spot, Patrick as chief of security and Joe as his assistant. Joe, who had needed the job more than Patrick, had never forgotten how his friend had gone to bat for him. If he could help Nick catch his killer it would be done in a heartbeat.

"I know you and I went over what happened that morning many times, but would you mind telling me what you know one more time?"

Joe nodded. "Sure." He collected his thoughts before speaking again. "Patrick was ending a double shift, as you know, filling in for one of his men whose wife had just had a baby. I was coming in. As he was leaving I teased him and told him to go get some sleep because we had a bowling tournament that night and I didn't want a zombie for a partner. He looked at me, mumbled something and walked out."

"Didn't it strike you as odd, that my father would act that way, instead of coming back at you with a snappy reply?"

"Well, maybe, now that you mention it. But when you've been working sixteen hours straight the way he had, you're not exactly Jerry Seinfeld. Know what I mean?"

"What happened after that?"

"I went to my office, which was next to his." He waved toward a closed door. "Minutes later, one of the bellboys ran in yelling that someone had been stabbed out in the parking lot and to call 911. I made the call, without knowing who the victim was, and then I ran out with the others." He clamped his lips together and looked down at the gray tiled floor.

"When I saw that it was Patrick, my heart stopped. He just lay there in a pool of blood. I ran to him and he opened his eyes, but I don't think he knew who I was. I told him to hang on, that help was on the way, but it was too late. He died in my arms."

Nick was silent, the image of his dying father vivid in his mind. "I know you said you didn't see any-one." His voice was tight with renewed grief. "But you're an ex-cop, Joe. You're trained to see what no one else sees."

"I know. And I probably would have seen some-thing, or someone, if it hadn't been Patrick lying there. I guess it was too much for me. By the time I did look up, the parking lot was so mobbed I couldn't have seen the killer if my own life had depended on it." He shrugged. "Whoever did it was long gone, Nick."

"And my father didn't confide in you about any-thing? He didn't mention finding some sort of incrim-inating evidence against Syd Webber?"

Joe just shook his head. He had been through the drill before and no matter how many times Nick had asked the question, the answer was always the same.

Joe walked over to the coffeepot and half filled a mug with the thick, dark brew. "That killing should have never happened. Your father was one of the best cops the Philadelphia PD ever had. He was tough, he was quick and he was smart."

He turned, mug in hand. "But he wasn't quick that morning, Nick. He was just tired and cranky. That's why he chose to put up a fight instead of giving that bum the damn wallet like he should have.''

Nick had said those exact words to himself a thousand times. They hadn't eased his suspicions. "Tell me about Syd and his reaction when he found out my dad had been killed.''

Joe repeated the same story he had a year earlier. ''They called him at his home in West Chester and he came down on the chopper. He was shook up, I can tell you that. He had hired Patrick himself and he thought the world of him.''

The feeling had been mutual. But then something had changed, and unless Nick found out what that was, his investigation would go nowhere. "One more question,'' Nick said. "Have you ever heard of a woman by the name of Magdalena Montoya?''

Joe's eyes narrowed in concentration. "Montoya. No, I can't say that I have. Nice name, though. Who is she?''

"Just someone I thought I'd check on. What about Enrique Vasquez? That name ring a bell?''

"Nope. Sorry, kid.''

Nick was disappointed, but tried not to show it. "Thanks, Joe. I've been a pain in the ass and you've been very patient.''

"Anytime, kid. I just wish I had been more helpful.'' The two men shook hands. Then, with that same old smile that reduced his eyes to slits, Joe added, "How's your sister?''

"Kathleen is fine. She and her husband are in Italy now, living the Dolce Vita."

"So Alex's still in the navy?"

"He had planned on getting out next year, but now with a baby on the way, he's decided to stay in."

"Good for him. Tell Kathleen I said hi next time you talk to her."

"I'll do that, Joe. Take care."

The old neighborhood on Brigantine Boulevard was exactly as Nick remembered—small, two-story houses built close together, well-tended yards, and compact cars that had seen better days parked along the curb.

Nick stopped his car in front of a little yellow Cape Cod and didn't try to prevent the memories that rushed at him like a tidal wave.

Patrick had been a widower when he had moved to Brigantine. Though Nick was a grown man with a place of his own, he had come down every Sunday, rain or shine, winter and summer, to spend the day with his father. Together they had taken long walks along the beach, fished off the pier or sat at the kitchen table playing cards. Joe, who lived three houses down, would sometimes join them and the three of them would watch football or baseball together, depending on the season.

Nick looked down the street at the Massinos' house, a white rancher with blue shutters and a blue awning over the front porch. Debris from last week's storm littered the front yard and some of the siding near the chimney had come off. Nick was surprised at the neglect. Joe had always been proud of his house and worked on it constantly, even after his wife, Dottie, died.

Across the street, old Josh Coburn stood in the middle of his driveway, squinting in Nick's direction. Josh was a retired fireman who had lived in Brigantine all his life. He, too, had been a good friend of Patrick's.

Not wanting to appear rude, Nick got out of the car and walked over to him. "How are you, Josh?"

The old man's face brightened instantly. "I knew that was you, boy." He tucked a stack of mail under his arm and offered a bony hand. "What in the world brings you down here? Taking a little trip down memory lane, are you?"

"I was in the area," Nick said with a shrug.

The old man looked around him. "The neighborhood's changing, Nick. Kids are growing up, people are leaving. I hardly know anyone on this street anymore. My daughter just bought a house in Cherry Hill and wants me to move in with her. I'm thinkin' about it. Now that Joe moved, the block's turning shabby—"

Nick looked at him sharply. "Joe Massino moved?"

"You didn't know?" Josh pointed a thumb over his shoulder. "He bought one of 'em big houses on Harbor Beach Boulevard."

Harbor Beach. Those were pricey homes—too pricey for Joe. "When did that happen?" And why hadn't Joe told him? Nick wondered.

"A year or so ago. Right about the time your father died, as a matter of fact." Josh shook his head. "The neighborhood lost two good people that year, but I guess Joe was due for a bigger place, what with three growing boys and all."

Nick thought back to the day Joe's wife, Dottie, had died and the concern in his father's voice after the funeral.

"I don't know how he's going to manage now that Dot's gone," Patrick had told him. "The two oldest boys can pretty much look after themselves but the young one can't. Someone's got to take care of him full-time. How's Joe going to afford that kind of help? Dot's illness bled him dry."

Josh bent to pick up a twig from the driveway. "I don't see Joe much anymore," he continued, sounding a little miffed. "He calls me once in a while and he keeps saying we'll get together, but we never do."

That, too, was strange, Nick thought. Joe wasn't the type to snub his old friends. "How are his kids?" he asked.

"The Massino boys are fine. The oldest, Danny, started college this year at Temple, in Philadelphia. Ron, the middle one, wants to be a cop like his old man, and little Tommy's five and a handful for his baby-sitter." He looked across the street. "I guess that promotion at the casino really came in handy, huh?''

Maybe, Nick thought, but the difference in salary still wasn't enough to pay for a new house on Harbor Beach Boulevard, a college tuition and a full-time baby-sitter.

So where had the money come from?

Only one person could answer that question—Joe himself.

Twenty-Two

This time when Nick walked into Joe's office unannounced, the ex-cop's smile was guarded. "Forgot something, kid?"

"I just came back from the old neighborhood," Nick said flatly. "Josh was there."

Joe's features tensed. "Then I guess he told you I don't live there anymore."

"He told me." Nick waited a beat. "The question is, why didn't you?"

Joe shrugged. "To tell you the truth, I didn't think of it." He raised a bushy black eyebrow. "Is that why you came back? Because I moved?"

"You know me. Always on the lookout for those little pieces that don't quite fit. And this one doesn't fit, Joe. A year ago you were flat broke."

"Dammit, Nick, I don't know what you're implying, but I resent your attitude."

"You know it's true, Joe. If it wasn't for my father spotting you a twenty every couple of weeks, you would have never made it from one payday to the next. Now you have a house on Harbor Beach, a son in college and a full-time baby-sitter for Tommy.

Quite a leap, don't you think, for a man who could never make ends meet.''

"The new job pays well."

"I know what the job pays, Joe. That's why I can't figure out how you've managed to do so well."

Joe pulled his shoulders back, his face pale and the expression in his eyes angry. "What the hell are you accusing me of?" he demanded.

"I don't know." Nick spread his arms wide. "Why don't you help me out and tell me."

"There's nothing to tell." Joe rose from behind his desk, his fists resting on the worn surface. "I don't know what's got into you, but you're way out of line here. I didn't do anything wrong and I don't appreciate you barging into my office with wild accusations—"

"What's going on in here?"

At the sound of the voice he knew so well, Nick turned around and found himself face-to-face with his old enemy. As always, Syd Webber looked as if he had just finished a fashion shoot for *Gentleman's Quarterly*. Everything about him, from the open neck of his crisp white shirt to the tip of his tasseled Italian loafers, spelled out success.

"It's okay, boss." Joe waved his hand. "We were just shooting the breeze, weren't we, Nick?"

"The hell you were." Webber closed the door and glowered at Nick. "What are you accusing my chief of security of, Detective?"

"That's none of your business."

"Wrong. This is my casino and when you come in here, disrupting work and upsetting my employees, it becomes very much my business. I gave you free rein of this establishment when you were investigating your father's death, even though you had no jurisdiction in Atlantic City, but I did it out of respect for Patrick, whom I admired very much."

"I have jurisdiction now, Webber." He hadn't planned on talking to him so soon, but the man was forcing his hand. "I'm investigating the disappearance of Jonathan Bowman." He didn't have to tell him the investigation was strictly unofficial.

"That doesn't give you the right to harass my people."

"He wasn't harassing me, boss, honest."

"Are you finished here?" Webber asked Nick.

Nick jammed his hands into his pants pockets. "I'm finished with Joe, but I'm only starting with you." He gave him a thin smile. "You got a place where we can talk?"

Webber turned around and walked out. Nick followed close behind him.

Nick questioned Webber for a solid hour, more to irritate the bastard than to learn anything new. The man was too smart to change the story he had told Kelly or to be caught in a lie. And though he admitted that Enrique Vasquez had performed at his Las Vegas casino, he claimed to have no idea where the entertainer was now. As for Magdalena Montoya, he'd never heard of her. He didn't even know Enrique had a sister.

Now, as Nick sped along the Atlantic City Expressway, he kept thinking about his conversation with Joe. Maybe he was reading too much into it. Maybe Joe had gotten one hell of a deal on the new house and a cheap loan for his son's tuition. The problem was, Nick just didn't believe it—any more than he had believed the Atlantic City police's version of his father's murder.

The one thing he did believe was his hunch about Enrique and Magdalena. The next background report, the one Quinn had requested from the Las Vegas PD, would shed additional light on the mysterious brother. With any luck, the new information might even establish a definite connection between Enrique and Webber. The thought brought a smile to his face.

He couldn't wait to nail that slick bastard.

"McBride! In my office. Now."

At Captain Cross's thunderous command, all six detectives in the room, including Nick, looked up.

"Uh-oh." Mariani chuckled as he walked back to his desk. "What have you done now, Nick?"

Nick pushed away from his computer, where he had been typing a report, and stood up. "I guess I'll soon find out."

Cross was standing in his office, waiting for him. "Did you tell the chief of security at the Chenonceau that you were reopening the investigation of your father's murder?''

Nick didn't flinch. "Who told you that?"

"Syd Webber just called. He said you barged into his chief of security's office and started throwing accusations at Massino."

"I didn't barge in. Joe invited me in. We talked."

"About what?"

"Jonathan Bowman's disappearance, at first."

"You had no business doing that. Didn't I tell you that your role was only to coordinate between the Miami PD and this department? Did you hear me say anything about going to Atlantic City and questioning Webber and his employees?"

"I have reason to—"

Cross banged his desk with his fist. "Dammit, Nick! I told you a year ago to leave Webber alone. You defied a direct order."

"The two incidents are connected."

"What the hell are you talking about?"

"Bowman's disappearance and my father's murder. I found a connection in a background check Quinn sent me. Magdalena Montoya, the woman who claims to be Bowman's mistress, has a brother, Enrique, who moved to Las Vegas in 1982."

"Your point?"

"Enrique was a celebrity impersonator. He performed at the Lido several times throughout the years."

Cross was beginning to calm down. "The Lido. That's Webber's casino."

"Precisely. Then, in 1991, Enrique killed his lover, Steve Marquant, and no one ever saw him again."

"How did you find out about that?"

"I didn't. Quinn did. He asked the investigating detective in Las Vegas to send me a copy of the police report. It should be here any day." He talked fast, wanting to get it all out before Cross found a reason to stop him. "Webber admits knowing Enrique, but claims he's never heard of Magdalena. I don't believe him. And I don't believe Magdalena's story that she's Bowman's mistress." He didn't tell Cross about the private investigator he had hired. He'd wait and see what Alan dug out before he did that. Cross started pacing his office, the way he always did when he had an important decision to make. "All right," he said after a while. "You can stay on the case, but on one condition. Until you have absolute proof that Webber is personally and directly connected to your father's murder, or Bowman's disappearance, you stay away from him. I won't have you use this department to settle an old score. Is that understood?"

Nick nodded.

Cross waved him out. "All right, you can go. But keep me informed, you hear? Of everything!" he shouted as Nick left the room.

Twenty-Three

Victoria looked like a new woman when Kelly returned to the Bryn Mawr house with Phoebe later that afternoon. She had shampooed her long, blond hair, letting it fall loose around her shoulders, and had changed into a black corduroy jumpsuit. She had even gone to the trouble of putting on a little makeup.

"How's my girl?" She smiled as she scooped up Phoebe from the floor.

Phoebe patted her stomach. "I'm full, Mommy. Don't give me any dinner, okay?"

Victoria laughed. "Did Connie make you a big lunch?"

"She made me my favorite macaroni. And then she gave me these." She held a small plastic bag filled with colorful, foil-wrapped chocolates. "They're called *gianduias*."

"What is this? You speak Italian now?"

Phoebe threw her head back and laughed. "No. Just when I want Italian chocolates."

"I see." Victoria put Phoebe down. "Why don't you go upstairs and change, honey? I'll put your *gian-*

duias in the candy jar. You probably had enough for one day.''

"'kay.'' Phoebe ran up the stairs, dragging her Pocahontas backpack behind her.

"I don't know how to thank you,'' Victoria said as she and Kelly went into the kitchen. "As much as I hate to be away from Phoebe, those few hours did me a world of good.''

"I can tell. You look wonderful.''

"She wasn't too much of a handful, was she?''

"Are you kidding? My mother practically cried when I told her I had to take her home. She agreed to let her go only after I swore to bring her back soon.'' She watched Victoria empty the bag of chocolates into a glass jar. "Have you received any more phone calls?''

"No.'' She took two small bottles of Perrier from the refrigerator. "I'm so sorry about the way I behaved earlier. Nick must think I'm a total bitch.''

"Nick understands. He's a…great guy actually.''

"Oh?'' A light smile touched Victoria's lips. "Great, huh?''

"You know what I mean. He's a good person.''

Victoria handed Kelly a bottle and sat down. "And what was that good person doing in your house early this morning while you were upstairs taking a shower?''

Kelly took a long gulp of her Perrier. "Please don't make any more of that than what it is. He had made an early appointment with Jack Templeton and I was still in my nightshirt, so—"

Victoria's eyes widened. "Kelly Robolo. Since when do you open your door in your pj's?"

"Will you stop it? The man practically dragged me out of bed."

Victoria leaned forward, her expression mocking. "And you have circles under your eyes. Didn't you sleep well? Not enough?"

"Both, as a matter of fact." Before Victoria could jump to any more conclusions, she told her about the two threatening notes she had received over the last couple of days.

"Oh, Kelly!" Victoria exclaimed. "That's terrible. Did you call the police?"

"Nick took both notes with him and will have them tested, but the chances we'll find anything useful are slim."

Victoria looked devastated. "God, I'm so sorry. It's my fault. If I hadn't asked you to find Jonathan—"

Kelly put up a hand, palm out. "Don't. We have no proof the notes are connected to Jonathan's disappearance." She took another sip of mineral water. "But that second note worries me, Victoria. It implied that others besides myself could be in danger."

"Like who?"

"Like people I care for. You, Phoebe, my mother."

"Phoebe?" Victoria's face paled. "What would they want with Phoebe? She's just a little girl. She hasn't done anything to—"

"Nothing will happen to her," Kelly said hastily. "We're going to make sure of that."

"How?"

"I think you should move in with your aunt and uncle. I know you don't want to disrupt Phoebe's routine, but you can make up a reason. Tell her it's a game, or a special time for your aunt and uncle and you want to be there with them. I'm sure Ward and Cecily will be more than happy to play along."

Deep concern was etched all over Victoria's beautiful face. "I suppose that could work."

"Make it work, Victoria. The Sanders' house is harder to get into than Fort Knox. Phoebe will be safe there. And so will you." She still had concerns about Ward and Cecily's reluctance to find Jonathan, but she was sure of one thing—they would never cause any harm to Victoria or Phoebe.

"What about you?" Victoria asked. "And your mother?"

Kelly leaned back against her chair. "Unfortunately, my mother wouldn't cooperate."

"Did you tell her about the threatening notes?"

"God, no. I took the coward's way out and asked Ronny to invite her to Atlanta for a couple of weeks." Kelly laughed, remembering her phone conversation with Ronny as she drove to Victoria's house. "Not only did my mother tell him no, but she became suspicious and started to grill him, demanding to know if I had anything to do with that sudden invitation."

Victoria stifled a laugh. "Oh, no."

"It's a good thing Ronny is a better liar than I am or she would have seen right through him."

"But if she won't go to Atlanta, then what will you do?"

"It's already done. Besides being a good liar, my wonderful brother is also a quick thinker. When Ma turned him down, he called my Uncle Gino in Napa Valley. It so happens that it's the slow season in the wine country right now and he was looking for an excuse to come to Philadelphia."

"Your mother won't find that suspicious?"

"No. Uncle Gino is long overdue for a visit. She said so herself not too long ago. She'll never suspect a thing. And she'll be totally safe with Uncle Gino there twenty-four hours a day."

Victoria kept watching her. "You didn't answer my other question."

"What other question?"

"Who will take care of you?"

Kelly walked into the laundry room where Victoria kept the recycling bin and tossed her bottle into it. "*I'll* take care of me. You worry about yourself and Phoebe." She came back, stopping by Victoria's chair. "Deal?"

"Promise you'll be careful?"

Kelly nodded just as Phoebe bounded back into the room. "Mommy, can I watch a video?"

"A short one. After that we'll go to Aunt Cecily's house."

"'kay."

As Phoebe disappeared again, Kelly rubbed Victoria's back. "How did it go yesterday with Ward?" she asked, keeping her voice low.

"I'm still in shock over the thought that Jonathan tried to borrow that kind of money." Her voice took on that bitter edge that was becoming familiar. "I suppose Magdalena Montoya is proving to be more expensive than we realized."

"What about Ward?" Kelly asked. "Is everything all right between you two?"

Victoria nodded. "I was upset with him at first for not telling me about all this sooner, but I understand now why he didn't."

Kelly was relieved. She wouldn't have felt right sending Victoria to the Sanders' if there had been any kind of tension between her and Ward. She gave her friend a hug. "I'm glad everything's all right. Now, if you don't mind, I'll leave you to your packing. My masterpiece is waiting for me at home."

They walked toward the door, arms around each other. "I take it you mean your bathroom wall," Victoria said. "How's that coming?"

"Let me put it this way, I'm seriously considering calling a real artist to finish the job."

"Why don't you ask Nick to come over and help you? He looks like a man with hidden talents."

"What is this? A conspiracy?"

"What do you mean?"

"First my brother accuses me of having the hots for Nick, and now you start with your innuendoes."

"Do you?" Victoria pulled the door almost shut so Phoebe wouldn't hear.

"Do I what?"

"Have the hots for Nick McBride."

"Oh, for God's sake." Then, because she didn't know how to answer that question without sounding totally like a phony, she kissed Victoria on the cheek and hurried to her car.

It was almost seven o'clock when Nick was finally able to walk out of the Roundhouse. Acting on a hunch, he turned right on Sixth Street and headed in the direction of Society Hill. With any luck, Kelly hadn't eaten yet and would agree to have dinner with him. Maybe he'd take her to Bards, where the crowd was lively, the Guinness cold and the Irish stew authentic.

As he drove, the image of Kelly standing naked in her bedroom kept replaying in his mind. He had felt like a damn fool afterward, a Peeping Tom. It was a wonder she had been so cool about the intrusion. Not angry, just shocked and then amused. That was the part that made him feel so stupid. And guilty, like a little kid getting caught with his hand in the cookie jar.

He wondered if he was falling for her. Or if this constant vision of Kelly was just a case of healthy lust. It had been so long since he was in love he probably wouldn't recognize the signs if they hit him in the face. Looking back at his relationship with his ex-wife, Nina, he wasn't sure he had truly loved her. They had met in high school, two teenagers with raging hormones and a passion for adventure. They had married right after graduation, much to his father's displeasure.

Sex—*great* sex—had been the only reason their marriage had survived those fifteen tempestuous years. Then one evening Nick had come home from work and found the house empty, Nina's things gone. On the kitchen table, propped against the salt and pepper shakers, was a note informing him she had left for Los Angeles with her kickboxing instructor. She wasn't coming back. That was six years ago.

There had been other women in Nick's life since then, attractive, intelligent women whose company he had enjoyed. But none had been able to stir in him the kind of passion he felt was essential to a lasting relationship. These days when one of his friends tried to fix him up with "the perfect woman," Nick just laughed and told him to introduce Miss Perfect to someone else.

He had just turned the corner into Delancey Street and was looking for a parking space when the door to Kelly's town house opened. He started to honk the horn to catch her attention, then stopped when he realized she wasn't alone.

Holding her elbow and acting as though he owned her was Syd Webber.

Nick brought the Taurus to a stop and watched them step into a stretch limo the size of a football field. When the car pulled away, Nick let his foot off the brake and followed them without hesitation.

Twenty-Four

A few minutes later, the limo stopped in front of an unassuming restaurant on Lombard Street. Webber came out first and extended his hand, which Kelly took gracefully. With the same possessiveness Webber had showed earlier in front of the town house, he took Kelly's arm and they walked into the restaurant together while the limo drove off.

Cursing the absence of valet parking, Nick circled the block a few times until he found a space to squeeze into. By the time he walked into the restaurant, the place was packed. Kelly and her companion were comfortably settled at a candlelit table, a bottle of champagne in a silver bucket next to them.

Nick looked around him. The restaurant may have looked unassuming from the outside, but inside it was a study in quiet elegance and comfort. A far cry from the little Irish pub where Nick had planned on taking Kelly.

"Do you have a reservation, sir?" A slender, attractive woman with Asian features smiled at him.

"No." He gestured toward the crowded bar. "I'll just have a drink."

"Very well."

He positioned himself near the window so he could have a clear view of the dining room, and ordered a Samuel Adams.

Kelly looked sensational. A sleeveless dress in a deep burgundy shade skimmed her slender figure, accentuating her round breasts. She had pulled her hair back in an elegant twist, leaving a few wisps to frame her face. Except for a pair of pearl earrings and a watch, she wore no jewelry. The effect was simple and stunning. Judging from the way Webber kept leaning across the table, Kelly's mesmerizing beauty wasn't lost on him either.

What the hell was Webber telling her that was so damn amusing? Nick wondered as he heard Kelly laugh. Didn't she realize she was making a fool of herself? That all that jerk wanted from her was information?

And what about you, old chum, Nick asked silently. What do you want from her? And what the hell are you doing here, spying on them and acting like a voyeur?

Common sense told him to leave. Forget the woman, forget Webber and get out of here before you make a fool of yourself.

But Nick seldom took his own advice. His eyes on Webber's back, he drained his beer and ordered another.

Kelly sipped her champagne and smiled as Syd talked about his early days as a bouncer in a Las

Vegas casino. He definitely had a gift for storytelling, and as he went from one anecdote to another with the ease of an accomplished raconteur, she wondered what lay beneath all that charm.

She had been at home, putting away her paint supplies when Syd had showed up at her door, a bouquet of red roses in his hand and a big grin on his handsome face. Behind him, a stretch limo stood waiting.

"I took a chance you'd be free and hungry," he had told her, handing her the flowers.

Her first impulse had been to turn down both the roses and the invitation. Now that she and Nick had joined forces in their search for Jonathan, going out with a man the detective not only despised but suspected of having killed his father made her feel disloyal.

On the other hand, spending an evening with Syd in relaxed surroundings would give her an insight into the man and his business she wouldn't have otherwise. That thought and the possibility that she could learn something vital about Jonathan had finally changed her mind.

So far she had no regrets. Syd Webber had turned out to be a wonderful dinner companion. He was entertaining, attentive and the perfect gentleman.

"I just can't imagine you as a bouncer," she commented when he told her about his humble beginnings.

He laughed. "It was a job. Lucky for me I wasn't

very good at it. When the manager realized I had an affinity for numbers and could do bookkeeping, he moved me into the administrative office. That's how I met Alister Graham.''

Kelly already knew about Graham and how he had taken the rather wild, impetuous youth, tamed him and then taught him everything he knew about the casino business. Graham's instincts about Syd Webber had been right on the money. Eighteen years after landing in Las Vegas, with five dollars in his pockets and a head full of dreams, Syd had turned his boss's casino into one of the most profitable on the Las Vegas strip.

As a reward, Graham had made him half owner of the establishment, and when he died he'd left everything he owned to his protégé.

"Do you miss Las Vegas?" Kelly asked.

"To tell you the truth, most of the time I'm too busy to realize I'm *not* in Vegas." Syd reached for the bottle of Veuve Clicquot and refilled their flutes. "Have you ever been there?"

"Once, when I was visiting my uncle in Napa Valley."

"What did you think?"

"Honestly?" She leaned forward and spoke in a conspiratorial whisper. "I hated it and couldn't wait to get out of there."

He laughed. "Thank God not too many people feel the way you do, or we'd all go bankrupt."

Now seemed like a good time to ask about another

facet of his life—his controversial friendship with the infamous Tony Marquese.

"Yes, I know Tony," Syd said when she brought up the name. "And I treat him the way I treat all my high rollers. I give him unlimited bar and restaurant privileges along with a penthouse suite. I even send his girlfriends gifts. What else am I supposed to do? The man spends more money in my casino in a year than all my other high rollers put together. Don't you think he has the right to expect the star treatment?"

"Some people say you've been closer to him than you should be."

"They don't know what they're talking about. When I arrived in Atlantic City in 1992, all the press was talking about was that I had my picture taken with Tony Marquese, that we were buddies. Soon the rumors turned into speculations and before I knew it, I was one of Tony's boys. That's bull." He tapped his chest with his fist. "I'm my own man. I belong to no one."

His voice had risen only slightly but she could hear the anger in it. Either she had been overly influenced by Nick and Cecily and totally misjudged the man, or he was one hell of an actor.

Unsure of what to say next, she started to take another sip of champagne. Her hand stopped in midair.

Standing at the bar, watching her, was Nick McBride.

"Something wrong?" Syd asked. He started to turn

around but she stopped him. "No, please. I'll handle this."

She made her way around the tables to the crowded bar, stopping a few inches from Nick. "Just what do you think you're doing?" she asked in a furious whisper.

Instead of looking embarrassed, Nick took a nonchalant sip of beer. "Keeping an eye on you. As I recall, you have a habit of getting yourself into situations you can't get out of."

"This is not one of those times, Nick. You're ruining everything. Please leave."

"What am I ruining? A romantic tête-á-tête?"

"Just leave, okay?"

Nick put his glass down. "Don't you see what he's doing?"

"No, why don't you tell me?"

He waved his hand. "This fancy restaurant, the expensive bubbly, the jokes you seem to find so amusing, are just his way of pumping you for information."

"Gee, thanks, Nick. And here I thought he was enjoying my company."

"Is that what he told you?"

"What he told me is none of your business. But since you seem determined to make it your business, you can relax. Syd has been the perfect gentleman. Now will you leave?"

"Not until you and Casanova do."

"God, you're exasperating!" They were beginning

to attract attention. Kelly spun around and marched back to her table.

Syd was livid and already on his feet. "That man needs to be taught a lesson."

Kelly stopped him. "No, Syd. We'll just leave."

"Then we'll go somewhere else."

"No."

"I'm not going to let him ruin our evening."

"It's already ruined." She grabbed his sleeve and gave a tug. "Come on, let's not make a scene." As she led the way toward the door, she stayed between Syd and the bar. She wouldn't put it past either man to provoke the other. But while she was signaling the coat-check girl for their coats, Syd pushed her aside and headed straight for Nick.

Visions of tomorrow's headlines flashed in front of Kelly's eyes: Casino Tycoon And Hot-Tempered Cop In Bar Brawl. She ran after Syd, but she wasn't fast enough. He had already reached Nick.

"I warned you once, McBride." Syd's voice was low and menacing. "This time you're going to find out that you're way over your head."

Nick climbed down from his stool. He towered over Syd by nearly a full head. "Are you trying to intimidate an officer of the law?"

"And what would you do if I did?" Syd laughed. "Cuff me? Or hit me maybe?"

"Don't tempt me, pal. I've got a short fuse."

"Go ahead, flatfoot, hit me." Syd took a step forward, his chin defiant, his whole demeanor so insulting, Kelly wondered how Nick managed to keep his cool.

"Syd, please." Kelly pulled his sleeve again. "Let's go."

Syd wasn't listening. "Go ahead," he taunted. "Do it. Maybe a big fat lawsuit charging you with police brutality is just what you need to get you out of my face."

"I wouldn't dirty my hands on a sleaze like you. Get out of here, Webber, before you give this fine restaurant a bad name."

Terrified at the look of dark fury on Syd's face, Kelly grabbed his arm. "I have our coats. Let's go."

But Syd had to have the last word. "You're nothing, McBride, you hear me?" he said between clenched teeth. "Nothing. I can crush you like a bug. All I have to do is give the word."

Only then did he allow Kelly to pull him away.

Twenty-Five

Back in her living room, Kelly took off her coat and threw it on the sofa along with her purse. If she hadn't been so concerned about not making a scene at the restaurant, she would have wrung Nick's neck.

What in the world had possessed him? Sure, he hated Syd with a passion and suspected him of having killed his father, but to follow them into a restaurant and watch them from the bar? What was that all about?

Reaching behind her head, she pulled out the pins that held her knot in place and shook her hair loose. If she didn't know better, she'd swear he was jealous.

She was scoffing at that thought when she heard the doorbell. "McBride," she muttered. "If this is you, I swear you're a dead man."

Her heels clicked angrily on the hardwood floor as she marched to the door. "Yes?" she said without opening it.

"May I come in, please?"

She refused to let Nick's apologetic tone sway her. "If you do, I'll probably kill you. Since I have no intention of spending the rest of my life behind bars, the answer is no, you can't come in.''

"What I did was stupid. Give me a chance to apologize.''

"You just did. Good night, Nick.''

She left him standing there, talking to the door. In the kitchen, she debated over making herself a sandwich. But thanks to Nick, not only had her dinner been ruined, so had her appetite. Oh well, it wouldn't be the first time she went to bed on an empty stomach. She flipped off the lights and headed upstairs.

Nick was still at the door when she walked by, alternating between knocking and ringing the bell. She ignored him. The temperature had dropped to a very uncomfortable seventeen degrees. He'd go away soon enough.

In the cozy comfort of her bedroom, her irritation began to ebb. Tomorrow, when she was calmer, she would talk to Nick. His sister, though Kelly had never met her, was right. Nick was obsessed with Syd Webber, and sooner or later this obsession would get him in serious trouble. It almost had last year, but apparently he hadn't learned his lesson.

Stifling a yawn, she undressed, took a pair of clean pajamas from her dresser drawer and went to the bathroom to get ready for bed. As she brushed her teeth, she thought of Victoria and Phoebe safely tucked into the Sanders' house and of her Uncle Gino who must have landed by now. The people she loved were safe.

She was safe. Or would be, as soon as that maniac downstairs gave up and went home.

With that thought in mind, she walked back into her bedroom, yawning. The big four-poster bed, with its puffy white duvet and fluffy pillows, looked warm and inviting, but instead of climbing into it, she walked over to the window, which overlooked the street. Please, God, she prayed, don't let him still be there.

He was. He sat on the stoop, gazing into the night, the collar of his suit jacket pulled up against the bitter wind. The fool hadn't even had the common sense to wear a coat.

Furious, she threw on a robe and pounded down the stairs. "All right," she said after opening the door. "You win. Come in."

This time he was the one who led the way to the living room, rubbing his hands to warm them. She hadn't planned on a confrontation at this time of night, but since he was here she might as well get it over. "Are you totally insane? Following me into a restaurant full of people, making a scene—"

His gaze stopped on the roses on the coffee table but he didn't comment on them. "I didn't make a scene. I was minding my own business, having a beer—"

"Bull. You were doing anything but minding your own business. You followed us. Why? What were you hoping to accomplish?"

"What about you? What were you thinking, going out with him?"

"Syd showed up at my door and invited me out to dinner. I accepted. What's so wrong with that?"

"It's stupid. He's using you, Kelly. He wants to pump you about the investigation."

"Boy, you really do know how to deflate a girl's ego, don't you?"

"Don't turn everything I say into an insult. You looked gorgeous tonight and you know it. So did Webber, but your good looks aren't the reason he's interested in you."

"I'm thirty-five years old." How often did she have to remind people of that? "Can't you trust me to know the difference between a man who is genuinely attracted to me and one who is using me?"

Something in his eyes changed. Before she could decide what that was, he grabbed hold of her shoulders, yanked her to him and crushed his mouth on hers.

For an instant, only an instant, she was too stunned to react. Then, as his mouth plundered hers, she felt hers opening, responding. Her arms coiled around his neck, her body, either by instinct or need, leaned into his. Every nerve in her body, every cell, seemed poised, ready to burst. She couldn't think or reason. She could only feel. So many sensations—heat, need, pleasure. She knew now why none of her relationships had worked. No one had ever kissed her with such passion before.

She didn't know how long the kiss lasted, or who let go of whom first. She was aware of being suddenly released and, as she lost her balance, of being steadied by two strong hands.

She cleared her throat, determined not to let him see how deeply that kiss had affected her. "Well, are you glad you got that out of your system? You feel better now?"

"Yes. Because now you do know the difference between being wanted and being used." He started to turn away.

"Wait!" The word was out before she could stop it. She didn't want him to leave, not like this. Had he said *wanted?* Did he really want her? Or had he just been trying to make a point? She wasn't ready to hear the answer to that question.

He turned, his gaze questioning.

"Something happened today, didn't it?" she asked quietly. "That's why you came looking for me in the first place.

"Webber didn't tell you?" Nick's tone had an edge to it.

"No. This may come as a shock to you, but your name never even came up. That is," she added, "until I saw you hiding behind the potted palm."

"I wasn't hiding."

She sat down. "Did something happen?"

He nodded.

She felt herself softening. For a tough guy, there were moments when he didn't look so tough. This was one of those moments. "You want to tell me about it? You might as well," she added with a smile as she settled onto the sofa. "I'm wide awake now."

Elbows on her knees, her chin resting on her fists, she listened while he told her about his father's friend, Joe Massino, the conversation they'd had earlier and the discovery that the Chenonceau's new chief of security was living well above his means.

"I don't know, Nick," she said when he was finished. "Just because Joe moved his family to a better neighborhood doesn't mean he was bought."

"He could never afford what he has now on his salary. Even with his pension added to it."

"Maybe he won the lottery."

"He didn't."

"But how could he spend that kind of money and not send a signal to the IRS?"

"There are ways. Webber could have arranged to give him a personal loan with the understanding that Joe would pay him back in monthly installments, except he's not paying him back. Or Webber could give him the money in the form of a bonus."

"All right, let's suppose that your friend Joe does have something on his boss. Why would Syd pay him off? Why not have him killed, the way he did your father, if indeed that's what happened."

"Because he couldn't afford to have two casino employees, both working in security, die of a suspicious death."

"But letting him live is just as risky. What if Joe had turned him in instead of taking his money?"

Nick couldn't stand still. He jumped up and paced up and down the small space. "You forget that Webber is an excellent judge of character. He knew my father couldn't be bought but Joe could."

"How will you prove that?"

"I can't yet, but there's more." He reached into his breast pocket and took out a thick business-size envelope. He handed it to her. "Take a look at this."

"What is it?"

"That background check on Magdalena Montoya."

Holding the document so the table lamp shone on it, Kelly read the three-page report. Much of it corroborated what Magdalena had told them about herself. What came as a surprise, however, was the information about Magdalena's brother and his ties to Syd Webber.

When she was finished reading, Kelly looked up. "Magdalena's brother killed a man?"

"He not only killed a man, he escaped so quickly the cops figure he had to have had help."

She glanced at the last page again. "And you think that help came from Syd Webber? Is that it?"

"That's a very strong possibility. They knew each other, and Webber had the connections. He could have gotten Enrique a new identity within forty-eight hours."

"But why would Syd help Enrique escape a murder rap?"

"Maybe we should put that question to Enrique."

"You have to find him first. Unless..." Her eyes narrowed. "You already know where he is."

"I have a hunch."

"Where."

He stopped pacing. "Where it all began—Miami."

Kelly shook her head. "The Las Vegas police must have combed that city from one end to the other. If they didn't find him, what makes you think you will?"

He leaned over and tweaked her nose. "Come on, Robolo. Show a little faith, will you?"

She understood now why he was so good at his job. It was the passion he brought into it, the excitement he generated as he faced a new challenge. She had no idea what his plans were, or if he would succeed. For all she knew, this obsession of his could prove to be his downfall. He didn't seem to care. And at this moment, neither did she.

He was smiling as though he knew exactly what she was thinking. "What do you say, Robolo? Will you help me catch a killer?"

Twenty-Six

At first Kelly thought she was dreaming. But as she opened her eyes, the sounds she thought were from her subconscious became more distinct. Someone was outside her house, in the garden.

Wide awake now, she lay very still, holding her breath. Nothing. Could she have imagined it? Then she heard it again, the unmistakable sound of gravel crunching beneath slow, careful footsteps.

She tossed aside the duvet and got out of bed, throwing on a robe as she ran down the stairs. By the time she reached the sliding glass door in the living room, the sounds had stopped again. With a steady hand, she took a corner of the heavy rose-colored draperies and lifted it slightly. A three-quarter moon cast a pale light on her garden, which could easily be accessed from the street.

And then she saw it, an indistinct figure in a bulky parka, bent over and moving furtively around the small space. A furry hood concealed the hair, so she couldn't see if the intruder was a man or a woman. Nor could she tell what he or she was doing.

Kelly didn't take time to think about the possibilities. In a single motion, she reached for the burglar alarm panel near the window and hit the panic button.

A loud siren tore through the air and the outside floodlights seemed to explode over the little patch of green.

The intruder spun around, looking like a trapped animal. It wasn't until the hood slipped off, exposing shoulder-length brown hair, that Kelly realized her late-night visitor was a woman.

Kelly threw the sliding door open and lunged, throwing her arms around the woman and wrestling her to the ground. "Who are you?" she asked, straddling her. She had to shout over the strident sound of the siren. "What are you doing on my property?"

To her surprise, the woman didn't put up a fight. Or try to escape. Instead, she turned her head away from the blinding lights and sobbed helplessly.

Taken aback, Kelly unstraddled her but stayed crouched beside her in case she tried to make a run for it. "Who are you?" she repeated.

The woman continued to cry. "Come on." Kelly helped her to a sitting position, propping her against the stone wall that separated Kelly's garden from her neighbor's. Still sobbing, the woman glanced apprehensively toward a rhododendron bush.

Kelly followed her gaze. "What the…" A red can, the kind used to store gasoline for a lawn mower, stood beside the bush, the cap still on. Scattered throughout the garden were a half-dozen rags.

The woman had tried to set fire to her garden.

The compassion Kelly had felt for her a moment ago vanished. "You tried to burn my house? Why? What have I done to—"

When the woman looked up, Kelly stopped abruptly and sat down on the gravel, hard. She didn't have to ask any more questions. She knew who the woman was and why she was here. "You're Nicole Santos."

Nicole Santos was the wife of one of the men arrested in the Chinatown protection racket a few weeks ago. Shortly after the indictment, Channel 10 had interviewed Nicole from the couple's Roxborough home. Unlike Matias's wife, who had refused to talk to the press, Nicole had been quite vocal, especially about Kelly whom she claimed had destroyed her life by taking away the father of her unborn baby.

"You'll pay," she had screamed at the camera. "You'll burn in hell for what you've done to my Miguel."

"It was you," Kelly said. "The threatening notes, the vandalism to my house and to my car. That was all your doing."

In the distance, a police siren began to wail, grew louder, then stopped as a cruiser screeched to a halt in front of the house and two officers spilled out of the car, their guns drawn. "What's going on in here? Miss Robolo, are you all right?"

Well, well, how quickly things had changed. "I'm fine." Kelly quickly ran inside to shut off the alarm. "Nothing happened," she added when she returned.

The two men looked at the prone woman. "Who is she?" one officer asked.

"Her name is Nicole Santos. She's the wife of Miguel Santos who was charged with extortion five weeks ago. She may be having some kind of nervous breakdown."

The young officer slid his gun back into its holster and crouched beside the crying woman. "What are you doing here, ma'am?"

While he tried to coax an answer out of her, the other officer walked around the brightly lit garden. It wasn't long until he found what Kelly had already seen. "Hey, Tim, check this out." He pointed at the gasoline can. "Looks like we caught ourselves a firebug."

"She didn't have time to do anything," Kelly insisted. "The cap is still on the can."

"It's still attempted arson, ma'am." The officer, whose name tag read Blair, turned back to Nicole. "Mrs. Santos, did you try to burn Miss Robolo's house?" When the woman didn't answer, he took her arm and helped her up while the other officer collected the evidence. "We'll have to take her in," he told Kelly. "You, too, Miss Robolo. Maybe not tonight, but first thing in the morning you'll need to sign a statement."

"I'm not pressing charges."

"Don't matter." Officer Blair shook his head. "Attempted arson is a felony."

Leaning against the wall, her eyes closed, Nicole

Santos had finally stopped crying but seemed oblivious to what was going on around her. "Will you at least take her to a doctor and make sure she's all right?" Kelly asked. "I'm afraid I may have hurt her."

Blair looked at Nicole from head to toe. "She seems fine to me."

"She's pregnant, Officer. She ought to be checked out."

"Oh. I didn't know." He nodded. "We'll take her to the emergency room."

"Thank you." She nodded at the other officer, who had returned from the patrol car. "Thank you both."

A small crowd had gathered out in the street. Neighbors, some concerned, others just curious, watched as the two officers escorted Nicole Santos to the squad car.

"Everything's under control," Officer Blair said in answer to a shouted question. "Please go home." His arms spread wide, he forced them off Kelly's property, back toward the sidewalk. "Come on, people, go. It's cold out here."

Reluctantly, one by one, they moved on. Taking the officer's advice, Kelly hurried back into the house, locking the sliding door behind her.

The phone, an invention Kelly was beginning to despise, jolted her awake. It was Nick. He had heard about last night's incident and wanted to make sure she was all right.

"I'd be a lot better if I were allowed to catch up on my sleep," she grumbled.

As usual, he was in a sickeningly good mood. "Stop being such a grouch and be happy you have people around you who care."

"How did you hear?"

"Officer Blair briefed me this morning, though he didn't have to. Your pretty face is on all the TV channels, courtesy of the early-morning news."

That meant her mother had heard as well. Great. "How's Nicole Santos?"

"She checked out fine, at least physically. Mentally, she's a mess."

"When is her bail hearing?"

"In a couple of hours. The D.A. already indicated he won't fight bail, provided she's put under psychiatric care."

"I'm glad."

"There's one more thing. Nicole admitted to the vandalism, but denied sending the notes. I don't think she was lying."

Kelly was silent. Her suspicions had been right, then. The threats had nothing to do with Chinatown.

"Kelly, did you hear me?"

"Yes, and since I know where you're going with this, the answer is no. I will not be put under any kind of police protection."

"Kelly, be reasonable—"

Her call-waiting signal beeped in her ear, saving her from further discussion. "That will be my mother,

Nick. I'll talk to you later." She clicked a button and threw herself into another fire. "Hello, Ma."

"Don't you 'Hello, Ma' me," Connie snapped. "Just tell me why I had to hear what happened to you last night from that Monica Malpass?" Monica Malpass was the TV 6 morning anchor and, like many Philadelphians, Connie called the local broadcasters by their first names, as though they were family.

"Nothing happened to me last night, Ma. I'm fine." Maybe if she kept repeating those last two words, like a mantra, people would start believing her.

"A crazy woman tries to set fire to your house and you call that nothing?"

"She didn't know what she was doing."

"I can't believe you're defending her."

"She's also three months pregnant."

That stopped her, as Kelly knew it would. "Pregnant? *Madonna mia.* Is she all right? Did she get hurt?"

"Nick McBride just called to say she and the baby checked out fine. Nicole should be out on bail sometime this morning. She's agreed to—"

"Nick McBride? That nice young man I like so much?"

Kelly sighed. What had she done? "That McBride, yes, Ma." She wanted to change the conversation and find out if her uncle had arrived but didn't know how to ask without giving herself away.

"You should bring him over, honey." Her good mood miraculously recovered, Connie was suddenly all sweetness and charm. "I'm sure your Uncle Gino would love to meet him."

"Uncle Gino is here?" Kelly did her best to sound both surprised and happy.

"He arrived last night. You didn't know?"

"No, of course not. I haven't talked to him in weeks. What's the occasion?"

"No occasion. He says things are slow at the winery and he felt like a visit. But I don't know." She made a *tsk* sound with her tongue. "He's been acting strange."

Unlike Ronny, Uncle Gino had never been much of an actor. "Strange how?"

"He drove me crazy last night, checking all the doors and windows before we went to bed, and this morning he told me I should install a burglar alarm."

"That might not be a bad idea."

"It's a stupid idea, and a waste of money." She paused. "And talking of stupid ideas, your brother called yesterday, just after you and Phoebe left."

"Ronny?" She was beginning to sound as phony as she felt.

"Yes, Ronny. How many brothers you got?" Her tongue clicked again. "He wanted me to go to Atlanta for a couple of weeks. Can you believe that? They're buried under two feet of snow down there."

"I guess he misses you."

"Hmm." She sounded even more skeptical. "He didn't tell you about it?"

"I haven't talked to Ronny either." One of these

days she would grow horns for lying so shamelessly to her mother.

In the background, Kelly heard her uncle's booming voice. "Gino wants to see you," Connie said. "He says to come for dinner. He'll cook something special. Oh, and bring Nick."

Nick? "I can't bring Nick, Ma. He—"

Connie had already hung up.

Twenty-Seven

"What the fuck do you think you're doing?"

Nick closed the door to Captain Cross's office and faced his enraged boss. It didn't take a genius to know what had put him in such a state. "Don't tell me. Moneybags called you again."

"Not me, Nick," Cross yelled. "The police commissioner. Webber went straight to the top this time, complaining not only about you but about me as well. You want to know what he said?" The captain leaned forward, his jacket pushed back, his fists on his hips, bringing his angry face inches away from Nick's. "He said I was incompetent, that I couldn't control my men and that I should be replaced. How do you like that?"

"I wouldn't worry about Webber," Nick said coolly. "The man's full of hot air."

"And you're one fucking thorn in my side, McBride. First you harass the man in a state where you have no jurisdiction and then you stalk him." Cross hit his forehead with the palm of his hand. "What were you thinking?"

"I'm conducting an investigation—"

"I told you to stay away from Webber! And what do you do? You tail him while he's on a date."

"He was not on a date."

"I don't give a shit what he was doing. You were supposed to stay away from him, not shadow him. The man's got connections, Nick. And he knows how to use them."

"Just because he has connections doesn't mean he should be given preferential treatment. And as long as Jonathan Bowman is missing—"

"Bowman is alive and well."

Nick frowned. "How do you know?"

"Cecily Sanders called. Bowman talked to his wife on the phone and told her he wasn't coming home. Ms. Sanders wants her niece and Jonathan to work out this domestic dispute privately and quietly, and I agree."

It was Nick's turn to lose his temper. "For Christ's sake, Captain. I was there when the call came through. That wasn't Bowman on the phone. It was an impostor."

"You have proof of that?"

"Not yet, but I will. Just give me a few more—"

"I'll give you zip. Not only are you off this case, but you're suspended for two weeks." On that last sentence, his wide shoulders sagged a little and his voice dropped. "I'm sorry, Nick. I didn't have a choice in this."

Nick was silent. He didn't blame the captain. He knew the orders had come from above, and for Cross to defy them would be professional suicide. Quietly, Nick took out his badge, removed his gun from his shoulder holster and placed both on Cross's desk. Then, without a word, he walked out.

Rouge was a small, elegant restaurant on Rittenhouse Square, half a block away from Victoria's shop. At this noon hour, the place was already crowded, but Victoria, who knew the hostess, had managed to secure a table by the window overlooking the park.

"Sorry I'm late," Kelly said as she brushed her lips against her friend's cheek. "The traffic was horrendous." Victoria looked good, Kelly noticed. Eyes bright, hands steady. And she had reopened the shop, which was a good sign.

"No problem. I've ordered us some wine—chardonnay, because I figured you'd want the fish. Is that all right?"

"Just what I need." Kelly took a sip of her wine, which was cold and fruity.

"Have you had a chance to see the news yet?"

"Briefly. As always they blew the incident out of proportion."

"How can you say that, Kelly? The woman had a half-dozen rags strategically placed throughout your yard and a five-gallon can of gasoline. Your house would have been engulfed in flames within moments if you hadn't stopped her."

"But I did stop her, so let's not talk about it anymore, okay?" Kelly shrugged off her coat and let it fall across the back of her chair. "How's your stay at the Sanders' Palace?"

Victoria picked up her menu and scanned it. "Cecily is a little overwhelmed by the constant noise and activity. It's one thing to have our little family over for Sunday dinner, and another to have a rambunctious five-year-old underfoot all the time, asking thousands of questions, making remarks no one quite knows how to take and jumping on priceless antiques."

Kelly laughed. "She's not."

"I'm exaggerating. But Phoebe's a handful. Adrian's doing his best to keep her under control, but it's obvious he's never been around children. He doesn't have a clue what it takes to either please or quiet a child. She, on the other hand, already has him pegged and knows exactly which button to push. He's probably attending church services right now, praying to his Rumanian God that our stay will be a brief one."

Kelly looked at Victoria from above the rim of her menu. It felt good to see her that way, relaxed and cracking jokes. They'd had a long phone conversation this morning and Victoria had told her that as long as Jonathan was alive, she would make no decision, and give her husband the benefit of the doubt until he told her, to her face, that he no longer loved her.

Victoria closed her menu. "Have you heard from Nick?"

"Early this morning. He found out about the incident at the town house from one of the officers on call.''

''You haven't heard from him since?''

''No. Why?'' Kelly asked as the waitress came to take their orders. She ordered the grilled salmon, Victoria the potato-crusted halibut, then waited until they were alone again. ''What's the matter with Nick?''

''He's been suspended.''

''*What?*''

''God, Kelly, where have you been? The news is all over town.''

''Why was he suspended?''

''Syd Webber. According to Action News, your other admirer called the police commissioner this morning and told him Nick was stalking him. You can guess the rest.''

''Oh, God.'' Kelly leaned back against her chair. ''I was afraid something like that would happen, but I never thought Syd would actually pull strings to get Nick suspended.''

''Maybe Nick has been right all along in suspecting that Syd was involved in Patrick McBride's death,'' Victoria said in a low voice. ''And that's why Syd wants him out of the way.''

''Hmm.''

''You don't agree?''

''I don't know what to think. Nick is a very persuasive man, and he makes a compelling case, but his hatred for Syd is so fierce, at times I wonder if he's being rational.''

"He has good instincts, Kelly. You told me so yourself."

Kelly looked up from her plate. "You didn't think so yesterday."

Victoria shrugged. "Just because I don't agree with his theory about Jonathan's phone call doesn't mean that I don't respect his judgment." She smiled. "Most of the time."

The waitress arrived with their food. Once again, Kelly waited until she was gone before speaking. "So, you still want Nick to help find Jonathan? Even though he's been suspended?"

"Absolutely." She speared a flaky piece of halibut with her fork. "I trust him, Kelly. You should, too."

The ring of a cell phone interrupted their conversation. Out of habit, Kelly reached for hers, but it was Victoria's. During the brief discussion, Victoria said nothing, murmuring only a weak "thank you" at the end.

When she looked at Kelly, her eyes were glistening.

Kelly put her fork down. "Victoria, what is it? Who was that?"

"Detective Quinn." Tears ran down her cheeks—tears of joy, judging from her luminous smile. "The teeth on that burned body don't match Jonathan's dental record." Her hand gripped Kelly's so hard she was afraid Victoria would break it. "He's alive, Kel," she said in a fierce whisper. "I knew it. My husband is alive."

Twenty-Eight

Syd Webber's voice was filled with concern. "Kelly, I just heard the news on the radio. Are you all right?"

Switching the phone to her left ear, Kelly drove out of the restaurant's parking lot and turned left on Manning Street. "Perfect," she said curtly. "Thanks for asking."

"I also found out you had been the victim of vandalism over the last few weeks. Why didn't you tell me?"

At her request, and with Nick's help, the vandalism hadn't been made public. How had Syd found out? "Because that's my business, Syd, not yours."

"I could have had you protected."

"How? By putting a three-hundred-pound bouncer outside my door?"

"If that's what it takes."

"I don't think so, Syd. My neighbors wouldn't take kindly to that sort of disruption. But thanks for the offer."

"If you won't take my help, then let me take you out to lunch." His tone turned playful. "You owe me a rain check, remember?"

"Sorry, I'm busy."

"With what? You're no longer investigating Jonathan's disappearance, are you? Not now that his wife heard from him."

So he knew about that, too. His private news network was even more efficient than she had realized. "Don't believe everything you hear, Syd."

There was a slight pause. "What does that mean?"

"Nothing. Look, Syd, I've got to go."

"You're upset with me. I can hear it in your voice. What is it, Kelly? What have I done?"

Kelly let out a short, brittle laugh. "I don't believe you. You really don't know?"

"Know what?"

"Okay, I'll tell you. I didn't appreciate you going to the police commissioner and having Nick McBride suspended. That was low, Syd."

"I had no say on McBride's suspension. The commissioner acted on his own, with no prompting from me."

"And just what did you expect he would do? Give Nick a slap on the wrist? No, Syd. You knew exactly what would happen. That's why you went to the commissioner and not to Cross."

"For Christ's sake, the man wouldn't leave me alone. Was I supposed to let him walk all over me? Sorry, Kelly, that's not my style."

"Obviously not. Goodbye, Syd."

"Kelly, wait! Let's talk about this."

She pressed the off button.

* * *

Alan Braden stretched his long legs in front of him and took the can of Samuel Adams Nick offered him. A few months shy of his sixtieth birthday, the private investigator looked ten years younger, with brown hair worn in an old-fashioned buzz cut and sharp hazel eyes. At six-four, he was too tall for a man whose profession required total anonymity, but somehow he managed to get the job done. The two men had met several years ago, during a crime spree that had spread along the entire East Coast, and had been friends ever since.

"Give me good news, Alan." Nick sat down and took a sip of his beer.

Alan laughed. "I'll start with the good and save the bad for last. First of all, you were right. That photograph on Magdalena's mantel is a phony. These days, thanks to computer technology, pictures can be doctored fairly easily, with a minimum of know-how. You can put two people in the same shot in about two seconds, using special software."

"Is that what happened?"

Alan nodded. "The man I took the photo to could tell right away. The first giveaway was the different light on the subjects. There was also a fine crop mark in the middle. You can't see it with the naked eye, but it's there."

Nick nodded. "Good work, Alan." He let a few seconds tick by. "And the bad news?"

"Magdalena is gone. She skipped town in the middle of the night."

Nick sat up. "What the hell do you mean she skipped town? You told me you were putting your best operatives on her."

"I did. She must have suspected she was being watched. Or maybe she was just being cautious. John had the second shift and was in his car all night. He never saw her coming out of the building."

Nick waved the explanation away. "Any idea where she went?"

"John talked to the maid, Marisol, but she was as surprised as he was. She arrived this morning and found Magdalena gone. No note, no special outgoing message on the answering machine. *Nada*."

Nick moved over to the window. A light snow had begun to fall, sticking to the little patch of grass outside his northeast Philadelphia home. It would change to rain soon, before another storm front moved in. "Somebody must have called her, told her the heat was on."

"They didn't do it through the house phone. The only calls that came through that one were from her masseur, her hairdresser and a couple of girlfriends calling to make a lunch date."

"No one visited her at the condo?"

"Nope. I'm sorry, Nick. We should have been more careful."

Nick shook his head. "It's not your fault. She gave

you no reason to suspect she'd do something like that.''

"I can find her if you want me to."

"No, that's all right. Let those bastards think they're safe. It will make my job easier if they're not on their guard."

"You'll let me know if you need me?"

Nick nodded. "When the time comes."

After Alan left, Nick called Quinn to tell him about Magdalena's quick exit and found he already knew. As in all bombing cases, the FBI had now taken over the investigation and one of the first persons they had wanted to question was Magdalena. They never got a chance.

Nick walked back to the table where Alan had left his typed report and sat down to read it.

Kelly's first call when she returned home from her lunch with Victoria was to Nick. "I thought you might need a little cheering up."

"You heard."

"No thanks to you, Nick. You should have told me."

"You have enough problems of your own."

"And this is one of them. I feel responsible. If I hadn't gone out with Syd, none of this would have happened. I'm so sorry, Nick."

She heard him chuckle. "I was suspended, Kelly, not terminated."

His good humor was contagious. "Does that mean you don't need cheering up?"

"Depends. What did you have in mind?"

"Are you playing hard to get?"

"No, I just like to know what I'm getting into, that's all."

"Smart-ass." She matched his playful tone. "Just for that I should withdraw the invitation."

"Now we're talking. What kind of invitation?"

"To dinner. At San Remo. I tried to bail you out of it, but my mother wouldn't let me."

"Good woman, your mother. I'm cheered up already."

"Good." Kelly's teakettle let out a loud whistle and she walked over to the stove to take it off the burner. "I had lunch with Victoria earlier. While we ate, Detective Quinn called."

"He told you there was no match?"

"He told Victoria. She's ecstatic, Nick. That call made her even more convinced that she and Jonathan will be able to work things out." She dropped a tea bag into a mug and poured hot water over it. "I'm afraid she's setting herself up for a bad fall."

"You mean if Jonathan is dead."

Nick was the only person with whom she could openly discuss this depressing possibility. "He would never treat Victoria that way if he was alive."

She heard him sigh. "I don't know him, so I can't comment one way or another, but I agree it doesn't look good for him, now less than ever."

"Why now?"

"Alan Braden, the private investigator I hired, just left my house. The photo on Magdalena's mantel is a fake. Beyond that, she left town in the middle of the night, destination and duration of her trip unknown."

Kelly's cup hit the tiled counter so hard that tea spilled over. The dancer had lied to her—to all of them—after all. But why? And equally important, who was behind that elaborate scheme? "Will you try to find her?"

"The feds will do a better job of that than I would. Besides, I'd rather concentrate on Enrique. But not tonight." She heard the smile in his voice. "Tonight I'd rather concentrate on you."

Kelly's heart picked up a beat. "You might be disappointed."

He laughed, as if remembering some private secret. "Not a chance. What time do I pick you up?"

"It'd be too much out of your way," Kelly replied. "Meet me at San Remo instead. Around seven?"

"Seven it is."

"And bring your appetite. My uncle is cooking."

Standing in the bedroom, Kelly studied her reflection in the full-length mirror and made a face. If blue was her color, as Victoria claimed, then why did this dress, for which she had paid a fortune, make her look so washed-out and prim?

It's the neckline, she decided, her fingers running

over the demure boatneck. It just wasn't…sexy enough. The word brought a smile to her lips. Since when did she try and look sexy for Nick McBride? Rather than answer the question, she unzipped the dress and started flipping through her closet again in search of something a little more appropriate for tonight's occasion—like a pair of jeans and a sweatshirt.

Her fingers stopped on a black dress she had worn at the Sanders' thirtieth wedding anniversary party last December. It was close-fitting without being tight, with spaghetti straps and a low square neckline that made her small breasts look bigger.

She turned to check her profile in the cheval mirror. Was Nick partial to big breasts, she wondered, or small ones? Small ones, she decided with a nod. After all, she hadn't seen any disappointment on his face the other morning when he had caught her naked in her bedroom. Just lust.

She let the blue dress slide off her body and slipped into the black sheath. Then, standing back, she nodded approvingly. Nick would definitely prefer this dress. It was a tad much for San Remo, but so what? It wasn't every day that she went out with a hunk like Nick McBride.

Suddenly feeling as giddy as a young girl on her first date, Kelly picked up the bottle of Magie Noire from her dresser, sprayed a little of the intoxicating fragrance behind her ears and walked out of the room.

* * *

"Princess!"

Kelly had barely come through the kitchen's swinging door when her uncle lifted her off the floor and spun her around as easily as he used to when she was a little girl.

"Uncle Gino!" She laughed hysterically. "Put me down."

"Say *prego.*"

She laughed harder, remembering their old game. *"Prego."*

He set her down and held her at arm's length. "Your mother was right. You are too beautiful for words."

"So are you."

She meant it. At sixty-two, Gino Robolo was still a handsome man, with big, laughing brown eyes and that thick Robolo hair, though his had turned snow white years ago. Seeing him here, in her father's old apron, brought a wave of memories. She could still see the two brothers in this very kitchen, looking over each other's shoulder, smelling, tasting and arguing whether or not to put a pinch of sugar in the tomato sauce or how long the osso buco should cook.

Gino glanced behind her. "Where's your beau?"

"He'll be here soon. And he's not my beau."

"It's not what I hear from your mother." He leaned forward and lowered his voice. "Everything okay, princess? You haven't gotten any more threats, have you?"

"No. And thanks for coming to the rescue, Uncle Gino. I feel so much better knowing you're here."

"You don't have to thank me. And don't worry about your mother, okay? I'm gonna take good care of her."

Connie looked up from a tray of ravioli. "What are you two whispering about over there?"

"I'm just telling your daughter she's beautiful, like her mother."

"Enough with the compliments already. Get your rear over here and check your stuffed peppers. I think they're done."

Kelly left them to their banter and walked back into the dining room to wait for Nick.

Twenty-Nine

Nick arrived just as Connie was bringing out a tray of bruschetta, crusty slices of toasted bread topped with chopped tomatoes, melted mozzarella, basil and a drizzle of olive oil.

"These are for you," he said, handing Connie a bouquet of yellow roses and a box of Godiva chocolates. "And don't tell me I shouldn't have, because I never know what to say when a beautiful woman tells me that."

Connie gave Nick's arm a playful tap. "Oh, you." She brought the fragrant flowers to her face. "Thank you, Nick. I love yellow roses."

"Kelly told me."

She waved her hand toward a booth that was already set with candlelight, a tiny pot of African violets and a bottle of sangiovese. "Sit down, please. You, too, honey. Have some bruschetta. And don't bother looking at the menu, Nick. Gino insisted on preparing something special, just for you." She leaned over the table. "Just don't tell the customers, okay?"

"My lips are sealed, Connie."

They sat down and Nick's eyes skimmed over Kelly's face, her hair and the revealing neckline as he poured the wine. "You look lovely."

"Thank you." Mentally she substituted the word *obvious* for *lovely* and felt herself blushing. She should have stayed with the blue dress.

The kitchen doors swung open again and Gino walked out, a big grin on his face. The two men hit it off right away, talking about everything from the art of making wine to the Philadelphia Eagles, which Gino still cheered for even though he now lived in 49ers territory.

"Your uncle is quite a guy," Nick said after Gino left.

"He's wonderful. Next to my dad, he's the sweetest, most generous, most loving man I've ever known. You see that piano over there?" Nick nodded. "I took lessons when I was little, but I hated it, and played only to make my mother happy."

"I didn't know you were musically inclined."

"I wasn't, but Uncle Gino refused to let me give up. He would sit with me sometimes and start playing the tunes I loved rather than the pieces I was supposed to practice. Soon I was playing right along with him, and loving it."

"He plays the piano, makes wine, cooks, serves." He watched Gino pass by, four huge bowls of pasta balanced on his arms. "Is there anything he doesn't do?"

"You forgot singing."

"No kidding?"

"No kidding. He and my Uncle Stefano used to sing at weddings and communions when they were teenagers. South Philly loved them."

"Where's Stefano now?"

"Somewhere in Mexico. He's a ringmaster for a traveling circus. Before that he was a trapeze artist and a sword swallower."

Nick laughed. "You have a very unusual family."

"You should see when they all get together. It's a real circus."

She was glad she could make him laugh and forget his troubles, if only for a few hours. He hadn't said anything about his suspension, or how he planned to catch Enrique now that he no longer had a badge, but she knew the matter was on his mind. A two-week suspension wasn't something a cop took lightly.

"Hey, Gino!" a customer called out as her uncle came out of the kitchen again. "How about a song?"

"Who do you think I am?" Gino replied. "Pavarotti?"

"Aw, come on, Gino." One of the restaurant's regulars clapped his hands. "It's Saturday night. At those prices you charge, customers are entitled to a little entertainment."

Connie appeared through the swinging doors, smiling as usual. "What's all the racket about?" she asked. "Gino screw up the orders again?"

"He won't sing!"

In the same theatrical manner Kelly remembered

from her childhood, Gino raised his hands up in the air and waved them above his head. "Okay, okay, one song. No more." He waited for the cheering to stop before adding, "But only if my lovely sister-in-law will accompany me on the piano."

Connie bowed, then, making a big production of stretching and flexing her fingers, she sat down in front of the old piano and started hitting a few keys. Gino waited, mike in hand, and winked at her.

"They're up to something," Kelly murmured more to herself than to Nick.

She was right. As Connie's fingers moved lightly over the keys, Gino turned to the booth where Kelly and Nick sat. "This song is dedicated to that cute couple over there—my beautiful niece, Kelly, and her handsome date, Nick. Hit it, Connie."

As her mother started playing the old neighborhood favorite "That's Amore," Gino's rich voice filled the dining room, waving at the crowd to join in with the famous refrain.

Kelly picked up another bruschetta. "I'll kill him. I'll kill them both."

Nick threw her an amused glance. "You don't like the song?"

"Can't you see? They planned this. Both of them." She saw him chuckle. "And you're enjoying it, playing right into their hands."

"What can I tell you? I'm a romantic."

When the song ended, the crowd rose to its feet, clapping and whistling and demanding an encore.

Gino walked from table to table, accepting compliments, shaking hands, laughing with old friends.

A few minutes later, he stopped at their table. "Did you like that, children?" He beamed at them.

"Yeah, Uncle Gino." Kelly rolled her eyes. "Real subtle."

"Don't blame me. Your mother put me up to it."

"Bad-mouthing me again, Gino?" Connie gave him a shove with her hip and put two salads in front of Nick and Kelly. "You can't trust anyone anymore, not even family." She tugged Gino's sleeve. "Come on, leave those two alone. I need you in the kitchen."

Gino threw his hands up again and followed her. "How does she manage without me the rest of the year?"

As they ate, drank and talked, Kelly found herself relaxing and opening up to Nick in ways she had never opened to anyone before. He was easy to talk to and, almost without warning, she found herself telling him about her two failed relationships.

"What kind of men were they?" Nick asked.

"Oh, God." She laughed, feeling suddenly self-conscious. "Let's see, first there was Johnny, a South Philly boy my mother introduced me to."

"What was wrong with him?"

"Me. Everything was wrong with *me*—at least as far as Johnny was concerned. I was too tall, too independent and too strong-willed. And he didn't like my job either. He thought investigative reporting was a man's job. Oh, and I was living in Center City. No self-respecting Italian girl would ever live in Center City."

"What did you ever see in him?"

"Charm. He oozed it. Whenever I was mad at him, he would serenade me outside my window and make all my girlfriends jealous."

"Hmm. Does that mean I should start taking singing lessons?"

"Don't you dare."

"What happened to your troubadour?"

"I couldn't take the criticism anymore, so I broke off the engagement."

Nick sipped his wine. "And number two?"

"Number two was a girl's dream. He was handsome, successful and supportive. Unfortunately his family was filthy rich and thought I was after his money."

"What did *he* think?"

"He must have agreed with them, because three weeks before the wedding he asked me to sign a seventeen-page prenuptial agreement. I got offended, told him where to stick his prenup and gave him back his ring."

Nick threw his head back and laughed, drawing warm glances from the people at the next table. "Good for you, Robolo." He refilled their glasses. "And there's been no one else since?"

"No, I've sworn off men."

He leaned across the table. In the candlelight his

blue eyes shimmered. "That's not what it felt like last night."

"Maybe we should forget last night."

He pulled back, pretending to be offended. "Was I that bad?"

Oh, no, Nick, she thought, you were that good. That's what worries me. "Stop fishing for compliments and eat your cannoli, or my mother will accuse you of eating like a bird."

They talked for another hour and never realized it was snowing again until a customer opened the curtains and pointed it out.

"Why don't you let me take you home?" Nick offered, standing up.

Kelly shook her head. "I want to stay and help my mother with the cleanup. That will give me a chance to spend a little more time with my uncle."

She didn't add that if he took her home, she would probably toss caution to the wind and ask him in. And that, she knew, would be a mistake. She liked him too much to spoil their new friendship with a romance that was bound to fail.

But Nick wasn't a man who was easily discouraged "In that case, I'll help your mother with the cleanup and you visit with Gino. After the feast he cooked for us, that's the least I can do. Then I'll take you home."

"I can drive in the snow, Nick. I've done it every winter since I got my learner's permit."

"I don't like the idea of you driving home alone

at this time of night. You won't take police protection, but at least let me do this."

"Stop it. You're making me sound helpless and I don't like the feeling."

He threw up his hands in surrender. "All right, all right. Let me say good-night to your family and I'm out of here."

By the time he came back the restaurant was empty. "Thanks, Kelly," he said as they walked to the door. "You did cheer me up. You and your wonderful, zany family. I'll have to get all three of you over to the house before Gino leaves and make you my mother's famous Irish stew."

"You cook?" Wonders never ceased.

"Not too badly. It's one of my favorite hobbies."

"Do me a favor, will you?" She lowered her voice. "Don't tell my mother."

"Hmm. Maybe I should. She might put in a good word for me with her daughter." Gently, he took her face between his hands and kissed her. This time, his lips brushed hers gently, sensually, in a side-to-side motion that threatened to melt down every ounce of resistance she had managed to hang on to so far.

"Nick—"

"Shh. Don't talk. And don't tell me to stop."

She shut her eyes and let herself go. How could she tell him to stop when she was the one who couldn't tear away from him? When images kept flashing through her mind, images of Nick carrying her up to her bedroom, laying her on the big canopy bed and making love to her all night.

But she did let him go, reluctantly. "Good night, Nick."

"Good night, Kelly."

She stood at the restaurant's bay window until he had disappeared into the snow. Then, her fingers on her moist lips, she turned and walked back into the kitchen.

"I'm taking you home," Gino declared after they had put the last dish away.

Kelly tucked the sponge into the dishwasher basket. "Don't be silly, Uncle Gino. I'll be fine. And anyway, how would you get back?"

"You ever heard of cabs?"

"In this weather? On a Saturday night?" She glanced out the kitchen window. The snow had intensified, though it wasn't sticking to the road yet. "You've been away from Philly too long, Uncle Gino. You forgot that in this city cabs are never where you want them when you want them." She leaned forward, her tone conspiratorial. "And you have to stay with Ma."

"Nick knew that, too, so how come *he* didn't take you home?"

"Because I wouldn't let him. Now go, before Ma asks what we're whispering about."

"All right." He kissed her cheek. "But you drive carefully, you hear?"

"I always do, Uncle Gino."

Outside, the wind had picked up and fat flakes fell on her bare head. The streets were slippery, and walking in her two-inch heels was a challenge she wasn't accustomed to. In the CVS Pharmacy parking lot, the bright blue Beetle sat waiting. She wondered if an overzealous traffic cop had left a little present under the windshield wiper. The sign had clearly said CVS Patrons Only, but she had ignored it. Parking in South Philly was tough, but the traffic cops were even tougher. Maybe tonight, because of the snow, they had made an exception.

The surprise snowstorm had sent Philadelphians scurrying home, and the neighborhood that had been so lively earlier was now deserted. At the intersection of Ninth and Catherine, Kelly started to cross the street. She was halfway to the other side when she saw the car. It moved slowly as though the driver was trying to read the street signs. Then, just when it should have stopped to let her go, it began picking up speed.

Kelly froze, momentarily blinded by the bright headlights. Her mind screamed at her to get out of the way, but she stayed rooted in the middle of the street, incapable of taking a step in either direction as the car hurtled toward her.

In that microsecond her instincts took over. Fighting for survival, she ran back to the curb and lunged behind a minivan. A blast of exhaust fumes hit her as the car roared by, its back fender scraping the mini-van.

Kelly tried to catch a glimpse of the person behind the wheel. All she saw was a cap pulled low over the driver's forehead, and long, blond hair. The license-plate light was out, making it impossible to read the numbers, but the car was familiar. From the back it looked like either a Mercedes or a Lexus.

She watched it zigzag down the street, tires screeching. It was a Lexus. A black Lexus.

Kelly leaned against the minivan and took big gulps of air. Her head began to pound. Someone she knew owned a black Lexus. Someone with long, blond hair.

Cecily Sanders.

Thirty

Her head lowered, her hands on the back of the minivan, Kelly waited for her heart to stop pounding and her breathing to return to normal. She felt drained. Her entire body shook uncontrollably but strangely enough her mind was clear.

Someone had just tried to kill her. Not just someone, but Cecily Sanders. Philadelphia's golden girl. Her best friend's aunt.

Chest still heaving, she looked up. The street was quiet once again and San Remo was more than three blocks away, her mother and Gino ignorant of the drama that had unfolded outside its walls. And that's how it would stay.

After another minute, Kelly took a step, then another, testing her legs. Nothing was broken or sprained. Her knees were bleeding from hitting the concrete, but other than that she was fine, at least physically.

Within moments she was inside the Beetle, the heater fan on high, her arms wrapped around herself as she waited for her nerves to settle. *Cecily had tried to kill her*. The words kept dancing in Kelly's head, ludicrous one moment, terrifying the next. Maybe she was wrong. Or she was so anxious to get to the truth that she was seeing things that weren't there. Like a Lexus. Yes, Cecily had acted strangely these past few days, even irrationally. But could she be a cold-blooded killer? It was a long, long stretch.

Sufficiently warmed, Kelly turned down the heat and slowly backed out of the parking lot. She didn't think the Lexus would come back, but why chance it?

As she drove, she thought of Cecily's reluctance to let Kelly search for Jonathan. From the start, she had cited a number of reasons—fear of scandal, the tarnishing of the Sanders' name, harassment from the press.

Kelly hadn't believed her. And she had sent Victoria and Phoebe into that house.

Oh, God, what had she done?

It wasn't until she merged onto the Schuylkill Expressway that she realized she was heading for the Sanders' house.

Nick's phone was ringing when he opened his front door. He picked up the receiver a split second before the machine did. "McBride."

It was Doreen, the detective who had been assigned to handle Nick's cases during his absence. "A special-delivery package arrived for you today," she said in her familiar Southern drawl. "It's from Las Vegas and it's marked urgent. I would have called earlier but some jerk buried it under a pile of paperwork. If I hadn't been looking for your notes on the Clover case, I wouldn't have seen it.''

Nick silently thanked Quinn for putting a rush on that police report. "Where is it now?" he asked.

"I have it with me. I didn't want anyone to get their hands on it.''

"You're a doll, Doreen. Do me a favor, will you? Keep it safe until—''

"I'll do one better. I'll drop it off at your house after my shift.''

"Not in this weather you won't.''

"Your house in on my way, Nick. Just sit tight, okay?''

Nick grinned. "Yes, ma'am.''

The special-delivery package contained a six-page police report and a videotape labeled Enrique Vasquez Live—The Lido—January 1989.

Seated in his comfortable easy chair, Nick picked up the report first.

The file contained basic information, some of which Nick already knew, some he didn't. Enrique's impersonations included superstars such as Cher, Diana Ross, Ann-Margret and Tina Turner. Sergeant Harrison had included a color photograph of Enrique in full costume as well as a couple of black-and-white glossies. Without the heavy stage makeup and fancy threads, the performer had been a handsome man with black curly hair, dark, sultry eyes and a fine, almost feminine jaw.

Until the moment Enrique had plunged a kitchen knife into his lover's heart, he had been an exemplary citizen without as much as a parking ticket to his name. But on the night of December 30, 1991, neighbors had heard Enrique and Steve arguing in their apartment on Decatur Avenue. Marquant, an attorney, had accused Enrique of infidelity and Enrique had retaliated by claiming his lover was neglecting him. One of the neighbors had been about to call the police when the shouting finally stopped.

The following day, alerted by a concerned co-worker, the police had gone to the couple's apartment and found the attorney in the bedroom, the knife still in his chest. Prints on the knife had identified Enrique as the perpetrator, but Enrique was nowhere to be found.

Nick continued to flip through the pages, reading every interview, every statement from friends and co-workers the Las Vegas police department had accumulated. But it was Syd Webber's statement that held his attention.

The casino owner was said to have been shocked to learn that one of his main attractions, a man whose performances he had watched and enjoyed time and time again, was wanted for murder. Unfortunately, he hadn't been able to offer any clue as to his whereabouts.

With a couple of questions still unanswered, Nick

called Sergeant Harrison in Las Vegas. "I just received your package," he said after identifying himself. "Thanks for sending it so quickly."

"Interesting stuff, huh?"

"I've only read the report so far, and I'm curious about something. How could Enrique have slipped out of town so easily? According to the report, he didn't own a car, and none of the airlines, bus lines or train lines had him on their manifest."

"My guess is that he had a friend here in town, someone well-connected who helped him buy a new identity."

"Any idea where he could have gone?" Nick still thought his destination might have been Miami, but he wanted to know if Harrison felt the same way.

The detective confirmed Nick's suspicions. "Miami seemed like a good idea, so we started there. We thought he might get in touch with his sister, but Enrique never showed. From what Magdalena told us, their split some years ago was anything but amicable. To put it in her own words, she didn't give a rat's ass if her brother was alive or dead. Nor was she surprised to hear he was wanted for murder."

"Why not?"

"She resented Enrique's lifestyle—meaning his homosexuality—and felt he'd end up badly someday."

But if Nick's hunch was right, Magdalena and Enrique had patched up their differences long ago.

"Thanks, Sergeant. If you ever need a favor from this side of the world, just holler."

"I'll do that. Good luck, Detective." He laughed. "And let me know if you find our man."

After hanging up, Nick walked over to the entertainment center and inserted the video into the VCR. As the strings of "Ain't No Mountain High Enough" filled the room, Enrique walked onstage wearing a black beaded gown that hugged every curve, real or otherwise. Voluminous black curls framed his perfectly made-up face and earrings as big as chandeliers hung from his earlobes.

Nick leaned forward. Even in close-ups, Enrique's resemblance to Diana Ross was so uncanny that if he hadn't known he was watching an impersonator, he wouldn't have guessed. Even the voice, though an octave lower than the former Supreme on the high notes, was astoundingly similar.

The next hour and a half brought out several transformations—Ann-Margret, Barbra Streisand, Billie Holliday, Cher and Tina Turner. Each time, the crowd greeted the new impersonation with thunderous applause, bringing Enrique back at the end of the performance for three curtain calls.

After the tape had finished rolling, Nick sat a long time, lost in his thoughts. From the coffee table, he picked up Enrique's most recent photograph. "Where are you, Enrique?" he murmured.

It had to be Miami. Just because the Las Vegas police department hadn't found him didn't mean he wasn't there. And after nine years, Enrique might have dropped his guard a little. All Nick needed was to come up with a flawless plan.

Nick ran the tape one more time. Halfway through Enrique's impersonation of blues singer Billie Holliday, a thought came to him. It was a long shot, one he rejected at first, but the more he thought about it, the more he thought it'd be worth a try.

Too upset to even force a smile, Kelly walked right past the Sanders' butler. "Good evening, Adrian. Is Mrs. Sanders in?"

"Not yet." If the well-mannered butler was put off by Kelly's late visit or her brusque attitude, he didn't show it. "She's in town, attending a DAR meeting."

It would have been easy enough for her to skip it, Kelly thought, or to leave early due to the weather. "What about Mr. Sanders?"

"He's having dinner with his father." Adrian glanced up the broad curving staircase. "Mrs. Bowman is in, but she retired an hour or so ago. I could—"

Kelly waved in dismissal. If necessary, she'd find a way of getting Victoria and Phoebe out of the house. "No, don't disturb her. It's Mrs. Sanders I've come to see. I'll just wait for her in the drawing room, if you don't mind. I'll keep my coat. I'm a little chilly tonight."

"Very well, Miss Robolo." He followed her into

the room. "Could I bring you some tea? Or coffee? I have some of that Hawaiian Kona you like."

She didn't think she could get anything past her throat. It was a wonder dinner had stayed down. "I don't care for anything, Adrian, but thanks just the same."

He bowed and retreated quietly. Once alone, Kelly felt a sudden nudge of panic. What if she had made a mistake and Cecily was not the driver of that Lexus? What if the highly respected Daughters of the Revolution all swore that Cecily had been present at their meeting? Kelly would look like an absolute fool. She might even lose Victoria's friendship over this.

If only she could be certain before she accused Cecily. She looked around her, not sure what she expected to find. Her gaze came to rest on a door that had been left ajar. Cecily's study. Victoria called it her aunt's inner sanctum, a sacred place where one entered by invitation only. In all the years Kelly had known Cecily, she had never set foot into that room.

Trying to appear casual, she approached slowly. Did she dare take a quick peek? It was risky. Adrian could come back at any moment to make sure she hadn't changed her mind about the coffee. How would she explain her presence in Cecily's office?

Her need to get to the truth outweighed her fear of getting caught. Or the brief guilt she experienced. Lou had once told her, "When an opportunity presents itself, seize it and worry about the morals of your actions later." It wasn't the most ethical advice she was ever given, but in this case she felt justified to take it.

With that thought in mind, she entered the room. Except for a low-wattage lamp on the desk, the study was in darkness. Even so, she could see that it was a lovely room, with deep burgundy walls, an ornate desk that was almost an exact replica of the one in Cecily's Center City office, a secretary and a built-in mahogany bookcase occupying an entire wall.

She searched the desk first, ready to move on if the single drawer was locked. It wasn't. As she pulled it open, she tried not to look at the framed photograph of a smiling Victoria and Phoebe facing her. If her friend ever found out about this she'd never speak to Kelly again.

The contents turned out to be disappointing. Other than the standard items found in a desk drawer—paper clips, letterheads, pencils and a stapler—she found nothing of interest. A quick search of the secretary proved just as futile.

That left the wall-to-wall bookcase, which was filled with beautifully bound books, old classics she knew well. She tilted her head sideways and read the spines—*Anna Karenina, Great Expectations, La Joie de Vivre.*

She moved from section to section, not touching, only reading the titles. Each book was so tightly pressed against the next that it would have been impossible to fit even the thinnest sheet of paper between them. Except... Kelly stopped. Except right here, between *War and Peace* and *Little Women*. There was a slight gap, hardly noticeable, but undeniably there.

With her right hand, she pulled out Tolstoy's masterpiece and slid her other hand through the vacant space. Her fingers came into contact with something hard and slick to the touch. Another book?

Puzzled, she took it out, walked back to the desk and held it under the lamp.

Her heart gave one solid thump.

It was a book of nursery rhymes.

Thirty-One

Kelly read the title again—*Mother Goose's Book of Nursery Rhymes*—before starting to flip through the pages. They were all there, the verses that had delighted her early years.

She kept turning the pages in search of two specific rhymes. Then she found them. Tweedle-Dum and Tweedle-Dee was on page nine. Her lips began to move as she read the near-forgotten rhyme. *Tweedle-Dum and Tweedle-Dee resolved to have a battle. For Tweedle-Dum said Tweedle-Dee had spoiled his nice new rattle.*

On the next page, she found the other rhyme. *Mary, Mary quite contrary...*

"Kelly!"

As bright light exploded into the room, Kelly jumped. Ward stood in the doorway, the expression in his eyes a mixture of bewilderment and displeasure.

For a few seconds, Kelly couldn't find her voice. She was lost for words, fumbling to say something that wouldn't sound stupid.

Ward's gaze remained fixed on her. She wasn't

even sure he had seen the book. "Ward...I can explain."

"Then please do." His gaze shifted to the book in her hand. "What is that?"

"A book I found..." She turned toward the built-in mahogany bookcase. "A book of nursery rhymes."

He looked puzzled. "In here?"

"Yes."

"What are you doing in Cecily's study? You know she doesn't allow anyone in here."

Kelly took a deep breath, like a high diver about to take the plunge. Once she started there would be no turning back. "Someone tried to kill me tonight."

"Dear God! Are you all right? Did you call the police?" His anger forgotten, Ward walked quickly toward her, his eyes inspecting her from head to toe.

"No...I mean, yes, I'm all right, just bruised, and no, I didn't call the police."

"Why not?"

"Because..." She waved toward the drawing room. "Is it all right if we go in there? I need to sit down."

"Of course." His irritation had vanished. He was once again the warm, concerned Ward she knew.

Once they were seated in front of the fireplace, Kelly placed the book on her lap.

"How did it happen?" Ward asked. It was obvious he was now more interested in Kelly's recent ordeal than in her reason for being in Cecily's study.

"A car tried to run me over." Kelly saw the look

of horror in his eyes. "I had just left my mother's restaurant and was about to cross Ninth Street when this car came at me at full speed."

"Are you sure it was intentional? It's been snowing rather heavily. Couldn't the car have spun out of control?"

"It was intentional."

"You should have called the police. In fact—" he rose "—if you won't, I will. It's not too late to catch whoever—"

"No!" She took another breath. "Please, Ward, don't call the police. Hear me out first."

He sat down again.

"This attempt on my life tonight…it wasn't a total surprise."

"What do you mean? Have there been other attempts?"

"No, but I've been receiving threatening notes. Two, exactly. The first was put in my mailbox on Tuesday, in broad daylight, the second just two nights ago."

"Who would want to do that?" He frowned. "Unless it was the same woman who tried to burn your house last night? Nicole Santos?"

Kelly shook her head. "No. Nicole is a likely suspect, but it wasn't her."

She glanced at the book on her lap while Ward waited patiently for her to continue. She couldn't bring herself to look at him, to tell him that the wife he loved so much, the woman he had been married to for thirty years, might be a cold-blooded murderer.

But even Ward's patience had its limits. "Will you at least tell me what you were doing in Cecily's study?" He looked at the book on her lap. "With a book of nursery rhymes?"

"The notes..." She felt miserable at the thought of the pain she was about to cause him. "The notes were written in the form of nursery rhymes."

He stared at her for a few seconds and she could tell from his blank expression that he hadn't immediately made the connection between her statement and the book on her lap. Then, as the meaning of her words finally sank in, he shot out of his chair. "What are you saying? That Cecily wrote those notes? That she's the one who tried to kill you tonight?"

"No, I...I'm not accusing anyone. I only came here for answers."

"How could you suspect Cecily of doing something so vile?" he continued. "So cold-blooded? She's never done anything but show you and your family the deepest affection. And this is how you repay her?"

"I just want to hear what she has to say, that's all." She glanced down at the book again, this damn book she wished she had never found.

"For your information," Ward said a little stiffly, "this book does not belong to Cecily."

Kelly looked up, confused. "It doesn't?"

"No." Ward squared his shoulders. "It's mine."

Kelly felt her mouth hang open. And then it hit her. He was covering for Cecily. He was taking the blame for something she had done, knowing damn well what the consequences would be. "I don't believe you."

"That's your problem," he said brusquely.

"Are you admitting that you sent me those two threatening notes?"

"I'm admitting nothing of the sort. Finding a book of nursery rhymes that I've had since Victoria was a small child doesn't mean I used it to write threatening notes. Or that I tried to kill you. I was nowhere near San Remo tonight. I was at the Striped Bass having dinner with my father. Call him if you wish."

She didn't have to. Ward drove a silver BMW, not a black Lexus. "This book isn't yours, Ward."

"How do you know?"

She opened a page. "Because it has a 1996 copyright. You couldn't possibly have had it when Victoria was small."

"Then I must have bought it for Phoebe."

She studied his face for a moment, trying to read his expression. What if all this was an act? What if Cecily and Ward were accomplices and he was just trying to confuse her?

"Aren't you curious about the car that tried to run me over?" Kelly asked, her voice shaky. "Or whether I was able to read the license plates?"

This time he turned pale. "Did you?"

"No. But I did recognize the make of the car. It was a Lexus. A black Lexus."

Ward's throat constricted as he swallowed. "There must be dozens of Lexus in the Philadelphia area."

"The driver was a woman with long, blond hair."

Ward's shoulders slumped. In the space of a few minutes he had aged ten years. No ordinary man could be that good of an actor. "Dear God," he murmured.

In the back of the house, a door opened then closed. Quick footsteps clicked against the marble floor. Kelly and Ward looked up. Cecily, wrapped in a black wool coat with the collar turned up, stopped when she saw them. She started to smile.

"Adrian told me you were here, Kelly." Her gaze shifted to her husband. "What's going on?" She removed her gloves. "Ward, what is it? You look ghastly."

"Sit down, Cecily."

Looking mildly bewildered, she tossed her gloves on a chair, shrugged out of her coat and lay it on that same chair. "Victoria is all right, isn't she?"

"She's fine," Ward said dully. "So is Phoebe."

Cecily's gaze returned to Kelly, who hadn't said a word. "Kelly? Would you mind telling me what you're doing here, looking so morbid?"

Without a word, Kelly turned the book of nursery rhymes over so Cecily could see the cover. The reaction was instantaneous, and so unmistakably finger-pointing that Kelly had difficulty taking her next breath.

"Where did you find that?" Cecily asked.

"Don't you know?"

Cecily glanced at her husband, who was watching her intently. There was a look of total resignation about her now. "Yes," she said in a whisper. "I do."

"Is it yours?"

Cecily nodded.

"And did you use this book to send me threatening notes?"

Cecily took a moment to answer. When she looked at Kelly again, her eyes were bright with tears. "I never meant to carry out those threats, Kelly, you must believe that. I didn't know what to do. You wouldn't stop that damn investigation and frightening you seemed like the only way to make you back off, but that's all I meant to do."

"Why, for God's sake?" Ward asked. "Why would you do something so irrational, so potentially dangerous?"

"Because I was scared. I was convinced that Jonathan was involved in something illegal. I still am. I was afraid of what that news, if it came out, would do to all of us."

"So you decided that the only way to stop me was to kill me," Kelly said.

"*No!* Of course not. I told you I had no intention of carrying out those threats. Oh, Kelly, how could I ever kill you? You're like a daughter to me."

"But you did try to kill me, Cecily. This evening, as I was coming out of my mother's restaurant."

Despair vanished, replaced by shock. "Me?" She shook her head in disbelief. "No, Kelly, no. You're wrong. I was at a meeting, my DAR meeting in the city. My God, how could you think that I—"

"The car that tried to run Kelly over was a Lexus," Ward said, his voice so flat, so devoid of intonation that Kelly could barely recognize it. "And the driver was a woman with long blond hair," he added.

Cecily gave him a horrified look. "You believe it, too." Her hands flew to her mouth. Her eyes, wild now, went from Ward to Kelly. "And you. You both think I tried to kill you." She shook her head, blond hair flying. "I didn't. I was at my meeting. Go ahead, call Melvina. She'll tell you."

"Where was the meeting held?" Kelly asked.

"Same place as always, the Union League."

The Union League was on Broad Street, a short drive from South Philly. "Were you there all night?"

"I...I left early, when I realized it had begun snowing."

"Then you should have been home long ago," Ward pointed out. "What kept you?"

"The roads were slippery. I couldn't drive much more than twenty miles an hour. And I had to stop for gas."

Kelly watched her closely. "What station?"

"I don't know! I can't remember. Kelly, you must stop this. It's insane. Ward, make her stop."

Kelly stood. "May I see your car, Cecily?"

Her eyes widened. "My car? Why?"

"Because the Lexus that almost hit me scraped a minivan that was parked at the curb. There should be some damage to your car, a dent, a scrape, something."

Ward had also risen. "Kelly, can't that wait until morning? Cecily is exhausted—"

He was still trying to protect her, even now, knowing what he knew. "I'm sorry, Ward. Believe me, I hate this as much as you do, but it's my life we're talking about." When no one moved, she spoke more firmly. "I have to see the car. Now."

Cecily sighed. "Let her see the car, Ward. It's in the garage."

Ward threw Kelly an angry look, then went ahead of them, his mouth set in a tight line. Adrian, still up and in the kitchen, watched them go by. His face showed no expression.

In the oversize garage, all three vehicles were impeccably aligned—the Land Rover Cecily and Ward used on weekends at the far end, Ward's silver BMW and Cecily's black Lexus, still wet from the snow, closest to the door.

Kelly walked around the car, took a deep breath and released it slowly.

There was no dent on either fender, or a scrape. Not even a blemish. Only a perfect, unmarred, glistening surface.

Thirty-Two

Cecily was already seated at a small, secluded table when Kelly arrived at the Four Seasons the following morning. She had called Victoria's aunt earlier and asked if they could meet for brunch. As if sensing a showdown was inevitable, Cecily had agreed, suggesting the Fountain Restaurant at the Four Seasons.

Cecily's face was pale, her gaze steady, as Kelly made her way across the room, but underneath that perfect poise was a despair only those who knew her well could recognize.

She waited until Kelly sat down before asking, "You haven't changed your mind, have you?"

"About not telling the police about the notes?" Kelly picked up the silver coffeepot on the table and filled her cup. "No. I gave you my word I wouldn't."

"Then why are we here? What do you want?"

"Answers."

"Kelly, I've told you—"

"You told me that your reason for not wanting Jonathan found was that you feared a scandal. That you were afraid the Norton board of directors would ask you to resign. I don't believe it, Cecily. You're much too valuable for them to dismiss you over something that is totally out of your control. At the very most, you might suffer some embarrassment, but that's it.''

"You don't know the Norton board."

"No, but I know how the system works. And I know when I'm being lied to. I let you off the hook last night because of Victoria. She loves you very much and until I know exactly what it is that you're hiding, I don't want to hurt her any further."

"I'm not hiding anything."

"Yes, you are. You don't want Jonathan found because you are *afraid* and I want to know what it is that you're afraid of. I'm not trying to be nosy, Cecily. The reason I'm pushing is because I have a nagging suspicion that what you're hiding could be related to Jonathan's disappearance. And I'm not leaving here until I find out if I'm right."

This time Cecily didn't look away, or play with the accessories on the table, or try to distract Kelly in some other way. She just sat there, with that same resigned look she'd had last night. "Jonathan was blackmailing me."

Kelly stared. *"Jonathan?"*

"Maybe 'blackmail' isn't the right word. Let's just say that he knew something about me and threatened to use it."

Imagining Jonathan as a blackmailer was even more difficult than imagining him as an adulterer. "Threatened *how?* What did he want?"

"For me to stop interfering in his marriage, to accept him for what he is and to stop treating him like a second-class citizen. Those were his exact words."

"Is that all?" Kelly thought of the hundred thousand dollars he had tried to borrow from Ward. "He didn't ask for money?"

Cecily shook her head. "No. He was only interested in family harmony. He claimed that my negative feelings toward him were upsetting Victoria and would soon start upsetting Phoebe."

"What did you tell him?"

"I agreed, of course. What choice did I have?"

"You make it sound as if he'd asked you for some monumental favor," Kelly commented.

"I just don't like being blackmailed. A woman in my position shouldn't be subjected to such humiliation."

Kelly could see why Jonathan had jumped at the chance to take Cecily down a peg or two. She was a good woman, but when she put some effort into it, she could be sickeningly obnoxious.

"If the two of you reached an agreement, why were you afraid I would find him?"

"It's the nature of what he knows that worried me. Jonathan is not terribly sophisticated, you see, and to my knowledge, he's never kept a secret from Victoria." Her voice was stronger now and her cheeks had regained some color. "I was afraid he might let it slip."

"It doesn't bother you that he could be dead?"

"Of course it does! I never wished this on him, but if he is alive and wants to stay away, that's perfectly fine with me."

"Regardless of what that would do to Victoria?"

She didn't reply.

After an extended pause, Kelly asked, "What did Jonathan have on you?"

A tuxedoed waiter came to take their order, then left. When Cecily spoke again, her voice was strained. "I had an affair."

Kelly was only mildly surprised. The thought of an extramarital relationship had already crossed her mind.

"It's not something I'm proud of," Cecily continued. "I broke it off eventually."

"Who was the man?"

"Syd Webber."

Kelly dropped back against her chair, wondering how many shocks she could sustain in only one week. Syd Webber, a man Cecily had openly despised.

"You're shocked," Cecily said. "And rightly so."

"I don't understand. You have nothing but contempt for that man."

"I still do."

"Then why...?"

Sadness and regret veiled her eyes. "Weakness. He offered me something I never had before and it went to my head." She paused. "Do you remember Victoria and Jonathan's fourth wedding anniversary party two years ago?"

Kelly nodded.

"Jonathan invited Syd. I tried to talk him out of it, but he insisted. Apparently he had mentioned the party to Syd and Syd had expressed an interest in coming."

"Is that when...?"

"Yes. It was all very calculated on his part, of course. He had tried to meet me socially once before, but when I found out he was going to be there, I bowed out of the event. I couldn't bow out of this one."

Cecily picked up a silver teaspoon from the table and twirled it between her fingers. "Looking back, I can't remember exactly what happened to me that day. I'm not easily charmed, as you know."

Kelly could understand why she would be. She had experienced that same magnetic pull toward Syd Webber herself. "I thought you and Ward were so happy."

"We are, in our own way. We love each other, in our own way." She lifted the spoon at eye level, studying it. "But there's no passion in our lives. Sex was unimportant to me."

"And Syd changed all that."

She laughed, a laugh that was filled with self-contempt. "He made me come alive. He walked into that ballroom that night and my life was changed forever. Suddenly it no longer mattered how I felt about him, or what he stood for. When he asked me to dance and I stepped into his arms, I already knew nothing would ever be the same. And I was right. He exposed a side of me that terrified me." She paused, sighed. "And thrilled me at the same time. "

"How long did the affair last?"

"A year. It took me that long to get my head back in place." She put the spoon back. "But it was already too late. The harm was done."

Totally caught up in the story, Kelly leaned forward. "What do you mean?"

"A couple of months ago, just before Christmas, Syd came to my office. I was furious with him for taking such chances. If anyone from the board had seen him there..." She shuddered.

"What did he want?"

"To tell me that he had just finished talking to the head of the GOP, whom he knows very well. Without my knowledge, or my permission, Syd had presented my name to the nominating committee for the mayoral elections in 2003."

"He wants you to be mayor of Philadelphia?"

"He not only wants me to be the next mayor, he'll make sure I'll win the election."

"How?"

"Money, what else? He's going to personally finance my campaign—not overtly, of course, but through various companies and businesses, even individuals."

"What did you tell him?"

"I laughed in his face. I told him he had wasted

his time and mine. I had no intention of running for mayor. I was happy where I was.''

Kelly believed her. A few years ago, a reporter for the *Philadelphia Globe* had hinted that Cecily would make an excellent politician. The following day, letters to the editor had poured in, agreeing with the article. Cecily had cut short the public's speculation, declaring she had no intention of seeking public office. Ever.

''How did he react?''

''Oh, he was very cool, very confident, almost as if had expected me to turn him down. Then came the coup de grâce. He walked over to the VCR on my bookcase, inserted a tape and told me to watch and enjoy.''

Kelly didn't have to ask what was on the tape. She had already guessed.

Several seconds ticked by. ''It was a video of some of the times we had spent together, in his office and at his home. I was horrified and so terribly ashamed. I never knew, never suspected he was taping us while…while…''

For a moment Kelly thought Cecily would burst into tears, but she didn't. Through great effort, she pulled herself together. When their food arrived, Cecily smiled at the waiter and murmured a quick thank-you before turning to Kelly again. ''He told me that if I didn't agree to run for mayor, he would send copies of that tape all over the state of Pennsylvania—to the newspapers, television stations, Ward, and of course, the Norton board.''

Kelly's heart went out to her. ''Oh, Cecily, I'm so sorry. Could he have been bluffing?''

''Why would he? He has nothing to fear. He's not married. An affair, even with a married woman, would do nothing to him, but an affair with a casino owner who is suspected of having ties to the mob would destroy me.''

''I still don't understand why it's so important for him that you become mayor.''

''Part of the deal was that once elected, I would agree to support river gambling and campaign heavily for it.''

River gambling. The controversial referendum Pennsylvanians had voted down a few years ago. One mayor alone might not be able to make much difference, but if that mayor was articulate, popular and powerful as Cecily was, she could influence millions of voters throughout the state.

''Was Jonathan aware that Syd was blackmailing you as well?''

''I told him. He didn't care. All he wanted was for our two families to live in harmony.''

''How did he find out about you and Syd in the first place?''

She drew her lips into a tight smile. ''Doing something you might appreciate, Kelly. Snooping. He was unhappy with the security at the Chenonceau. He wanted to make changes, even though that wasn't his department. You know how he is, always getting involved. He didn't give me any details, but he found the tape and made a copy.''

"Without Syd's knowledge?"

Cecily nodded. "Syd would have killed him if he…'' Her eyes filled with horror. "Oh, my God, do you suppose that's what happened? Syd found out and…''

"I don't know. But I agree with you that if he did, Jonathan could be in serious trouble.'' Nick had been right about him all along. The man was a sleaze. Her thoughts flashed back to last night's ordeal. "By the way, do you know what kind of car Syd drives when he's not using the limo?''

Cecily shook her head. "I've never seen him in anything but his chauffeur-driven limousine. Or the helicopter.''

Kelly made a mental note to find out about that later. Right now she wanted to hear the rest of Cecily's story. "What happened after you saw the tape?''

Cecily's gaze followed an elderly couple as they were led to a table by the window. "I had no choice but to agree to his terms. But I swear to you, Kelly,'' she added, meeting Kelly's eyes again. "I never intended to run for mayor. I only let him think I was in order to give myself time to figure a way out of this mess, without hurting the people I love.''

"Maybe I can help,'' Kelly said gently. "I don't know how yet, but if we put our heads together, I'm sure we'll think of something. We have plenty of time."

"You would do that? Even after I..."

Kelly, who hadn't touched her food, pushed her plate aside and covered Cecily's hand with hers. "You were desperate. I know that now. I'm sorry I was so rough on you a moment ago, but I'm also glad you told me about Syd. It helps me get a better perspective on the man. I don't think I fully realized what kind of person he was until now."

A light smile touched Cecily's lips. "I'm glad we talked, too. And thanks for being so kind. I wish Ward was as understanding as you are."

"Is he very upset?"

"Yes." Her eyes filled with tears again but she was able to hold them back. "I'm afraid he's terribly disappointed in me. I don't know what he'll do when he finds out about my affair with Syd."

"You don't have to worry about that for a while," Kelly reminded her.

"You're right." Cecily's smile was shaky but she held on to it. "Would you mind very much if we left?"

"Not at all."

Cecily took a fifty-dollar bill from her purse, dropped it on the table and stood up.

Under the hotel portico, she and Kelly gave the valet attendant their respective parking tickets and stood silent for a while. The snow had ended sometime during the night and the sun was shining, melting the thin coating of ice on the roadways.

Cecily took a deep breath. "Strange, isn't it?" she said. "This is one of the darkest days of my life and yet I feel as if a huge black cloud had just been lifted from over my head. I'm not afraid anymore, Kelly, just ashamed. And so very sorry for what I did to you."

Those words, spoken so sincerely, went straight to Kelly's heart. On impulse, she turned and threw her arms around Cecily.

Thirty-Three

The news of Matt Kolvic's involvement in the Chinatown racketeering had been made public on Friday afternoon, in a brief press conference held at the Roundhouse. By then, most of the wives had already found out and in a show of support and solidarity had come to Patti's house, offering whatever help she needed.

Fear of an onslaught on the part of the press had prompted Patti's decision to leave at dawn on Sunday and Nick had agreed that a quick exit was best. Frustrated by the lack of news on Jonathan Bowman's disappearance, the press was hungry for something new and hot.

While Nick had helped the Kolvic family pack, he had tried to keep their spirits up, especially the girls', who were heartbroken at the thought of leaving their friends behind. He had taken care of a few financial details as well, selling Matt's old MG and most of his tools. Without Patti's knowledge, he had added a thousand dollars of his own money to the proceeds. He had tried earlier to give her some extra cash but she had been too proud to take it, assuring him that

Matt's life insurance more than covered their needs, but Nick knew better.

The family's house on Torresdale Avenue would be shut down until Patti made a final decision on whether to sell it. In the meantime, Nick had offered to keep an eye on the place, air it out from time to time and mow the grass as needed.

The girls, woken at five this morning, clung to Nick as if sensing they might not be coming back. "I'm going to miss you, Uncle Nick." Tricia's big, mournful eyes locked with his, bringing a lump to his throat.

He picked her up and carried her to the packed Blazer in the driveway. "You won't have time to miss me, sweetheart. I'll come up to see you very soon. How's that?"

"What about my birthday in July?"

"I'll be there. I wouldn't miss the biggest party in town, now, would I?"

As he put her in the front seat, Tricia folded her arms across her chest and made a pout, the way she always did when she was unhappy. "My friends won't be there. They're all here."

"You'll make new friends. You'll see. A couple of days from now, you'll be on the phone telling me all about them."

"No, I won't."

"Want to bet?"

She seemed to give that question some thought. "How much?"

Nick laughed. "Not money, you greedy little thing.

We'll bet...let's see...your birthday cake. If you win and you make no friends between now and your seventh birthday, you buy the cake. If I win, I find the biggest, most beautiful cake in the city of Philadelphia and bring it with me to Dayton."

The pout disappeared and the arms unfolded. "You forgot the sparklers. Sandra Hughes had sparklers on her birthday cake."

"I'll make sure your cake has sparklers. So? Do we have a deal?"

She nodded and threw her arms around him just as Patti walked out of the house, carrying Ashley, who was still half-asleep. Nick helped her put the four-year-old into the car seat in the back and then it was time to go.

When both girls were buckled up, Patti turned to Nick. "About the money," she said, looking into his eyes. "I know that thousand dollars you tried to give me a couple of days ago is in here." She took a thick envelope from her purse. "I can't take it, Nick. You've been suspended—"

He stopped her. "I wouldn't do it if I couldn't afford it."

"Yes, you would. You'd go hungry if you had to but you would do it."

He laughed. "It won't come to that, I promise. Take the money, Patti, for the girls. I don't need it." It was true. His father, a frugal man and a savvy investor, had left him a substantial inheritance that Nick had put into a mutual fund and watched soar over the last twelve months.

Patti hugged him fiercely. "How can I ever thank you for all you've done?"

"By taking good care of yourself."

"I'll do that. You will, too?"

He nodded. "Call me as soon as you get there, okay? I had the car checked from one end to the other. You shouldn't have any problem with it, but I'll feel better once I know you've arrived safely."

There were more hugs, more tears. A few neighbors had come to say goodbye, which delayed departure for several more minutes, then they were gone. Nick's chest felt tight as he walked to his car. God, he'd miss them, especially the girls.

By the time he had reached the end of the street, he had already made plans to drive to Dayton for the Easter break.

"All right, all right!" Kelly put down a book of fabric swatches and marched down the hallway. "Don't knock the house down, I'm coming." She didn't have to look into the peephole or ask who was on the other side of her front door. That loud, persistent knock could only belong to Super Cop.

"Why don't you just move in?" she said as she opened the door.

"Why, Robolo." Nick planted a kiss on her lips. "Is that your way of saying you can't live without me?"

"It was just a figure of speech." In the living room, she pushed more sample books aside and sat down.

Nick did the same, a sudden concerned expression on his face. "Okay, what is it now? And don't tell me nothing. I'm starting to know you pretty well."

"You think." She stared at one of the books, trying to find a way to tell him what had happened last night after he left San Remo. The aftermath of the ordeal had hit her shortly after she'd returned from brunch, and she was afraid that if she let herself, she'd break down completely. "Someone tried to kill me last night."

Nick's smile vanished. "What did you say?"

Hugging a throw pillow against her chest, Kelly told him everything, including finding the book of nursery rhymes at Cecily's house. There was no way of avoiding that. He had to know or he would comb the earth trying to find the culprit.

"And you didn't call the police?"

"She's not the one who tried to kill me."

"The woman is a psycho. She sent you threatening notes."

"She had no intention of carrying them through. You said so yourself. Less than two days ago you stood right here, in this living room, and told me killers didn't bother sending threatening notes... they...just..."

She began to tremble. Still determined not to cry, she tried desperately to hold herself together and couldn't do it. The tears rushed out like a torrent, with no warning. Then arms hard as steel wrapped around her and she collapsed against Nick's chest, sobbing and heaving.

After an eternity, she realized his jacket was soaked. "I'm sorry..." She spoke between sobs. "Your jacket..."

"Don't worry about it." His voice was soft and gentle and came out a little muffled because his mouth was in her hair.

She relaxed then, went limp against him. He felt good. Steady, safe. So safe.

After a while, her sobs stopped and her head came up. Her eyes, wet and blurry, met his. He pushed a damp strand of hair away from her cheek and tucked it behind her ear.

"Feel better?"

Later she would wonder what had gone through her mind at that very instant. Where the boldness had come from. For the moment she just let her instincts take over. "Not yet." She cupped his face between her hands and kissed him passionately.

To her surprise, he held her back. "Kelly, darling. Now may not be a good time."

"Now is a perfect time." She kissed him again.

"You're upset." His voice had turned husky. "Vulnerable. It wouldn't be right."

An honorable man, through and through, she thought. But a man just the same. "Do you want me, Nick?"

He closed his eyes briefly. "God, yes."

"Good, because I want you." She bit his lower lip, gently, teasingly. And heard him groan. "I need you." Another nip. "You're not going to deny a woman in need, are you, Nick McBride?"

"You're not playing fair," he said against her mouth.

"I know." Her hands moved down his chest, to his waistband. "Make love to me, Nick. Make love to me right now."

A ray of sunshine found its way through the bare trees outside Kelly's window and came to rest on their naked bodies. They lay on the throw rug, in front of the fireplace, warm from the flames, hot and sweaty from their lovemaking.

Exhausted, sated and not quite ready to look into his eyes, Kelly buried her face in Nick's shoulder. She had been all over him, hands and mouth, a woman possessed, shameless, greedy. She hadn't even given him time to take her upstairs. Instead, she had dragged him to the floor and practically torn his clothes off.

As the fire roared, he had kissed her gently, deeply, and when his lips had stopped on her scar, on their way to her breasts, the softness of his touch had brought fresh tears to her eyes. Driven by a need they could no longer control, they had made love at a hasty, almost furious pace. The second time was different, slow and delicious as they discovered each other's pleasures.

"Any regrets?" His hand slid up her thigh and came to rest on her hip.

"One." She snuggled closer. "That you didn't seduce me sooner."

"I seduced you?" He laughed. "You've got it a little backward, don't you think?"

"Are you complaining?"

His hand slid between her thighs, caressed her gently. "Do I look like a man who has something to complain about?"

A low, husky laugh rolled out of her throat. "No, not at all."

They showered together, turning each other on again and finding a new way of making love. Later, dressed and with the fire roaring, they ordered a pizza—half pepperoni, half anchovies—and sat at the breakfast counter, eating and talking about the events of the previous night. Nick was surprised to find out about Cecily's affair with Syd but not shocked to hear of the casino owner's plan to control Pennsylvania's politics.

"Men like him never have enough," he said. "And trying to rig an election is right up his alley. The trick is to make sure he doesn't get away with his dirty little scheme and is put away for good. Unfortunately, the latter won't be easy. The man is slick as a snake."

"Cecily said she'd go public with her announcement."

He shook his head. "That won't do it. It's her word against his."

"Then what do we do?"

He looked up. "Did he know you and I were going to be at San Remo last night?"

"I don't see how. I mentioned it to Victoria at lunch, but that's it."

"Could she have mentioned it to the Sanders?"

"I suppose so, but Cecily would never discuss something like that with Syd. She hardly speaks to him anymore."

"What about Ward?"

"They've only met socially, a couple of times."

Nick selected another slice of pizza loaded with anchovies. "In that case, we'll have to proceed with 'the plan.'" He spoke the two last words very distinctly.

Kelly quirked a brow. "The plan?"

He took a healthy bite and spoke with his mouth full. "How good are you at pretending to be someone you're not?"

Kelly laughed. "Are you kidding? I'm an investigative reporter. Make believe is my game."

"That's what I hoped you'd say."

He looked like the proverbial cat who swallowed the canary. "What are you up to now?"

"I was talking to Sergeant Andy Harrison of the Las Vegas police earlier. He was the detective in charge of the murder of Steve Marquant."

"Enrique's lover."

He nodded. "Harrison sent that police report Quinn

had requested, along with a videotape of Enrique's Vegas act."

"How is that going to help us prove Syd Webber is a killer?"

He nodded at a thick manila envelope he had brought in earlier and put on the counter. "Go ahead, open it. I know you've been dying to."

Kelly opened the clasp and took out the contents of the envelope. Besides a thick report, there were photographs of someone she presumed was Enrique and a video. The color shots showed the entertainer in various costumes and looking enough like the stars he impersonated to fool even the most discerning eye.

Kelly looked at a black-and-white shoulder shot. "Is that him, too?"

"At twenty-three. And this one—" he pointed his pizza to another photograph "—is Enrique ten years ago."

She studied the more recent picture. The man's face had matured and his hair was shorter, but he had the same dark, smoldering eyes and fine jawline.

"Look like anyone you know?" Nick asked.

"Magdalena," she said under her breath. "With a little work he could look exactly like her." She looked up. "My God, you don't think…"

"I thought about it, too." He shook his head. "Unfortunately, the fingerprints don't match. Enrique and Magdalena are definitely two different people." He dropped the rest of his pizza onto his plate, took the video and walked over to the VCR. "Come over and watch this."

For the next hour and a half, Kelly sat, totally mesmerized by the man on the screen. His resemblance to the divas he impersonated was uncanny, and so was his voice, rich and mellow one moment, high and powerful the next.

Nick glanced at Kelly, watching her reactions. "Good, huh?"

"He's incredible."

"Now watch this." He froze a shot. The last number was over and Enrique stood looking at the cheering audience. "Look at the expression on his face, his eyes, his posture as he takes his bows."

"He obviously loves what he does."

"It's more than that. Much more." He fast-forwarded the tape then stilled another shot. "This is curtain call number three. Look at the way he opens his arms, as if to embrace the audience. Look at the way his eyes shine as they roam over the crowded room."

"I don't understand. Where are you going with this?"

"The man *lives* for the applause, the adulation, the fame."

"You can tell all this from one tape?"

"The interpretation of body language is basic cop training."

"Okay, so Enrique thrives on fame. I still don't see—"

"Must have been tough," he mused, staring at the frozen shot, "leaving it all behind."

"He didn't have much choice, did he? It was either that or face life in prison, maybe even death."

Nick turned to look at her. "Do you suppose he'd ever consider returning to showbiz?"

"And risk being arrested the moment he stepped onstage?" Kelly shook her head. "I don't think so."

Nick leaned back in the chair and stretched his long legs in front of him. "Not even for the gig of a life-time?"

Kelly's eyes narrowed. "And what would that gig be?"

"One single, lavish, live performance that would be broadcast all over the world to millions of view-ers."

"But that would be suicide. If he was as famous as the police report claims, he'd be recognized right away."

"It wouldn't matter, because by the time the show aired, several weeks later, Enrique would be far, far away."

Enrique's swan song. How clever. "One last bril-liant performance," Kelly murmured. "One that will last him the rest of his life."

"Precisely."

"It's good," she admitted. "There's just one hitch."

He leaned over to steal a kiss. "You're such a pessimist, darling. But I'll humor you. What's the hitch?''

"Who's going to offer Enrique that fabulous gig?''

He grinned and spread his arms wide. "Meet Richard Trumbull, executive producer of Trumbull Productions, a small, very hip London-based production company with an office in New York City. Among our most ambitious plans for this millennium year is a huge, glittering, Las Vegas-style extravaganza that will feature today's hottest celebrity impersonators.''

Kelly gaped. "You're going to pretend to be a TV producer?''

"Not me alone. You're in this, too, as my assistant.''

"Assistant," she said with a sniff. "As in gofer?''

"My partner, then.''

Kelly was silent for a moment. The plan was creative but full of flaws. "I don't know, Nick. Enrique is no dummy. In fact, he had to be pretty smart to have eluded a nationwide search all these years.''

"So?''

"So won't he have that phony production company of yours checked?''

"That, too, has been taken care of. First thing tomorrow morning, my friend Alan will have another phone line installed in his office. When and if Enrique calls to check on us, Alan will fill in the blanks, explaining this will be Trumbull's first U.S. production and that we want to capture the market in a big way. That's why we're only looking for the very best. He'll also tell each caller that our stay in the U.S. will be short—twenty-four hours. Unless Enrique moves fast, he'll miss his golden opportunity."

Kelly was still skeptical. "Won't he be suspicious to hear that we're looking for him?"

"We won't. We'll be going from club to club, auditioning performers."

Once again, Kelly found herself wishing she had thought of this plan herself. "You want Enrique to come to you rather than the other way around."

"By George, she's got it!" Nick exclaimed in his best British accent, which wasn't bad. Not bad at all.

"How will Enrique know we're auditioning?"

"He'll find out. Entertainers form a very close-knit community, no matter where they are—New York, Las Vegas, Miami. They also have a strong news network. Whatever Enrique is doing now, when he hears about the TV special and how safe it will be, he won't be able to resist it."

Grinning, Kelly stretched toward him like a cat. "Did anyone ever tell you that you have a wicked, wicked mind?"

"All the time." Grabbing her by the waist, he lifted her and sat her on his lap so she straddled him. "It's part of my charm."

Thirty-Four

Nick didn't visit his parents' grave often. Occasionally, spurred by guilt or need, he'd buy a bouquet of red carnations and drive to the Holy Sepulcher Cemetery on Cheltenham Avenue for a visit, and would just sit there for a while.

The McBrides' grave was in section P, but as Nick approached, flowers in hand, he stopped. His parents already had a visitor. Joe Massino.

The former detective had one knee on the ground. Assorted flowers wrapped in clear cellophane lay on the earth against the headstone.

"Joe?"

The older man's head snapped around. His eyes were red, as though he had been crying. "Hey, kid." He stood up, grunting a little as he did. "Small world, huh?"

Walking slowly, Nick closed the distance between them. "You all right?"

"Sure." Joe took a white handkerchief from his pants pocket and blew his nose. "I miss the old son of a gun, that's all."

"I didn't know you came here."

"I haven't since the funeral and I was in the area, so..."

Nick didn't believe him. The man had guilt written all over his face.

"Look, Nick, about the other day—" Joe put his handkerchief back in his pocket. "I'm sorry it turned out the way it did. I never meant to get you in trouble. You got to believe that."

Nick lay the carnations beside Joe's flowers. "Is there something you'd like to tell me, Joe?"

"I told you all I know."

"Then why do I have this feeling in the pit of my stomach that you're holding out on me?"

Joe waved an impatient hand and started to walk away. "Don't start with that again."

Before he could take another step, Nick grabbed Joe's arm. "Wouldn't you do the same, Joe? If something didn't look kosher to you, wouldn't you keep digging until you got to the truth?"

"Take your hands off me."

As Joe tried to free himself from Nick's grip, Nick increased the pressure. "Do you remember what I said the other day about the pieces not fitting? Guess what? They're beginning to fit, Joe, one by one."

"Good for you. Now let me go."

"The bitch of it is," Nick continued, "that the more the pieces fall into place the less I like what they add up to."

"I don't know what you're talking about."

"Oh, I think you do. That's why you're here. You

feel guilty for letting my father down. What were you hoping to get from visiting his grave, Joe? Guidance? Absolution? What?''

Joe gave another jerk. It was as useless as the first. "You're pushing your luck, kid."

"Someone tried to kill Kelly Robolo last night." Nick watched the startled look on the older man's face. "You know anyone who would want to do that?"

"Why would I?"

"First my father is killed, then Jonathan Bowman disappears. Now they're after Kelly. When is it all going to end?"

"I'm sorry about your friend, Nick." Joe shook his head. "But I had nothing to do with the attempt on her life. Now let me go or I'll be forced to deck you."

Even though he said that last sentence in a joking tone, Nick knew that if push came to shove, Joe would do what he had to do. Or try to. "Your loyalty to your boss is commendable." Nick let go of his friend's arm. "But he doesn't deserve it."

Joe shrugged. "We all have our faults, kid."

"He had me suspended. Did you know that? He couldn't lick me fair and square so he pulled strings and called the Philadelphia police commissioner."

Joe already knew. "I'm sorry, Nick. Really I am."

Nick decided to take advantage of Joe's genuine regret to ask one last question. "What kind of car does Webber drive? I'm not talking about the limo."

"A Mercedes. Why?"

"Just curious." Nick was silent for a moment. A Mercedes looked a lot like a Lexus, especially from the back. Could Kelly have made a mistake in identifying the car? Taking into consideration her frame of mind that night, and the snowstorm? "What color is it?"

Joe's eyes narrowed but he answered the question. "Black."

Nick took a deep breath and gazed into the distance, past the row of graves.

Joe lay a hand on Nick's shoulder and squeezed it. "Let it go, kid. Please." Then, with one last glance at Patrick's grave, he walked away, his hands jammed into his overcoat pockets.

When he had disappeared, Nick turned back toward his parents' headstone and lowered himself on one knee. "I'm going to find out who put you here, Dad," he murmured, "if it's the last thing I do."

Thirty-Five

It had taken Kelly the rest of the day but she had finally found an appropriate wardrobe for her role as coproducer of Trumbull Productions. Explaining to the young salesgirl with the purple fingernails that the two micromini skirts in neon colors were for her was a little embarrassing, but in this business, feeling occasionally stupid was part of the job.

In another department, she had found a little blond wig in a short pixie style that made her look like the sixties' supermodel Twiggy.

Alan Braden, Nick's P.I. friend and willing accomplice, hadn't been idle either. He had spent the last few hours tracking Miami nightclubs that headlined celebrity impersonators and had faxed the list to Nick.

Nick had taken it from there, calling each establishment and explaining to the owner, in a perfect British accent, who he was and what he was looking for. With the exception of one, who had flatly refused, all had been willing to set up auditions for their respective stars.

Nick and Kelly left first thing on Monday morning and arrived in Miami at ten-thirty. After registering at the Eden Roc Resort Hotel in Key Biscayne and checking in with Detective Quinn, they had hopped into their rented car and gone straight to their first appointment—Club Noche on Miami Beach.

The owner, a man with the improbable name of Marco Polo, greeted them in person, wrapping his arm around Kelly's shoulders and escorting them to a front-row table. Doing her best to ignore Marco's glances at her legs and occasional winks, Kelly hitched her chair a little closer to Nick's and sat down to watch the show.

By four o'clock that afternoon, they had visited four clubs and watched a half-dozen performers within a twenty-mile radius. No one even remotely resembling Enrique had come to request an audition, and the hope that Magdalena's brother would find out about Trumbull Productions and come forward was getting more dismal by the hour.

Now as they sat on the Eden Roc's beachfront terrace, sipping frosty piña coladas and gazing at a cruise ship anchored in the distance, Kelly tried to stay optimistic, but deep down she was afraid that Nick's brilliant plan had failed. Either he had totally misjudged Enrique, or the man simply wasn't here but in some other city.

Nick, on the other hand, wasn't letting a couple of defeats destroy his hopes. "What time is that next audition?" he asked, glancing at the scheduling book at Kelly's elbow.

"Six. And it's not too far from here. If we leave now, we can walk and be there on time."

Nick pushed his chair back. "Then what are we waiting for?"

To Kelly's surprise, Club Antigua was a first-class supper club, with white tablecloths, soft candlelight and a five-piece band warming up as they arrived.

According to the owner, Carlos Fuentes had been the main attraction at Antigua for more than a year. Prior to that, he had performed around the country, taking his act to places like Aspen, New York, San Francisco, San Diego and Chicago.

He was also thirty-nine years old and more likely to know Enrique, who by their estimation had to be around forty-five years of age by now.

"He packs them in every night," the owner told Nick and Kelly. "You'll see why."

On cue, the room went dark and a single blue spotlight found its way to the center of the stage. As the band began playing "Hello, Dolly," a slender figure in a clinging, sequined gown and a blond wig glided forward. Kelly sat up, goose bumps crawling up her arms. The man looked enough like Carol Channing to be her twin sister. And when he started singing in that famous, lazy, scratchy voice, Kelly understood why Carlos Fuentes was such a huge success. He was incredibly talented, much more so than the other performers they had auditioned earlier.

"He's almost as good as Enrique," Kelly whispered in Nick's ear. "Do you suppose it could be him?"

Nick shook his head. "You've seen his picture outside. He doesn't look anything like Enrique. And he's too young."

Kelly kept her eyes on the stage where Carlos had reappeared after a short costume change, this time as the incomparable Tina Turner. Forty-five minutes later, having gone through three more costume changes and half his repertoire, Carlos joined Nick and Kelly at their table. Both shook his hand and complimented him on a great performance.

Under the heavy stage makeup, Carlos blushed and the way he looked at Nick left no doubt as to his sexual preference. Maybe that would come in handy, Kelly thought.

"I've just added two more impersonations to my act," Carlos told them as he sat down. "Cher and Celine Dion. They're not perfected yet." He laughed. "I haven't quite mastered Celine's French accent, but if you want, I'll be glad to give you a sneak preview."

In the tape Sergeant Harrison had sent Nick, Cher had been one of Enrique's most popular impersonations. If Carlos had just added the diva to his repertoire, he definitely wasn't Enrique.

"That won't be necessary," Nick said. "My associate and I have already decided that you are perfect for what we have in mind."

Carlos beamed and Kelly felt a pinch of guilt for raising hopes that would never materialize. Nick, on the other hand, didn't seem the least bit remorseful. He was on a mission. In the same way he had questioned the other performers, he started scratching the side of his nose. "We do have a problem, however."

Carlos looked crestfallen. "I thought you said you liked my act."

"Oh, we do. Don't we, Megan?" he asked, using the name he had chosen for Kelly.

Falling quickly into the part, which she now had down pat, Kelly nodded enthusiastically. "You were wonderful, Carlos. Your impersonation of Barbra Streisand was amazing."

Carlos only gave her a passing glance before returning his attention to Nick. "Then what's the problem?"

"The special we have in mind will be something in the order of a television spectacular that aired last year, *Divas Live,* with Cher, Tina Turner and Whitney Houston. Have you seen it?"

Carlos laughed. "Only about a hundred times."

"Good, because that's exactly the type of production I want to put together—lavish and glitzy. With one exception. I want two divas instead of three."

"So you need another impersonator."

"One as good as you." The compliment earned Nick another delighted smile.

"What about the other acts you saw today?"

Nick also seemed to have developed into his part well. He shook his head, looking regretful. "Frankly,

Carlos, we didn't see anything to rave about." He looked at Kelly, who took the cue.

"The kind of performer we're looking for," she said, leaning forward and trying to look intense, "has to be unique, and have a reputation that precedes him. Maybe even some big-time exposure, like Las Vegas."

Carlos, not at all stupid, looked from her to Nick. "So why don't you go to Las Vegas?"

"Too pricey. The few performers we talked to wanted a seven-figure salary. Too rich for our blood."

Carlos licked his lips. "How much are you willing to pay?"

"A flat five hundred thousand each plus residuals."

"Wow."

"Are you sure you don't know anyone who would fit our criteria?" Kelly pressed. She and Nick had agreed not to ask such leading questions, but time was flying by and she was getting a little desperate.

At the query, however, Carlos was thoughtful. "I know—*knew*—someone. I lost track of him, though."

Simultaneously, Kelly and Nick leaned forward. "Tell us about him," Nick said.

"Well, he had everything you're looking for—Las Vegas exposure, talent and an incredible rapport with the audience. He showed me a tape once. He was mind-blowing."

"What's his name?"

"Teddy Luna."

Kelly shot Nick a quick glance and saw that he,

too, had reacted to the Hispanic name. "Was he a close friend of yours?"

Carlos blushed again. "I wish, but he wasn't interested."

"When did you meet him?"

"About nine or ten years ago. He had recently returned from a farewell world tour and was looking forward to retirement. I was introduced to him at a party, when I was just starting in the business. Teddy and I started to talk and he gave some great pointers. He's the one who suggested I add Carol Channing to my repertoire."

"Do you know why he retired?"

"He said he was burned out. That happens in this business. Six months later he had left Miami."

"If you two hit it off so well," Nick said casually, "why didn't you keep in touch?"

Carlos shrugged. "Fate, I guess. He called me a few weeks later to apologize for leaving so abruptly. He wanted to know if I'd come up and visit him sometime." He let out a regretful sigh. "But by then I was with someone."

Kelly exchanged another wordless glance with Nick. "Do you suppose we could coax him out of retirement?" Nick paused. "That is, if you know where he moved to."

"Oh, sure I do. Teddy's in Atlantic City."

Thirty-Six

After Carlos's audition, Nick and Kelly returned to Eden Roc for a light dinner followed by a long walk on the beach. "Do you suppose Enrique went to Atlantic City to resurrect his career?" Kelly asked after a while.

"I don't see how he'd want to take such risks. But if he's connected to Syd Webber, then it's possible that Enrique is working at the Chenonceau in some other capacity."

"Such as what?"

"Oh, I don't know, waiter, parking attendant." He paused. "Killer for hire."

She looked up at him. "Do you really think that's a possibility?"

"As good as any." His arm tightened around her waist. "But to confirm it I have to find Enrique. I can't walk into the Chenonceau and start asking questions, but I certainly can check with the DMV and other licensing bureaus such as hunting and fishing, maybe even the unions, in case he's working in construction."

"If you so much as set one foot in Atlantic City,

you'll be terminated for sure," Kelly reminded him.
"I, on the other hand, can move about freely. And I
have contacts at the DMV."

Nick stopped walking and gripped her shoulders,
forcing her to face him. "You are not getting within
ten miles of that town, do you hear me? If my suspicions about Syd are correct and he's the one who
tried to run you down two nights ago, he won't hesitate to finish the job. In fact, as soon as we get back
to Philadelphia, I want you to go to San Remo and
tell your mother you'll be staying with her and Gino
for a while."

"What reason do I give her?"

"You're creative. Think of something." The pressure on her arms increased. "Do I have your word
you'll do as I said?"

"Did I ever tell you I don't take orders from the
men I date?"

"Learn." He shook her. "Do I have your word?
Or do I have to take you to my house and strap you
to the bed until I return?"

She narrowed her eyes trying to gauge if he was
kidding. "You wouldn't."

"Try me."

She held his gaze for a moment longer, saw that
he was dead serious and nodded. "All right. I'll stay
with my mother."

But in her mind, an idea was already taking shape.

Kelly closed her eyes and sank deeper into the hot,
swirling water. Above her, the sky was studded with

stars, and beneath it, the ocean, so blue earlier, had turned silver as it bathed in the glow of a full moon.

At first, Kelly had feared that the luxurious ocean-front cottage Nick had booked at the Eden Roc was an extravagance he couldn't afford and she had insisted on paying half. He had hushed her with a kiss.

"Put your money away, darling, or the staff will think I'm your boy toy."

The patio, where the hot tub was nestled, was surrounded by potted palms and climbing bougainvillea, and offered complete privacy from other guests.

After eating dinner under the stars, they had made love with the windows wide open and the sound of reggae music drifting in from the beach. Sleep had come easily afterward, but the tension of the day, combined with the realization that Enrique was closer than they had thought, had made Kelly restless. Rather than wake Nick with her tossing and turning, she had slipped out of bed and turned on the hot tub.

Her eyes closed, she thought of the plan she had devised to try to find Enrique and prayed she could make it work.

Though he usually slept soundly, Nick wasn't surprised to suddenly find himself wide awake. Kelly was gone from the king-size bed, where a few hours earlier they had made wild, passionate love.

From the open windows he heard a soft humming sound, and smiled. So that's where the little wench was. In the hot tub, all by her lonesome.

He got out of bed and walked over to the patio. Kelly sat in the foaming water, totally submerged. Her head rested against the edge and her eyes were closed. Any thought that she might have dozed off vanished when he heard her voice.

"Sleepwalking, darling?"

He came to sit on the edge of the tub, already aroused. "You planned this. You knew I would wake up, find you gone and come looking for you."

She let out a husky laugh. "Now why would I go to all this trouble?"

"Because you enjoy seeing me all hot and bothered."

"Are you?" She smiled coyly and allowed her breasts to bob above the surface. "Hot and bothered, I mean."

"As if you hadn't noticed."

Her wet hand came up and stroked his bare arm. "I'm a little nearsighted, darling. Why don't I take a closer look."

She gave his arm a tug, pulling him into the swirling water.

After returning from Miami, Nick had gone home to make a few calls and Kelly had driven to Victoria's shop to bring her up to date. When she told her friend what she intended to do next, however, Victoria stared at her in utter disbelief.

"You are planning to do what?"

"Shh." Kelly looked around the small, cramped

shop. In a far corner, a woman with an old-fashioned fur cape was inspecting a bronze Buddha. "Not so loud."

"I don't care if all of Rittenhouse Square hears me," Victoria replied in a fierce whisper. "Maybe someone will shake some sense into you, because I think you've gone totally bonkers."

"I didn't say I was *going* to do it. Just that I was thinking about it."

"Well, stop thinking, because I won't let you take such a risk."

"Just answer the question, please."

Victoria sighed and walked over to her desk. "All right," she said, sitting down. "Yes, there are security cameras throughout the Chenonceau, though according to Jonathan not nearly enough."

That was exactly what Kelly wanted to hear, since it reinforced what Cecily had told her about Jonathan not being happy with casino security. "Do you know where the cameras are?" she asked.

"Most of them are on the casino floor. A few are on the VIP floor and one camera is on the eighteenth floor where the administrative and executive offices are located."

"How are the cameras monitored?"

"That's the part Jonathan hates. At last count, there were ninety monitors in the security office and only two men to watch them."

"How do they keep track of all the activity?"

"That's just the point. They can't. If they need to

check something specific, they rely almost entirely on the tapes, which are changed daily. When they have a reason to monitor someone, as they did a few months ago when one of the dealers was suspected of stealing, the management will tell the guards to watch a specific monitor, but that's about it.''

Kelly could barely hold her excitement. ''Tell me about the executive floor. When I was there last week, I didn't notice any cameras, but then I wasn't particularly concerned about them at the time.''

''There's only one, directly across from the elevator. Jonathan thought each office should be equipped with one as well, but apparently Syd decided it was overkill and nixed the idea.''

''So the personnel office is clear?''

''As far as I know, but there's still that camera by the elevator. How will you get through it without being noticed?''

''With ninety monitors to watch, what are the odds the guard will be watching the executive floor? Especially at a time when all the action is in the casino itself.''

Though such reasoning made sense, Victoria was too much of a worrywart to admit it. ''I still don't like it, Kelly.''

''To tell you the truth, neither do I, but getting into those personnel files is the only way I can think of to find out if Enrique works for Syd.'' She glanced at the lone customer, who was now admiring a set of silver candlesticks, before adding, "Did you find Jonathan's spare set of keys?"

Reluctantly, Victoria reached in a drawer and brought out a key ring with a dozen or so keys looped through it.

"Which one belongs to the personnel office?"

"I have no idea." Victoria made no move to give Kelly the key ring. "Kelly, this is crazy. What if you're caught?"

"I'll say I got lost."

"All the way inside the personnel office? Come on, Kelly, who will believe that?"

Kelly snatched the keys from her friend's hand. "Why don't you wish me luck instead of looking for problems? I may need it."

"I'm going to tell Nick what you're up to."

Kelly leaned over the desk, her expression as stern as she could make it. "You do that and you may never find out what happened to Jonathan. Is that what you want, Victoria? To give up when we're almost there?"

Victoria shook her head. "No."

"Good." Kelly dropped the keys in her purse.

"Will you call me as soon as you're out of there?" Victoria asked.

Kelly squeezed her hand. "I will."

Wearing her Twiggy wig and holding a cup full of quarters, Kelly glanced nonchalantly around her before stepping into the elevator marked Staff Only. It was 1:00 a.m. and the lobby of the Chenonceau was bustling with activity. With any luck, no one had noticed the absentminded-looking tourist, and with greater luck, no one would spot her once she reached the eighteenth floor.

When the elevator doors opened again, Kelly immediately went into her act, looking nearsightedly around her before quickly moving out of camera range. A few seconds later, she reached the personnel office. Her heart thumped erratically in her chest but she ignored it, concentrating instead on finding the right key.

On the eighth try, the lock clicked open. Holding a pencil-size flashlight, Kelly swung the beam around the room in a slow arc. The personnel office was one large area with a half-dozen desks, some partitioned, some not, a computer on every desk and a bank of file cabinets along one wall. Kelly approached and saw that each cabinet was marked alphabetically, with the *L* section about halfway down.

She tried one key after another, dropping the ring at one time and cursing the loss of precious seconds. When the last key failed to unlock the drawer, she looked helplessly around her, searching for something with which to open the lock, a nail file, a paper clip, even a letter opener, if she could find one thin enough.

She had already reached the nearest desk when she heard a click, followed by an order.

"Stay where you are and put your hands up."

Thirty-Seven

Kelly froze in midmotion.

"Now turn around."

Once again, she did as she was told, slowly, avoiding any sudden movement. A large man in a security guard uniform stood in the doorway. Two very steady hands aimed the barrel of a gun directly at her chest.

"Well, well," said a familiar voice. "If it isn't the lovely Miss Robolo."

Kelly felt a flutter in her chest as Syd Webber stepped from behind the armed guard.

"You can put the gun away, Billy," he said to the guard. "I'll take it from here."

"Are you sure, boss?"

Syd nodded and watched the guard leave before turning to Kelly. He looked mildly amused as he took in the blond wig, the ski jacket and stirrup pants. When he saw the cup of quarters on the edge of the desk, he chuckled. "Not a bad getup for a Halloween party," he commented dryly. "But as far as I'm concerned, I prefer the original version of Kelly Robolo."

She didn't reply. What could she say? How could

she explain her presence in this office other than with the plain truth?

"Why don't you take off that silly disguise," Syd said. "Then we'll talk."

Kelly pulled off the wig and stuffed it, along with her cup of quarters, into her bag.

"That's better." Syd glanced around him, as if trying to guess what she had been doing in this room. "Now, would you care to tell me what this is all about?"

"I was looking for someone," she admitted. "A possible employee here at the Chenonceau."

"Who?"

"Teddy Luna."

She watched him closely and saw no reaction other than a lift of his eyebrows. "Never heard of him. Who is he?"

"A man you knew a long time ago under the name of Enrique Vasquez."

"Ah." He nodded. "Yes, the infamous Enrique Vasquez. Your friend Nick McBride was interested in him as well. Why are you calling him Teddy Luna?"

"Because that's the name he now goes under. Or at least it was when he left Las Vegas nine years ago."

"How do you know the two men are one and the same?"

"I went to Miami and found out."

He nodded and walked around the room, giving a passing glance at the file cabinet along the wall. "And so, because I once hired Enrique Vasquez to perform at my Las Vegas casino, you assumed he is now working for me here at the Chenonceau?''

Even with the experience she'd had getting caught in hopeless situations, she found it difficult not to fidget. "I was told he had moved to Atlantic City."

"I see." He took his lower lip between his thumb and forefinger and pulled on it lightly. "This Enrique Vasquez killed a man, if I recall."

Kelly nodded.

"And you think I would knowingly employ a fugitive from the law." He paused. "Then you must suspect me of some kind of conspiracy in that crime, am I right?"

Kelly swallowed. "Not in the Steve Marquant murder, no."

"In something else then?" He came to stand in front of her. "Jonathan's disappearance? Is that what this is all about? You think I had something to do with what happened to Jonathan?"

When she didn't reply he shook his head in disbelief. "Dear God, Kelly. What kind of man do you think I am? I thought you and I were friends. I thought you believed in me. At least that's the impression you gave me the other night." He waited for an answer. When there was none, he raised his arms by his sides and let them fall again. "What reason could I possibly have to harbor a man like Enrique Vasquez, a man wanted for murder?"

"I don't know."

"So you decided to sneak into my casino in the middle of the night to see how you could incriminate me?"

"I wasn't out to incriminate you, Syd. I just wanted to find Enrique."

"May I ask how you got this far?"

"Victoria found Jonathan's spare set of keys."

"Wouldn't it have been easier to just ask me to see the files?"

"I didn't think you'd let me."

"You're wrong." He dug into his pocket and brought out a set of keys similar to Jonathan's. He selected one and held it out to her. "This key opens every drawer. Go ahead. Search."

"Syd, I..."

He gave the ring an impatient jingle. "What's the matter? This is what you came here for, isn't it?"

She extended her hand, half expecting him to yank the keys away and yell "Gotcha." To her surprise, he let them go and leaned against the desk, folding his arms across his chest.

She felt completely awkward, but he was right. Getting into the Chenonceau's personnel records, was the reason she was here, so why not finish the job? Walking over to the file cabinet again, she opened the drawer marked L and walked her fingers through several files. Leonard, Lingstrom, Lombard, Lyndros. There was no Luna.

"You might want to check under the *V*s for Vasquez," Syd suggested in a mocking tone. "Just to be sure."

She did, not expecting to find anything there either. She felt like an utter fool. She had never suspected him in the first place, and now that she had, the whole thing was blowing up in her face.

"No one named Vasquez." She pushed the drawer shut.

"I could have told you that and saved you a lot of embarrassment. Not to mention a night in our city jail."

At the thought of sharing a cell with some of Atlantic City's criminals, she shivered. "Is that what you're going to do? Call the police?"

"Wouldn't you? In my place?"

She was tired and didn't feel like playing games. "I suppose I would."

"Then it's lucky for you that I'm not you, isn't it?" He took her arm and escorted her out of the personnel office, barely giving her time to grab her bag.

"You're going to let me go?"

"Not exactly." He didn't release her until they had reached his office. "I'm going to put you up in one of my best suites," he said, picking up the phone. "And let both of us have a good night's sleep. Tomorrow—"

"I can't stay here," she protested.

He gave her a steely look. "You don't have any choice, Kelly. *I* am calling the shots now."

Syd spoke into the phone. "Art, would you come to my office. I need you to escort a friend of mine to the Fleur-de-Lys Suite. But before you do, call Elaine at the boutique and tell her to send nightwear, for a woman, yes, toilet articles as well, and a change of clothes—daytime clothes." He glanced at Kelly, his eyes traveling up and down her body. "Oh, I'd say a size six. Thanks, Art."

Syd hung up. "I'll meet you in your suite at eight tomorrow morning—or shall I say *this* morning?" he corrected after glancing at his watch. "If that's all right with you."

As long as he was asking her opinion, she might as well give it to him. "No, it's not. I don't appreciate being held against my will."

"You should have thought of that before you broke into my personnel office."

She wondered if he was detaining her because he had to check with an accomplice before taking further steps. Tony Marquese maybe? "Why do you need six hours to decide what to do about me? Why can't you make up your mind now?"

"Because I've been on my feet for the last eighteen hours and I need some rest."

From the hall, they heard the *ping* of the elevator.

"That's my night manager. He'll take you up to your room. Your things will arrive momentarily, but don't hesitate to let him know if there's anything else you need." He smiled. "Good night, Kelly. I'll see you in the morning."

* * *

Standing in the middle of the luxurious suite, Kelly looked around her, and gave an angry kick to the desk. Not only was Syd holding her prisoner, he had also taken her purse with him, which meant she had no phone, no money, no car keys, no means to go home. One look outside the peephole had confirmed what she had already suspected. Another very large man, this one in a suit and tie, sat across from her door reading a current issue of *Wrestling World*.

She looked around her, searching for a phone. None. What kind of suite had no phone?

There was a light knock at the door, and she went to open it. A smiling, well-dressed young woman stood in the hall holding a garment bag. "Good morning, Miss Robolo. My name is Elaine. These are the items Mr. Webber asked me to select for you. Would you like to take a look? I'll be glad to exchange—"

Kelly took the garment bag from her. "I'm sure everything is fine, Elaine. Thank you, and good night." It was easier to accept the items than to ask her to take them back, which she probably was under strict orders not to do.

Inside the garment bag were a black pantsuit in light wool, an ice-blue turtleneck, black socks, a black shoulder bag, white panties and a pink lacy nightgown. In a zippered compartment, she found a toiletry bag with everything from toothpaste to Chanel bath soap and even perfume spray.

Kelly helped herself to the toothbrush, the toothpaste, the cake of soap and the panties. Everything else, including the nightgown, was left inside the bag. Tonight she would sleep in the raw.

If Syd thought he was going to win her over with a few expensive trinkets and a three-thousand-dollar-per-night suite, he was in for a rude awakening.

At exactly eight o'clock the same morning, there was another knock at her door. This time it was a room-service waiter pushing a table that held breakfast for two—coffee, a pitcher of freshly squeezed orange juice, fruit, croissants and an assortment of English preserves. Behind the waiter, looking well-rested, was Syd.

"I trust you slept well," he said when they were alone. He took in the charcoal stirrup pants and black sweater she had worn yesterday and frowned. "You didn't like the clothes Elaine selected? Were they the wrong size?"

"They were fine," she said, putting as much frost in her voice as possible. "I just feel more comfortable in my own clothes."

"I understand." He poured coffee for both of them and held out a cup to her. She thought about turning it down but didn't. She always thought more clearly with a shot of caffeine pumping through her system.

"Croissant?" He held up a plate. "I have them flown in daily from Poilâne in Paris."

"No, thank you." She took a sip of coffee, which was strong and hot. She noticed that he had brought back her purse. Had he gone through it? Not that it made any difference. Except for the tools of her trade—a miniature camera, a voice recorder and about a hundred dollars in cash—she didn't carry anything he'd find interesting. "Am I free to go?"

He tore a piece of croissant with his fingers and chewed it slowly. "You are, though I would love for you to stay. I was hoping we could spend some time together. There is still so much we need to iron out, don't you think?"

He was still charming, still the incorrigible seducer. It was easy to understand why Cecily had fallen prey to his charms. "Look, Syd, it was wrong of me to break into your personnel office and I'm sorry—"

He smiled. "Sorry you broke in, or sorry you got caught?"

"A little bit of both, I suppose."

"But you won't stay."

"No." She put her cup down, picked up her bag from the desk and walked out.

Thirty-Eight

Kelly stood under the Chenonceau's broad portico, deserted at this early-morning hour, and took a deep breath of frigid air. Seven hours ago, she had arrived here full of hope and bravado. She was leaving with nothing except a bruised ego. Syd was no murderer. If he was she would have been dead long ago.

Rather than let the valet take her car the previous night, Kelly had parked her Beetle in the Chenonceau's open lot on Missouri Avenue, the same lot where Patrick McBride had been stabbed.

Without questioning why, she let her steps take her toward the last two rows marked Security Employees Only. Her gaze swept over the parked cars, trying to visualize what had happened that morning. It would have been easy for someone to hide behind any of these vehicles, wait for the right victim to appear and pounce. But why that particular victim? And why kill him? If robbery had been the motive, why not just hold Patrick McBride at knifepoint, take his money and run? The police had assumed that Patrick was killed because he had put up a fight, but no one had actually seen him fighting off his assailant. Or even being attacked, for that matter.

A scraping noise behind her made her spin around. Nerves raw, she surveyed the lot, recoiling slightly as a pair of eyes peeked at her from behind a green Dumpster.

"Good morning." She tried not to sound nervous. This was broad daylight and traffic was beginning to pick up along Missouri Avenue. What could happen?

The eyes glanced away, and a man slowly stepped out from behind the Dumpster. He was thin and scruffy and rather harmless-looking. A knit cap hid most of his hair and a three-day stubble made him look older than what he probably was. A coat, two sizes too big for him, hung over his body like a tent. Scuffed shoes and wool gloves with the tips torn off completed the outfit.

He looked at the paper bag in Kelly's hands. Inside was a Danish she had bought at the Chenonceau's cafeteria before leaving, intending to eat in the car on her way home. Without a word, she held the bag out to him, even though what he really needed was a hearty meal, something that would stick to his ribs until the next handout. "It's a cheese Danish. Would you like it?"

When he didn't move, she set the bag on the trunk of a blue Buick. "Go ahead. Please."

The stranger took a tentative step, then another, watching her with distrusting eyes. Kelly felt herself relax. He was just a hungry man, most likely homeless, who went around the city from Dumpster to Dumpster in search of food. She remembered reading that at the time of the investigation, the Atlantic City police had questioned as many homeless men and women as they could find but had learned nothing. That wasn't surprising. Homeless people were as distrustful of the police as the police were of them, and made it a point to stay as far away from the authorities as possible.

Hoping to earn the man's trust, Kelly remained perfectly still while he continued to shuffle toward the Buick. Once he was within reach, his arm shot out and he grabbed the bag, tearing it open.

"What's your name?" Kelly asked gently.

He stuffed half the Danish into his mouth, pushing it with the palm of his gloved hand. "Ralph."

"Hello, Ralph. I'm Kelly."

He watched her as he chewed and said nothing.

"Do you come here every morning?" She kept her voice low and unthreatening.

He nodded.

"That's good, because I'm looking for someone who comes to this parking lot regularly."

"Why?" His voice was rough but not unfriendly.

"Because that someone committed a murder."

He tensed. "I ain't seen nothin'."

A defensive reaction, Kelly thought. If you didn't see anything, you couldn't get in trouble. "I don't mean today. I mean a year ago."

He took another bite of the Danish and continued to watch her.

"A murder took place right here, in this parking lot a year ago next month. A stabbing. Did you hear about it?"

She could see from the fearful expression on his face that he had. "I'm not saying you did it," she added hastily. "I'm here to try to find out what happened that morning. But to do that, I need help."

She rummaged through her purse and pulled out two twenties. It wasn't much, but for a homeless man it was a small fortune. "If you agree to answer a couple of questions, this money is yours."

"What d'you want to know?"

"Were you here the morning that man was killed?"

"No."

He was afraid. Or maybe he was telling the truth, in which case she had struck out. Again. "Are you sure, Ralph?"

"I didn't see nothin'. I wasn't here." He paused. Then, his tone bitter, he added, "Last year at this time I still had a job, food in my stomach and a warm bed to sleep in."

"I'm sorry." Her apology sounded hollow, and she read the disdain in his eyes. Kelly understood it. What did she know about the homeless except what she read in the papers?

Ralph shifted from one foot to the other. "But I know someone."

Kelly jerked to attention. "Someone who was here? At the time of the murder?"

He nodded.

Kelly started to walk toward him then stopped when he took a step back. "Why didn't that person tell the police?"

Ralph laughed. "The police. They treat us like we was criminals and they lock us up like we was animals. We tell 'em nothin'. Let 'em earn their keep, that's what I say."

A break. Maybe. "I tell you what, Ralph." She extended her arm. "You take this money. You've earned it. And if you take me to your friend, I'll give him some money, too."

"He won't talk to you. He's scared." He gave no sign of taking the two twenties.

"You tell your friend he has nothing to be scared of," she said, desperate not to lose this lead. "I'm not a cop."

"What are you?"

"A friend of the dead man's son. Together we're trying to find out who killed his father. Please tell your friend that. And take the money."

He did. She watched him as he lifted his coat and several layers of clothing underneath and stuffed the bills in a pocket. Then, glancing furtively around him to make sure no one was watching, he hurried away.

"Hey!" she called out. "You'll be back, right?"

He didn't answer. He just kept on running.

Kelly leaned against the Buick and cursed herself. How stupid could she be? Of course he wasn't coming back. And neither would his imaginary friend. She'd been had.

Common sense told her to leave. This was another

of those humiliating failures that were best forgotten. She wouldn't even mention it to Nick. He'd never let her live it down.

So why wasn't she leaving? Why was she standing there like an idiot, hoping that Ralph would come back. With his friend.

Half an hour later she was still there, watching the parking-lot entrance where Ralph had disappeared. Then she saw him, hurrying toward her, his head bent against the wind. Trying to keep up beside him was a short, heavyset man with grimy cheeks and thin gray hair going in a dozen directions. He looked as destitute as Ralph.

"This is Ben," Ralph said when both finally came to a stop. "Show him the money."

Kelly smiled at Tom Cruise's famous line coming from Ralph's mouth. Taking several bills from her purse, she let him see them. "Here's sixty dollars, Ben. That's all the money I have on me right now. If you give me the information I need, I'll see that you get more."

"You just said you didn't have no more."

"Not on me, but I can get it. I guess you'll just have to trust me." She held his hard gaze. "The way I trusted Ralph when he left with my money earlier."

Ben took the bills. "You a cop?"

Ralph gave him a nudge. "I told you she ain't no cop."

"I'm a friend of Nick McBride, the son of the murdered man." When Ben didn't answer, Kelly added,

"Ralph tells me you were here the morning Patrick McBride was killed. Is that true?"

"I don't lie," Ralph protested. Once again he nudged his friend. "Tell her I don't lie."

"He don't lie."

Ralph let out an exasperated sigh. "Tell her what you saw, stupid."

Ben looked toward the entrance of the parking lot. "I saw a man walk to that row of cars over there." He pointed a grimy finger somewhere above Kelly's shoulder.

Kelly said a silent prayer. Maybe, just maybe, her streak of bad luck was over. "Then what happened?"

"Someone was hiding behind a car, jumped up and stabbed the man."

Kelly frowned. This wasn't adding up. The police report had clearly stated robbery as the motive, but the way Ben explained it, the stabbing had taken place first. Was he lying to her? Telling her what she wanted to hear for a fast buck? "Didn't the killer ask Mr. McBride for his wallet?" she asked.

Ben shook his head.

She studied his face. Clear, unflinching eyes stared back. He was telling the truth. "Did you get a good look at him?" She kept her fingers crossed.

"Him?" Ben laughed, showing two missing bottom teeth. "It wasn't a him. The killer was a broad. A woman."

Thirty-Nine

Kelly stared at him. "Did you say *woman?*"

Ben nodded.

"Are you sure? No one said anything about a woman."

"Yeah, I'm sure," he said defensively.

"Can you describe her?"

"I didn't look at her. I was too damn scared."

"Please, Ben. You must remember something—her clothes, the color of her hair. Was she big? Small?"

"Not big, just strong. Stronger than that McBride was, that's for sure, and he was no slouch."

"What about her hair?"

"Can't say for sure. She had a hat on, one of 'em ski things pulled down low, but..." He squinted his eyes, deepening the lines around them. "I think I saw blond hair. Yeah, that's right." He nodded several times. "I'm pretty sure she had blond hair."

So had the driver of the black Lexus. "Had you ever seen her before?"

He shook his head. "No, and she wasn't one of us either. Them cops say a homeless man killed that casino employee, but it ain't true. Bastards always pin the stuff they can't solve on us.''

"Can you remember anything else? What she was driving maybe?''

Ben shook his head again. "She didn't hang around long. She stabbed him, pulled the knife out and started to leave. Then she came back, took his wallet and ran out.''

She had come back for the wallet. Not because she wanted it, but to make it look like a robbery.

"Ben.'' She hesitated, afraid her next question would send him running and she would never see him again. "Would you be willing to tell what you saw to Mr. McBride's son?''

He glanced around him, suddenly uncomfortable. "I don't know. What if she comes after me?''

"She won't. Nick will protect you.''

The suspicious look came back. "How can he do that?''

"Because he…he's a homicide detective.''

Ben gave a violent shake of his head and started to back away. "No, no way. I ain't talking to no cop.''

"Ben, listen to me.'' She put up her hand, but made no move to stop him physically. "Nick isn't like those cops who harass you all the time. He's different. He's a good man. All he wants is to find his father's killer.''

"Then how come he ain't here himself?''

"Because he's been suspended.''

Now he was more curious than suspicious. "What'd he do?"

"Some things he wasn't supposed to and the guys at the top didn't like it."

He seemed to relate to that and glanced at Ralph, who shrugged. Kelly took advantage of his indecision to pressure him a little more. "If you help us, Nick might be able to find you a job. Both of you," she added, including Ralph in her offer.

The shrewd eyes were suddenly filled with keen interest. "What kind of job?"

"You'll have to talk to Nick about that, but he knows a lot of people in Atlantic City and in Philadelphia. I'm sure he'd be willing to help find you something." Nick might not agree but what else could she do? In order to reopen the investigation of Patrick's death, the Atlantic City police needed to have something concrete to go on. And without Ben's testimony, they had nothing.

"Will you do it, Ben?" she pressed. "Will you talk to Nick?"

He took his time answering, fidgeting with the zipper of his faded blue parka and glancing around him apprehensively. After a while he nodded. "Yeah, I'll talk to him."

"Thanks, Ben. Where can I find you?"

He pointed behind him. "Under the boardwalk. Across from Bally. Just ask for Ben."

She thought of the three Encantado employees and how quickly they had disappeared. Could she trust

Ben not to run away? Or would he change his mind later? His expression revealed nothing. She would just have to take a chance that he was a man of his word.

Ten minutes later, she was back on the Atlantic City Expressway headed west to Philadelphia. As she drove, she thought of the blond woman Ben had seen and of his remark about her strength. How could a woman overcome a man like Patrick McBride? Granted, he had been caught by surprise, but still…

And then it hit her.

The shock caused her to swerve into the left lane, in front of a passing car. A long, angry honk snapped her back. She gave a twist of the wheel and got into her lane, then pulled over to the shoulder and stopped the car.

She sat there for several seconds as cars whooshed by. Why hadn't she thought of it before? The woman who had killed Patrick McBride and who had tried to kill her on Saturday night wasn't a woman at all.

It was Enrique.

Forty

Nick had just finished talking to his friend at the DMV and was about to try Kelly when his phone rang.

"How're you doing, kid?"

Nick almost shot out of his chair. "Joe?"

"Surprised, huh?"

Nick tried not to get too excited. "A little."

"I've been doing some thinking."

"I'm listening."

"I'll need some guarantees first, Nick. Not for me. For my kids."

Joe didn't scare easily, which meant that whatever he had to tell him was serious. "Tell me what you want."

"Safety for the three of them. Not tomorrow, not after I talk to you, but right away. This morning."

"That's a little short notice."

"Now, Nick. Or I don't talk."

Nick thought quickly. He had an idea but didn't know how well it was going to be received at the other end. "Do the kids have passports?" he asked.

"Yes. We got them a couple of years ago, when me and Dottie took the family to Mexico."

Nick remembered the vacation, the last one for Dot, who had been celebrating her forty-fourth birthday. "Good. Are you being watched? Is that why you're worried?"

"I'm not being watched. And my phones are clear. I just don't want to take any chances."

"All right. Give me a few minutes and I'll call you back." He took down Joe's cell phone number, and immediately called his sister in Aviano, Italy, where her husband was serving a three-year tour with the U.S. Navy. She sounded her usual cheerful self when she answered the phone but sobered instantly when he told her what he wanted.

"Oh God, Nicky," she groaned. "What have you got yourself into now?"

"It's all coming together, sis, I swear. But Joe won't talk until his kids are in a safe place."

"What about his niece? She loves those children as if they were her own."

"That's the first place Webber will go looking for them."

Another groan, a little weaker this time. "I don't know. Alex is at sea right now."

"Please, sis, you've got to help me out. You know I wouldn't ask you to do this if I thought you were in any kind of danger. Webber doesn't even know you exist, much less where you are."

A sigh reached him from four thousand miles

away. "All right," Kathleen said. "I'll do it. I'll take them in."

"Thanks, sis. I'll call you again after I've made the arrangements."

His nerves tingling as if he was on a caffeine high, Nick called Joe back. "It's all set, Joe. Where are the kids now?"

"Danny has a class at Temple, Ron's in school right here in Brigantine, and Tommy is downstairs watching TV."

"What about the nanny?"

"This is my day off so it's hers, too."

"Good." Nick was silent for a moment while his mind worked out the logistics. "What time does Ron get out of school?"

"Two o'clock. He usually gets here at about two-thirty."

"Take the two kids and meet me at Philadelphia International Airport, at the US Air terminal. If you leave right after Ron gets home, you can be there at about three-thirty. Don't pack anything. You can buy what they'll need at the airport. For now, act like you're taking the kids to a video store nearby. And don't forget the passports."

"What about Danny?"

"Call him and tell him I'll meet him outside Temple's main entrance at three o'clock. Make sure he doesn't tell anyone he's leaving."

"Where are they going, Nick?" Joe's voice was heavy with worry.

"To Italy. Kathleen has agreed to take them in until this mess is over."

"God bless her."

"Yeah, she's a good kid—and a sucker for people in trouble." Nick glanced at his watch. "I'm going to call the various airlines and see what's the earliest flight I can get. They'll probably fly into Rome and from there take a connection to Aviano."

"Thanks, Nick. I feel better now."

"Good. I'll meet you at the airport at five."

"You did *what?*" Nick bellowed over the phone.

"Don't shout." Kelly held her phone away from her ear as she drove. "You'll bust my eardrum."

"I'm going to do a lot more than bust your eardrum, Kelly. I'm going to skin you alive. You gave me your word you would stay away from Atlantic City."

"I did it under duress. It doesn't count."

"Dammit, Kelly."

"Are you going to keep on yelling at me? Or do you want to hear what I found out?"

He let out a long breath. "What did you find out?"

"I know who killed your father."

There was a long pause, followed by a single word. "Who?"

"Enrique."

She told him about her conversation with Ben and Ralph and why Ben had been afraid to come forward at the time of the murder. "He thought it was a woman, but it wasn't. It was a man all along, a man *disguised* as a woman. Considering how well Enrique can change his appearance, that wouldn't be very hard. He probably kept most of his paraphernalia.''

''And you're sure he wasn't in those files Webber let you see?''

''Positive. And Syd knew he wouldn't be there or he wouldn't have been so willing to let me look. Enrique's employed somewhere else, Nick. Maybe another casino?''

''I'll call Alan and ask him to check it out. In the meantime, if you're finished with your little escapades, I'd like you to—''

''Go to San Remo. I know. I'm on my way there now.'' She lowered her voice to a sexy whisper. ''Unless you want to come to my house and keep me under guard yourself.''

That remark brought out a laugh, his first. ''You wench.''

''Will you?''

''Wish I could, but Joe just called. I was right after all, Kelly. He knows something and it's big.''

Kelly slowed down as she approached the Ben Franklin Bridge. ''Does it concern Syd?''

''I'd bet a year's salary on it. The problem is, Joe won't talk until his kids are safely out of the way.''

She listened as he told her how his sister had come through for him and would take the children until all danger had passed.

''I'll call you when I know more, okay?''

''Sure. You know where to reach me, Nick.''

Forty-One

Nick's plan had gone off without a hitch, due mostly to the speed with which it had been executed and the cooperation from the entire Massino family, even five-year-old Tommy, who hadn't wanted to leave his dad at first but had finally agreed to get on the plane.

At boarding time, Nick had spoken to the senior flight attendant and explained that the boys would be met in Aviano by his sister, Kathleen Hargrove. The attendant had assured him she would personally escort them to the Alitalia terminal for their connection to Aviano.

After the plane had taken off, Nick and Joe drove back to Center City and went to a busy sports bar just off Broad Street. Half a dozen TV sets were strategically placed throughout the room and every eye was glued to the Temple versus University of Dayton basketball game in progress. Not a soul was paying attention to the two men sitting at a back table, sipping their beer.

Nick slid a card key across the small round table. "I made arrangements for you and me to stay at the

Doubletree. You're registered under the name of Thomas Parson.''

Joe tried a little humor. "You're afraid the boogeyman will get me?"

"Just a precaution."

"Okay." Joe pocketed the key. "But you're going to have to tell me how much I owe you for everything—the plane tickets, the clothes you bought for the kids, the room, everything."

"I'll send you a bill." The man was now officially unemployed and he would need every cent he had, but Nick didn't tell him that. "Are you ready to tell me what you know?"

Joe nodded. He hitched his chair closer to the table and spoke in a low voice. "Syd is hiding money. Illegal money."

Nick put his mug down. "You got proof?"

He shook his head. "No, but I'm sure it's in his office somewhere, maybe on his computer."

"How do you figure?"

"A week before your father died, he told me he'd overheard a phone conversation between Syd and someone else. Patrick could only pick out bits and pieces but it was enough to alert him that the boss was making loads of money through back-room gambling and loan-sharking, and laundering the cash through several phony businesses before transferring it to the Cayman Islands."

On the table, Nick's hands fisted. "Why didn't my

father come to me with that information? I could have done something. Maybe saved his life.''

"I told him to. He said he didn't have any proof, but he would soon. He was thinking of bugging the back room where he thought the illegal gambling was taking place.''

"Is that when he started to work the extra shifts?''

"Yeah. He figured he could do it after 4:00 a.m. when the casino closed for a few hours. I asked him if he needed help, but he said no. He didn't want to get me involved in case something went wrong.''

"And Syd found out?''

Joe's answer surprised him. "I don't know, Nick. I swear on my dear Dottie's grave I don't know what happened. That Thursday morning I expected your father to tell me the bug was in place, but instead he rushed out of there, with a mean look on his face. Next thing I knew, he was lying in the parking lot, dying.''

Nick wrapped his hands around his mug, needing something to hang on to.

"I was sick with grief at first, then I got angry. I went to Syd and told him what I knew.''

"What did he say?''

At the bar, loud cheers broke out as the center for Temple scored again. Joe waited for the noise to die down before saying, "He swore to me he had nothing to do with your father's death. He didn't even know Patrick had overheard his phone call.''

"So he didn't deny his illegal activities?''

"No. He knew that if he did and I went to the authorities, he'd be investigated. He couldn't risk that."

"So he bought your silence." Nick tried not to sound bitter.

Joe hung his head for a couple of seconds before looking up again. "I told him to go to hell at first. I told him I was going to finish the job Patrick had started. I even handed him my resignation. He wouldn't accept it. He kept reminding me I was broke and fifty-six years old. Who would hire me? On the other hand, if I stayed and kept quiet, he would not only promote me to chief of security but he'd make sure I had enough money to send Danny to college, pay for a full-time baby-sitter for Tommy and buy a bigger house in a better neighborhood."

"Were all those things that important to you?"

"No." Joe gazed at him calmly, as if he had been expecting the question. "What was important was my kids' safety."

"Did Webber threaten them?"

"Not in so many words, but he gave me some very strong hints. I would have been a fool to ignore them."

Nick didn't say anything. How could he blame him? If Syd had had Patrick killed, as Nick believed, and Joe had become a threat, he would have killed him as well, without hesitation.

"So I agreed to stay at the Chenonceau and keep quiet," Joe continued. "I wasn't proud, believe me.

Not a day went by in the last year when I didn't think of your father. I felt like a traitor, unworthy of his friendship, his trust. Yet at the same time I knew that in my shoes, he would have done the same thing. Someday, when you have children of your own, you'll understand.''

"Hello, princess." Gino kissed Kelly on the cheek. "I was wondering when you'd get here."

"How did you know I was coming?"

"Your young man called." He winked at her. "I think he's checking up on you."

At the other end of the kitchen, Connie was filling manicotti with a ricotta-and-spinach mixture. Benny was at the sink cleaning squid.

Knowing her mother would have seen through a lie, Kelly had told Connie the truth. The investigation was coming to an end and Nick hadn't wanted to take unnecessary chances with Kelly.

"I like that boy," Connie had said, giving Kelly a pat on the back. "You should marry him."

"Hey, Kelly!" Benny held out the phone. "It's Nick."

She walked over and took the wall extension from him. "Why didn't you call me on my cell phone?" she asked Nick.

"Because I wanted to make sure you were where you're supposed to be."

She smiled. It had been a long time since a man

had worried about her the way Nick did. "I told you I would be. What's the matter? Don't you trust me?"

"Not after the stunt you pulled yesterday. Besides, I called fifteen minutes ago and you weren't there."

"I stopped at Victoria's and filled her in on what took place in Atlantic City."

"You didn't mention Joe, did you?"

"Of course not. How's he doing?"

"Better now that the kids are out of harm's way. We'll wait until they've arrived at their destination before going to the police."

"What did he have to say?"

"I'll tell you everything when I see you tomorrow morning. Hopefully, by that time, this mess will be all over."

After Kelly had hung up, Connie came to stand beside her and wrapped an arm around her waist. "I heard you mention Victoria. Why don't you call her and ask her and Phoebe to come over for dinner?"

"I already did. She wants to spend a quiet evening at home with her daughter. Ward and Cecily will be at the Bellevue tonight, Adrian has the night off, and Phoebe can be as noisy as she likes."

"Oh, that's right." Connie bobbed her head. "Ward is getting an award tonight, isn't he?"

"The Benjamin Franklin Award." It was a prestigious honor bestowed on a single individual each year for his or her selfless efforts to make the city of Philadelphia a better place. This year Ward had been selected for financing the construction of a women's shelter through the Eastland Bank.

"How come you weren't invited?" Gino asked.

"I was. I declined in respect for Victoria. She's not going either."

Connie shook her head and went to check a pot on the stove. "Poor kid. She must be going crazy not knowing what happened to her husband."

Maybe she would soon, Kelly thought. Maybe Nick was right in saying this mess should be over by morning.

Kelly was taking a dish of lasagna out of her mother's oven when Nick called her back, this time on her cell phone. "Kelly," he said, talking over the loud static. "Something came up." He started to fade then came back. "Meet me…"

"Nick, I can barely hear you. Can you speak up?"

He did, though there was little improvement in the connection. "I didn't get that, Nick. Can you repeat—"

"I said to meet me in Weekstown."

"Where the hell is Weekstown?"

"South Jersey. Past Egg Harbor City."

"What are you doing there?"

"No time to explain…" More static. "Meet me there."

"Nick, Egg Harbor is an hour from here."

"Not if you take the expressway, then Route 50 to Route 563. Past Weekstown, and across Ocean

Yachts, you'll see a path. The cabin is at the end of that path. You got that?''

''Yes, but whose cabin is it?''

''Kelly...Kelly, are you there?''

''Yes,'' she shouted. ''Whose cabin is it?''

''We've got them, Kelly. It's all over.''

They were disconnected.

Kelly lay her phone on the counter. Connie and Gino were looking at her.

''What was that all about?'' Connie asked. ''Why would Nick want you to go to Egg Harbor at this time of night?''

Kelly glanced at her watch. ''It's only five o'clock.'' She walked over to the hutch and opened a drawer. ''You still keep a map of New Jersey in here? Ah, here it is.''

She spread it on the counter, located Egg Harbor and Weekstown and traced it back to Center City.

Connie looked worried. ''You want Gino to go with you?''

''I was about to suggest it,'' Gino said, already untying his apron.

''Guys, please.'' Kelly shook her head. ''I don't need a bodyguard. I'll be with Nick. You stay here, Uncle Gino.'' She gave him a knowing look and he nodded.

Traffic was heavy throughout Philadelphia and on the expressway, but began thinning along Route 50. Out of the city limits, Kelly had wanted to call Nick and had realized that in her haste, she had left her cell phone on her mother's kitchen counter. Whatever explanation there was for this sudden change of plans would have to wait.

As she passed Egg Harbor, she concentrated on her driving. This was unknown territory to her, but she knew the area was called the Pinelands, a million-acre pine forest lying roughly halfway between Philadelphia and Atlantic City. Some of the land was private, with beautiful summer homes built onto it, the rest was government-owned and had been turned into state parks.

At last, she spotted the sign for Ocean Yachts. The small, log-shingled cottage stood alone in the middle of a clearing. Tall pines surrounded it and kept it hidden from the road. Kelly stopped the car and stepped outside looking at the ramshackle structure and the single light that shone through the tiny window. Partially concealed behind the cabin were two cars. Why two? she wondered. Who else was here?

Apprehension swept through her as she studied the isolated cabin. Something about Nick's call had reminded her of something. Something she should know. But what?

"Kelly, is that you?"

Thank God. "Yes, Nick!" Relief bubbled out of her throat and she ran toward the cabin, pushing open the door. "I didn't know what to make of—" She looked around the room, bare except for an old rickety table on top of which stood a lantern. "Nick?"

"Nick isn't here," someone said from the depth of a hallway.

At the familiar voice, Kelly let out a strangled cry. "Jonathan?"

"Wrong again." This time the voice no longer sounded like Jonathan's. It was deeper, slightly accented.

The man stepped out of the darkness. A smile, rare for him, stretched his thin mouth. A gun was aimed at her. "Surprised, Miss Robolo?"

Kelly met his eyes, those dark, mysterious eyes that had never fully met hers. They did now, with a touch of arrogance.

"Yes, Adrian." She tried to control the fear hitting her from all sides. "Or should I call you Enrique?"

Forty-Two

Enrique met Kelly's gaze with stony dislike. "You were always too smart for your own good, Kelly. In fact, I'm surprised you didn't figure it all out sooner."

"Where's Jonathan?"

He made a motion with his hand but didn't take his eyes off her. "Buried back there in the woods. You'll be joining him soon."

Kelly closed her eyes in a silent prayer for the friend she had loved and lost. "Why?" she murmured.

He shrugged. "Like you, he stuck his nose in where it didn't belong and paid the price."

"He never went to Miami, did he? You did. You pretended to be Jonathan. You're the one who checked into that motel and you're the one who placed that call to Magdalena, knowing it would be traced to her. Jonathan never had an affair with your sister. You set him up."

"Bravo, Brenda Starr." Enrique laughed. Cool and relaxed, he was still very proper in his demeanor, but looked nothing like the Enrique Kelly had seen in the videos. Reconstructive surgery had totally changed his facial features, even his jawline. "You want to know why I'm laughing, Kelly? Because it was so damn easy."

Listening to him talk in Enrique's voice made her realize what had sounded so familiar about Nick's call earlier. The static on the line. Victoria had mentioned the same interference the morning Jonathan had called her from the airport. Kelly gave herself a mental kick. Why hadn't she remembered that? There hadn't really been static on the line. Enrique had created it in order to distract her. By concentrating on what "Nick" was saying, Kelly hadn't paid attention to the flaws in Enrique's imitation.

"Easy?" she repeated. "Easy to kill people? Easy to stab them to death and watch them die?"

"I do what I have to do."

"Who was the man in room 116 of the Encantado?"

"A bum who was only too happy to have a clean room for the night." There was no remorse in his voice, not an ounce of regret for the innocent people who had died.

"And the bomb? Was that your doing as well?"

He smiled at that. "No. A friend of mine did the job. The idea was to blow up the room in such a way that there would be nothing left of the body but scattered ashes, making identification impossible. The police would have believed the remains were Jonathan's and that would have been the end of a tragic story. Unfortunately, the charge wasn't powerful enough."

He leaned against the wall, the gun still steady in his hand.

"You're the one who called Victoria on Friday and pretended to be Jonathan. Why?"

"So she would realize he didn't want to come home and would ask you to drop the investigation."

"And when that backfired, you got scared and sent Magdalena away."

He gave her a brief, chilling smile. "I'm not scared of you, Kelly. I'm just a cautious man."

"Of course you're scared. If you weren't, you wouldn't have tried to kill me. It *was* you the other night, wasn't it? Hiding behind a woman's disguise?"

In the gleam of the lantern, his eyes glinted with a cold light. "That was the part I liked the best, catching that terrified look in your eyes."

"Whose car were you driving?"

"Syd's Mercedes. I parked it behind the house after I returned from my failed mission. And you never knew it. You were so intent on putting the blame on poor Cecily."

A Mercedes, not a Lexus. She had never been able to tell one from the other, especially from the back.

"It would have been so much better for you if you had died right there and then," he continued. "You would have had a proper burial, family and friends laying you to rest, saying wonderful things about you. But now..."

"So you do work for Syd Webber."

"And for me," another voice replied.

For a moment, Kelly thought the voice was another of Enrique's imitations. It had come from the same direction, but unless ventriloquism was another of his talents, she couldn't see how it could possibly be him.

When the other man stepped out of the shadows, her heart stopped.

He was dressed to the nines, in an impeccably cut tuxedo and a black overcoat he'd left open. Gold cuff links glinted at his wrists.

There was a look of regret in his eyes. "I tried to tell you, Kelly," Ward said in his quiet voice. "I even begged you to drop the investigation. You wouldn't listen."

"You." She was too stunned to say anything more. She thought of the conversations they'd had, his concern for her, for Jonathan, his bold lies. What a fool she had been, so gullible, so quick to accept what he wanted her to see.

"You're disappointed in me."

"You killed Jonathan."

Ward let out a long sigh. "It couldn't be helped, Kelly. He knew too much."

"I thought he was only a threat to Syd."

"I wish that were true. Unfortunately, when he found out that Syd was running an illegal operation out of the Chenonceau, he also found out that I was helping him transfer the money to Grand Cayman."

A money-laundering scheme through one of Philadelphia's oldest and most respected private banks. How perfect. "And that lunch you had with Jonathan before he disappeared? He never asked you for money, did he?"

"No." Ward brushed an invisible speck of dust from his sleeve. "He wanted to warn me that he was going to the authorities. He gave me forty-eight hours to come forward and publicly admit my involvement with Syd Webber. If I didn't, he would go to the police."

"So you killed him."

"It was nothing personal, Kelly. Just a matter of survival."

"Why that elaborate piece of theater in Miami? Why check him in a drug-infested motel, set him up with a mistress?"

"To detract attention. Thanks to Enrique's contacts there, and Magdalena's, we were very successful in doing that. But you wouldn't let it go, Kelly. You kept digging and digging."

"How did you lure him here?"

"We didn't. I told him I needed to discuss my press conference with him, that I wanted to confess but in a way that would be the least embarrassing for my family. He agreed and came to my house." Ward waved toward his accomplice. "Enrique did the rest."

Kelly's gaze shifted back to the man she and Nick had pursued so relentlessly. His eyes were cold and flat. The eyes of a killer, she thought with a shiver. She saw Ward glance at his watch and remembered he had an awards ceremony to attend. Ward Sanders, Citizen of the Year. A man whose last five years had been devoted to the betterment of the less fortunate. Had it all been a scam?

"Why did you do it, Ward? Why did you team up with a man like Syd Webber?"

The corners of his mouth lifted. "Money, of course."

"You already have money."

"Wrong, Kelly. My father has money, and all the prestige that goes with it. I'm nothing but the rich man's son. You would think that after all I've done for Eastland Bank in the last thirty-six years, he would at least make me an equal partner. Or leave me the bank after his death."

This time the corners of his mouth turned downward in a bitter expression. "You want to know who will inherit Eastland when Monroe dies? My brother Sean."

At Kelly's startled expression, he gave a short, harsh laugh. "That's right. My brother the stockbroker. It doesn't matter that Sean doesn't have the faintest idea how to run a bank. He was always Dad's favorite and because of that, the business will go to him.

"Thirty-six years of being at the old man's beck and call. *Yes, sir. No, sir. Whatever you say, sir.* And what do I have to show for it? Nothing. Ironically, the only thing I can really call my own is the award I'm being presented tonight. Even though the financing of the women's shelter came from Eastland money, the idea was mine. *I'm* the one, not Monroe, who saw the project to its completion. Tonight, I will finally be somebody."

A gust of wind rattled the small window and Kelly pulled her coat tighter around her. Neither Ward nor Enrique seemed to feel the cold.

"When did you and Syd became partners?"

"At Jonathan and Victoria's wedding. We had never met before that day, but he had done his homework. He knew how disenchanted I was with the business arrangement my father and I had, so he made me a deal I couldn't refuse, as they say. He asked me if I would be willing to occasionally transfer large sums of money to the Cayman Islands. For my services I would receive ten percent of every transaction.

"Now I'm a multimillionaire, Kelly. Before long, I'll have enough money to move to the West Indies, buy myself a villa, a boat and live like a king for the rest of my life."

Kelly kept watching him, wondering how long she could stall the inevitable. "What about Cecily?"

He laughed. "I only married Cecily because my father thought she'd be good for my career. As it turned out, she married me for the same reason. She never loved me. All she cared about was the Norton Trust and her position as CEO. Look what she did trying to protect it."

He didn't know about her affair with Syd, Kelly realized, or he would have said something. She glanced at Enrique again. Her executioner. "Where does he fit in?"

"He worked for Syd and Tony Marquese in Las Vegas. When he needed a place to hide after Marquant's murder, Syd got him a new face, a new identity and a glowing letter of recommendation as a Rumanian butler." He laughed. "Cecily was so ecstatic when she heard about him. She just had to have him."

Kelly shook her head. "I remember how reluctant you were to hire him. It was all an act."

He looked pleased. "I took drama in high school. Didn't you know? At one time I almost thought of becoming an actor. Then my father dangled that carrot in front of my nose and I became a banker instead."

He dragged his hand through his silver hair. "I'm truly sorry to have to kill you, Kelly. But you were getting too close. Another day or two and you would have cracked this case wide open. Breaking into the Chenonceau's personnel office last night convinced us we had to stop you."

He began buttoning his coat. "If it's any consolation, I liked you very much. So did Syd. He was quite smitten, actually. Did you know that?"

"That will be a comforting thought to take to my grave."

The small attempt at humor brought a smile to his face. "Goodbye, Kelly."

She stood in front of him, blocking his path. "You won't get away with this, you know. Too many people know I went to Atlantic City. They know Syd and a security guard caught me searching the personnel office. The investigation won't stop just because I'm dead.''

"Only one person can keep that investigation going, Kelly. Nick McBride.''

"Don't make the mistake of underestimating him.''

"Never. That's why he'll be taken care of as soon as Enrique has taken care of you.''

Kelly suddenly realized that Nick would soon suffer the same horrible fate she was about to face. Her emotions vacillated between fear and anger. "Won't that look suspicious? Two investigators killed within hours of each other?''

"It doesn't matter, because they'll never know who killed you. In fact, I doubt they'll ever find your bodies. This is government property. It hasn't been used in years." He spread his arms wide. "You see, Kelly, we thought of everything.''

No, Ward, not everything. You didn't think of Joe Massino spilling his guts to Nick. Please, God, she prayed. *Don't let Nick wait until morning to talk to the police. Let him do it right away, before Enrique catches up with him.*

"Time for me to go." Ward gave her one last look. "I wish it didn't have to end this way, but you understand." He nodded to Enrique. Then, without a look back, he walked out.

The powerful sound of the BMW engine filled the night. Within moments, all was quiet again. Enrique picked up the lantern and motioned Kelly outside.

Forty-Three

By five-thirty that evening, Nick had decided he had enough evidence to take to Captain Cross. Joe had agreed to go with him and sign a statement but not until they'd heard from Kathleen and the kids. That was fine with Nick. Webber wasn't going anywhere.

Too wound up to keep what he knew to himself until the following morning, he called Kelly on her cell phone. To his surprise, Connie answered.

"She went to New Jersey to meet you," Connie said. He could already hear the panic in her voice. "To a place called Weekstown."

Something in the pit of his stomach turned cold. "That wasn't me, Connie."

He heard a moan, a quick shuffle, then Gino's booming voice. "Nick, what the hell is going on? Where's Kelly?"

"She was tricked." Someone had pretended to be him, probably the same person who had pretended to be Jonathan. Who else could it be but Enrique, the man with the thousand voices? "When did she get that call, Gino? Did she say anything? Leave any clues?"

"She looked at a map of New Jersey and said something about a cabin across from a boatyard. I can't remember the name of the place. Something yachts, after Weekstown. She left right after that, so fast that she forgot her cell phone."

Nick couldn't remember a boatyard, but he knew the area. Weekstown was a few miles southeast of Batsto, the historic village in the Wharton State Forest where he used to go as a kid. "What time was that?" he asked.

"A little after five."

In clear traffic, the trip wouldn't take him more than forty-five minutes, less if he really pushed it. But Kelly had a twenty-minute head start on him. Even if he barreled down there at ninety miles an hour, he wouldn't be able to catch up with her.

At the end of the line, Gino was growing impatient. "Nick, what do you want me to do?"

"Stay by the phone, Gino. I'm going after her."

"You're going to need help."

"I'm bringing it with me. And I'm calling the police. Try not to worry."

Joe, who had heard the conversation, was already out of his chair. In the car, Nick dialed Captain Cross's home number and filled him in. Cross didn't say a word until Nick was finished.

"Stay on the line," he told him, "while I call the New Jersey State Police."

Within minutes, three squad cars had been dispatched to the small New Jersey town.

* * *

"What do you like to be called?" Kelly asked as she and Enrique walked through the thick brush. "Adrian or Enrique?"

"I don't give a shit," he replied. "Just keep walking."

She took her time, stepping over tangled laurel bushes, ducking under low-hanging limbs and trying to think of a way out. Behind her, the light from the lantern in Enrique's hand swung over the area, giving her an occasional glimpse of the deepening shadows ahead.

If only she could engage him in a conversation, she might have a chance. She might discover a weakness, a chance to escape.

"Why did you kill Steve Marquant?" She started to turn, but he poked her in the ribs with the barrel of the gun.

"That's none of your business."

Had she struck a nerve? She couldn't tell. "From what I gathered from the police report, you and Steve had been together for a long time. Four years, wasn't it?" He didn't answer. "A relationship like that doesn't end because of a little tiff."

"Steve was stupid."

"What did he do?" Kelly slowed her pace, hoping he wouldn't notice.

"He used me. I was his trophy wife, the glamorous star he liked to show off at parties."

"So he was proud of you. What's wrong with that?"

"He wasn't proud of me!" The light swung wildly. "He was screwing behind my back."

Kelly stopped abruptly, though not because of what Enrique had just said. She didn't give a damn about his love life. In front of her lay an open grave. Beside it was a pile of dirt with a shovel stuck into it.

"Oh, my God." Her stomach flip-flopped. Inside the hole she could see part of a trench coat, a pant leg, the point of a shoe. A briefcase. Nausea rose to her throat and for a moment she thought she was going to throw up.

"What's the matter, Brenda Starr?" Enrique put the lantern down on a tree stump. "Never seen a corpse before?"

She turned then. "What about you, Enrique? How many have you seen? How many people have you killed in cold blood?"

"You've got a big mouth, Kelly."

"Doesn't it bother you? Don't you think about it sometime? Have nightmares at night?"

"Shut up and get in the grave."

Kelly sucked in a breath. He was going to bury her alive. He was going to make her lie on top of a dead body and then shovel the dirt back on. The thought made her gasp for air. She wouldn't do it. He would have to kill her first.

The sound of a car engine approaching broke the

silence. She saw Enrique tense, then relax as the sound faded away.

"I said, get in the grave," Enrique repeated. "Or would you prefer I put a bullet through your leg?"

Kelly's mouth was dry but she kept on talking. "Did you warn Steve you were going to kill him?" she taunted. "Were you looking into the eyes of the man you loved when you plunged that knife into his chest?"

"Shut up!"

He was beginning to crack around the edges. Could he be feeling guilty about killing his lover? Had her stab in the dark hit a pressure point?

Aware she had nothing to lose, she pushed harder. "Do you ever wonder what went through Steve's mind in that last moment? The fear he must have experienced? The sense of betrayal?"

In the glow of the lantern, she saw his face contort in pain. She gave one more jab. "Did you watch him die, Enrique?"

"Shut up! Shut up! Shut up!" The gun still in his hands, Enrique covered his ears.

In the half second it took him to realize that was a mistake, Kelly yanked the shovel from the pile of dirt and swung it at Enrique's head with brute force.

The heavy blade caught him on the right temple. Blood gushed from the wound, streaming down the side of his face, his jacket.

He just stood there, looking half-dazed and surprised, as though he hadn't expected her to do that.

The gun was still in his hand. With what seemed like a monumental effort, he turned it back toward her.

Oh God. She hadn't hit him hard enough.

Words she couldn't understand spewed out of his mouth. Without warning, his legs folded under him and he fell like a disjointed puppet. The gun slipped out of his grip and dropped to the ground, but Kelly didn't dare pick it up, not yet.

When he remained motionless for several seconds, she edged away from him, circling the grave.

In the distance, the sound of another car grew closer, louder. Bright headlights tore through the trees. She ran for cover, afraid Ward had come back.

"Kelly!"

Nick was running toward her. Another man was with him, running just as fast. Behind them, a police cruiser had come to a stop.

With a strangled cry, Kelly ran into Nick's arms.

Forty-Four

The ballroom of the Bellevue Hotel glimmered with hundreds of lights, and was made even more brilliant by the glittering, bejeweled audience attending this special evening.

The dinner was over. So was the presentation of the Benjamin Franklin Award. The man of the hour stood at the podium, holding the inscribed plaque and preparing to deliver his acceptance speech.

From the threshold, Kelly watched him for a moment, then started walking toward him, Nick and two uniformed officers behind her. As all eyes turned in their direction, she recognized several dignitaries— the mayor, a Pennsylvania senator, several heads of corporations—people gathered to honor a man who only two hours ago had left her to die.

Shortly after her rescue, Captain Cross had given Nick his badge back and told him to handle Ward Sanders's arrest any way he saw fit. Nick had immediately turned to Kelly. "We can do it two ways. Quickly and discreetly, sparing Ward any public embarrassment, or we can do it right now at the Bellevue, in front of his peers. It's your call."

The choice had been so easy.

A charged silence fell over the room as Kelly continued to approach the podium. Even from this distance, she could see the color on Ward's face drain, his lips flutter as if he was trying to say something but couldn't get the words out.

She kept walking, her eyes upon the man on whom Philadelphia had just bestowed its most prestigious award. A few feet from him, she stopped. "What's the matter, Ward? You look as if you've seen a ghost."

He glanced behind her, then over his shoulder, where two more uniformed officers had appeared.

"If you're looking for a way out, don't bother. There isn't any."

Close by someone grabbed her hand. Kelly looked down and saw Cecily. Her face was white, her tone an angry whisper. "Kelly, for God's sake, what are you doing?"

Kelly's gaze shifted calmly from Cecily to the man sitting next to her. Monroe Sanders was watching her intently. He had never felt one way or another about Kelly. She was just a friend of Cecily's niece, nothing more. Tonight, though, his expression was one of clear hostility. She was the enemy who, for reasons still unknown, had come to disrupt their charmed lives.

Kelly left Cecily's question unanswered and returned her attention to Ward. "Why don't you tell these good people what you've been up to?" she said quietly. A deadly silence had fallen over the room. "I would, but you're so much better at telling stories than I am.

"Tell them how you lured me into the Pinelands this evening and ordered your butler to kill me because I knew too much. Tell them how you and Syd Webber had Jonathan Bowman killed because he, too, knew too much."

A gasp rippled across the room. Heads bent toward each other. "And while you're at it, tell them who you really are. Tell them you're not the generous, honorable, upstanding Philadelphian you pretend to be, but a corrupt, untrustworthy, ruthless swindler who's in bed with the mob."

Behind the podium, Ward remained frozen, his expression a mask she couldn't read. It didn't matter. She knew that this public humiliation was a crushing blow from which he would never recover.

It was a small payback for what he had done to Jonathan and Victoria.

"Too bad your timing was so poor, Ward," she said, managing a condescending smile. "If you hadn't been so greedy and eager to make one more million or two, you'd already be on that tropical island you bragged about."

As she saw him glance down at the plaque, she remembered what he had told her about the award being the one thing—the only thing—he could really call his own. Now he would have to give it back. How fitting.

The silence grew oppressive as each guest waited for the conclusion of this high-powered drama. They would have to witness it without her. Her job here was done. Kelly didn't want to look at Ward's face a second longer.

She turned in time to see Nick nod at the two officers.

"Ward? Ward had Jonathan killed?" Victoria stared at Kelly in horrified disbelief. "It can't be true. It's a mistake. Tell me it's a mistake."

Her grief at the news that her husband was dead had been painful to watch, difficult to soothe. Clinging desperately to Kelly, she had cried endlessly, while upstairs Connie and Gino did their best to entertain an unsuspecting little girl. Cecily was at the police station, intent on hearing her husband's confession with her own two ears, although Ward still wasn't talking.

Sitting in the Sanders' living room, Kelly shook her head. "It's not a mistake. I'm so sorry, Victoria. I kept hoping that things would turn out differently."

"I don't understand. Ward, of all people. I trusted him. So did Jonathan."

"It all boiled down to money." Kelly repeated what Ward had told her at the cabin, adding details she and Nick had learned later.

"If it's any consolation," Kelly continued, "Ward will be facing several charges—conspiracy to commit murder, conspiracy to attempted murder, tax evasion and conspiracy to illegally transfer a total of twenty-seven million dollars of undeclared money from the U.S. to the Cayman Islands.''

"And Adrian was in this, too? A man to whom I entrusted my daughter?'' Victoria's expression turned savage. "I wish you had killed him, Kelly. I wish that shovel had split his skull in two, instead of just giving him a concussion.''

She closed her eyes and let out a long breath. "That's all right. I'm sure he'll get the death penalty. And when he's executed, I want to be there. I want my face to be the last thing he sees before he dies.''

Kelly looked down at their interlaced hands. "That's not going to happen, Victoria. At least not in Pennsylvania.''

"Why not?''

"He and his attorney worked out a deal with the D.A. Enrique will tell all he knows about Syd's illegal dealings, on the provision that the Commonwealth of Pennsylvania agrees not to seek the death penalty. Of course, he's still facing a murder charge in Nevada, and whether the Las Vegas courts will agree to the same deal is another matter.''

"I hope their D.A. doesn't.'' Victoria picked up a photograph of Jonathan from the table beside her and ran her fingers lightly over the glass. "Jonathan never went to Miami, did he? And he wasn't involved with Magdalena.''

"No. That little brainstorm was engineered by Ward and Syd so the suspicion would be diverted from them. Enrique is the one who flew to Miami on Monday, using Jonathan's driver's license for identification. Apparently he managed to look enough like Jonathan to pass through inspection. Meanwhile, in Miami, Magdalena was buying the cooperation of her former boss at Salamander. You might like to know that she's been found at her aunt's house in Puerto Rico and is now in custody. So is the owner of Salamander."

"But the photo on her mantel...the snuff bottle..."

That had been one of the first questions Kelly had asked Nick when he had finished interrogating Enrique in his hospital room. "Enrique borrowed Cecily's keys, without her knowledge, of course, let himself into your house and searched through your photo album until he found exactly what he was looking for. Another friend in Miami did the rest."

"And the snuff bottle?"

"He took some risks there. Do you remember a woman by the name of Mrs. Cartright? She came into your shop on Friday afternoon."

Victoria nodded. "Yes, very well. She was interested in that Louis XIV clock I had in the window, but when I showed it to her, she said it wasn't exactly what she wan..." She stared. "*That* was Enrique?"

"Yes. In the time it took you to remove the clock from the window display, he had already stolen the bottle. He knew he needed something small that could easily be transported. The snuff bottle was perfect. Later, he called Magdalena and told her to find some miniature bottles for her phony collection. She did, and the stage was set."

"And Jonathan's trench coat?" Victoria blinked away new tears. "His briefcase?"

Kelly wished she didn't have to go into those gruesome details, but as long as Victoria wanted to hear them, she had no right to withhold that information. "Enrique put them in the grave earlier this evening, when he reopened it."

Victoria was silent for a moment, still struggling with her emotions. "You said Syd and Enrique knew each other well?"

"Very well. As it turned out, when Enrique arrived in Las Vegas the first person he befriended was one of Tony Marquese's men. Enrique was broke and in bad need of a job, so with his new buddy's recommendation, he became a collector for Marquese's loan-sharking operation—an operation Marquese owned in partnership with Syd Webber. That's how the two of them became acquainted. Later, Syd gave Enrique his first break as an impersonator and their friendship was sealed. Nick didn't elaborate, but I think Enrique continued to work for Marquese in one capacity or another even after he became famous. There's a dark side to Enrique that could only be satisfied by committing acts of violence. Marquese and Syd saw that and used it to their advantage."

As all the pieces slowly fell together, Victoria let out a long sigh. "So those allegations about Syd being connected to the mob were true after all. Jonathan thought they were the fabrication of jealous competitors.''

"They weren't. The competition may have tried to use the information to their advantage, but they didn't make it up. Syd fooled everyone, even the Casino Control Commission. It wasn't an easy thing to do, but Marquese knew enough people to make that happen.''

Victoria took a tissue from the box Kelly had brought earlier from the bedroom and folded it in two, then in four. "I want Syd to pay for what he did, Kelly.''

Kelly looked away.

"Kelly?" Victoria frowned. "He *will* pay, won't he?''

"Not exactly.''

"Why? Because of his high-powered friends? His battery of attorneys?" She gave a fierce shake of her head. "They're not going to bail him out this time, Kelly. I won't let them.''

"Syd is gone, Victoria.''

Victoria was very still for a moment, stunned into silence. "Gone?''

"Someone tipped him off. Maybe Enrique, though he denies it. But the fact is, when the police arrived at the Chenonceau, arrest warrant in hand, Syd had vanished.''

"But they're going to find him. The way they found Magdalena.''

"I'm not sure. People like that always have an escape planned in the eventuality they ever have to make a quick exit. He could be anywhere, under an alias, wearing a disguise."

"They can get him when he goes to claim his money."

"I'm sorry, Victoria, but I doubt that very much. He's too clever not to have already transferred his money from the Caymans to another location."

"Son of a bitch." Victoria put Jonathan's picture back and stood up. "That bastard killed my husband and got away with it." Tears ran down her face and she did nothing to stop them. "It's not fair, Kelly."

"I know, honey." Kelly walked over to her and wrapped her arms around Victoria's trembling shoulders. She held her for a while before saying, "What are you going to do about Phoebe?"

Victoria dried her tears. "I'll have to tell her. Oh, God, Kelly, I don't know how. She's only five years old. She doesn't understand death."

Kelly remembered Nick telling her how Patti Kolvic had explained her husband's death to her children. "You could tell her he's gone on a long trip to heaven to be with the angels, but that he loves her and will always watch over her. That's what Matt Kolvic's widow told her two little girls."

Victoria nodded and squared her shoulders, preparing herself for the ordeal ahead. Kelly watched her walk out of the room, then, with a heavy sigh, she sat down to wait for her mother and Gino.

* * *

Three hours later, Kelly was on her sofa, snuggled in Nick's arms, her back leaning against his chest. She gazed into the fire Nick had started after she'd come back from Victoria's house. Victoria and Phoebe had returned to Bryn Mawr as quickly as they could.

A lot had happened during her absence. Kathleen had called from Aviano to tell them that Joe Massino's boys were with her. They were fine, tired, a little confused, but in fairly good spirits. Each of them had talked to their father. They'd had a million questions for him and Joe had tried to answer them as best as he could without frightening them unnecessarily.

Unfortunately, Joe could still be facing charges of withholding information in exchange for money. But because of his recent cooperation, Nick and Captain Cross were trying to work out some kind of deal with the Atlantic City police so he wouldn't have to go to prison. Victoria and Phoebe were being looked after by Cecily, who had returned to Bryn Mawr to be with her niece and help her make the necessary arrangements for Jonathan's funeral.

Still deep in her thoughts, Kelly gently stroked the arms that encircled her. "When I think of Victoria and Phoebe in that house," she said. "All alone with that madman…"

Nick tightened his hold around her. "Enrique will be put away for a long, long time, Kelly. Stop thinking about him."

"I can't. I can't forget the way he looked at me in that cabin, with those cold, ruthless eyes. And the way he changed voices. It was creepy." She continued to watch the flames dance on the hearth. "How did he know *your* voice, Nick, when he had never met you?"

"Syd was in the habit of recording certain conversations that took place in his office. The one he and I had a week or so ago was in collection. All Enrique had to do was listen to the tape and practice. The static he created while talking to you was just a precaution."

"That static should have been a dead giveaway. I was so stupid."

"No, you weren't." He kissed the top of her head. "Enough of Enrique. That's an order."

"You're right." She stretched her legs on the sofa, crossing them at the ankles. "Actually, I have something more important to discuss with you. A confession of sorts."

"A confession, huh? Are you going to ask for immunity?"

Her spirits began to lift. "No. I'll take whatever punishment you want to give me."

"Tempting. What did you do?"

"I promised two friends of mine that you would find them a job."

"I see. Anyone I know?"

"You know *of* them." She paused. "Their names are Ralph and Ben. Ben is the man who witnessed

your father's murder. I know you don't need him now
that Enrique has made a full confession, but..."

"But you made a promise and you'd like to honor
it."

How well he knew her already. "Yes."

"Hmm. What do they do, those two friends of
yours?"

"I never asked, but I know they're good men, honest and proud."

She heard him chuckle. "You could tell all that
from one conversation?"

This time she turned so she could look at him.
"Cops don't have a monopoly on human intuition,
you know." She saw him smile and gave his arm a
little shake. "Is that a yes? You'll find them a job?"

"I'll look into it. How's that?"

She threw her arms around his neck. "You're wonderful."

"Not so fast, Robolo," he said, holding her back.
"You don't think I do favors without expecting something in return, do you?"

She gave him a wicked smile. "I was about to take
care of that, silly."

"That's not what I mean."

"You're turning me down?"

"No, I just want something more. Like...a commitment that you're going to make this relationship
work."

She threw her head back and laughed. "Is that
all?"

"Considering that you keep saying we're too much alike and are headed for disaster, it's a legitimate question."

"I thought *you* were the one with all the doubts."

"I never said that."

"You called me bullheaded."

"Only after you called me bossy."

"Well, you are." They held each other's gaze for a moment, then started to laugh and continued laughing until Nick kissed her.

As she lost herself in the kiss, she thought of telling him how much she loved him, how much she had come to depend on him, and how the thought of spending a single day without him scared her to death. But she didn't say anything. She would save that confession for another time.

"All right." Kelly pulled away just enough to gaze into those serious blue eyes. "If a commitment is what you want, you'll get it. As soon as you answer one question."

"Fair enough. What's the question?"

"Just how far do you want to take this relationship of ours?"

He cupped her face between his hands and brought it close to his. "How about...all the way?"

New York Times **Bestselling Author**

ELIZABETH LOWELL

GRANITE MAN

Mariah MacKenzie returned to the family ranch to search for a long-lost gold mine in the land of her ancestors. Cash McQueen was a distraction she didn't need, a temptation she didn't want—but the only man tough enough to be her guide on a bold quest for the legendary treasure.

Cash's passion for prospecting didn't run to beautiful women—not after the cruel blow the female species dealt him in the past. Trust wasn't in his vocabulary anymore...until temptation made him want to believe in something more precious than gold....

"I'll buy any book with Elizabeth Lowell's name on it."
—Jayne Ann Krentz

Available February 2001 wherever paperbacks are sold!

CHRISTIANE HEGGAN

66577   ENEMY WITHIN   ___ $5.99 U.S. ___ $6.99 CAN.

(limited quantities available)

TOTAL AMOUNT $_____
POSTAGE & HANDLING $_____
($1.00 for one book; 50¢ for each additional)
APPLICABLE TAXES* $_____
TOTAL PAYABLE $_____
(check or money order—please do not send cash)

To order, complete this form and send it, along with a check
or money order for the total above, payable to MIRA Books®,
to: **In the U.S.:** 3010 Walden Avenue, P.O. Box 9077, Buffalo,
NY 14269-9077; **In Canada:** P.O. Box 636, Fort Erie, Ontario,
L2A 5X3.

Name:_____
Address:_____ City:_____
State/Prov.:_____ Zip/Postal Code:_____
Account Number (if applicable):_____
075 CSAS

  *New York residents remit applicable sales taxes.
   Canadian residents remit applicable GST and provincial taxes.

MIRA®